WHY ~~WERE THEY PLAYING~~ DUMB, I WONDERED?

Toni, Sara, Brigitte. Each, quite obviously, hoping to make the most out of Berry's tragic demise. Each, in her own way, hardworking and deserving. And each, for whatever reason, holding back on me. Was it simply a practical business decision to pretend they didn't know Berry had decided to pull out of the Tantamount deal? The fact of the matter was, each had more to gain in the long term if the company was sold . . . than if it wasn't.

And more to the point, it dawned on me at last as I glanced again around the table, each had a lot more to gain with Berry dead.

---- ★ ----

SEVENTH AVENUE MURDER

SEVENTH AVENUE MURDER

Liza Bennett

WORLDWIDE®

TORONTO • NEW YORK • LONDON • PARIS
AMSTERDAM • STOCKHOLM • HAMBURG
ATHENS • MILAN • TOKYO • SYDNEY

SEVENTH AVENUE MURDER

A Worldwide Mystery/February 1990

ISBN 0-373-26041-5

To W.E.B.,
as always

ONE

SEVENTH AVENUE is called Fashion Avenue, yet it's one of the least stylish thoroughfares I know. It's an architectural hodge-podge: an uncomfortable marriage of dilapidated sweatshops and soulless new high rises, their tinted glass already pocked with grime. The wind whips cruelly around the corners of the cross streets, and no green thing seems capable of survival. The large cement tubs planted at the base of one of the newer office towers contain balding stumps of what had once—for a week or so—been evergreen shrubs. No amount of care could coax them to live. That afternoon, as I hurried past, I noticed that their skeletal shapes were draped with blinking Christmas tree lights. A rather pathetic homage, I thought, to a season that represented at least one-quarter of this district's annual sales to retail outlets.

I turned south into the wind, burying my neck tortoiselike into the animal warmth of my mink-lined duffle. A birthday gift from my mother, Theo. Well, actually, I'd returned the one Theo had originally sent me for this more practical model. Leave it to Theodora Goodenough to pick out a floor-length iris blue. Perfect for lithe czarinas racing in open troikas through the snow-laden streets of Saint Petersburg. A little less useful for a slightly overweight and not particularly graceful Manhattan advertising art director. Though that's not to say that I don't have a certain full-bodied allure. That afternoon, for instance, with my unruly mop of black curls jouncing around my well-padded shoulders and my stiletto-heeled snakeskin boots adding a tasty two inches to my usual five foot six, I felt the eyes of more than one Midtown male slide back for a second take on the merchandise.

My mother, one of America's leading abstract expressionist painters and an early pioneer of feminist thought, would have returned such looks with a withering gaze. I, on the other hand, her far-less-demanding only child, tend to react with Pavlovian eagerness to even the smallest display of masculine approval. And the truth of the matter is, I still haven't mastered the native New Yorker's congenital ability to maneuver down the most crowded avenue without once making eye contact with another human being.

"Sweet young thing," a deep bass insinuated just behind me as I reached the corner of Seventh and Forty-third. I turned to find myself staring up at the tallest, tannest and most attractive man I'd ever seen outside of a photo shoot. Piercing blue eyes, bleached white brow, hard but sensuous lips. He could have been thirty-five. Or sixty. Here was the kind of man whose age had never mattered. He wore a white leather jacket, skintight cream-colored corduroys and buckskin boots with tassels that snapped around his ankles as he walked. This eye-grabbing getup was topped off with a genuine Stetson—adding another six inches to his six-foot frame. The rich, honeyed voice was as un-New York as the ensemble. And, as if to confirm that he was a stranger to these parts, the gorgeous giant gave me a quick, knowing up-and-down look and—if you can believe it— a wink! He then strode past, whistled down a cab on Broadway and typically—just like most of the promising men one encounters—disappeared.

I sighed and hurried on through the streaming crowd. It was not quite four-thirty, but a bleary-looking sun was already staining the side streets Popsicle orange. When I turned west at Fortieth, the usually shadowy street was lighted with a supernatural glow. The grime-covered storefronts of the wholesale fabric merchants blazed with a color vibrant enough to appeal to the most tasteless buyer. The gutters seemed to run with gold. But by the time I reached the colonnades of the Zabin Building, halfway down the block, the illusion had faded. The sun— a thread of color stretched above the high rises of New Jersey—dropped suddenly. Darkness fell with a renewed swoosh of wind, helping me push through the heavy, revolving doors of the building that had recently become my second home.

The turn-of-the-century mercantile grandeur that the Zabin Building had once boasted was now long gone. The marble had yellowed, the gilded ceilings blackened. Years ago the inlaid tile floor had been covered with linoleum. A cheap metal lectern sat uncomfortably in the middle of the small lobby, manned by an ever-changing sentry who usually spoke no English. I'd been in and out of the place at least a dozen times during the past few months and had yet to see the same face twice. And I'd yet to discover the exact function of these surly looking men in their poorly cut gray fatigues. Although there was a sign-in sheet, no one ever asked my name or destination. Tonight, the small, balding gentleman on duty—again, someone I'd never seen before—didn't even look up from his *El Diario*.

I pushed the worn, gummy button for the elevator and wondered if I should have called ahead to let Berry know I was coming. The trip had been pure impulse. Peabody & Quinlan, the multibillion-dollar Madison Avenue agency that owns my soul, was in the final stages of preparing a major new brand-labeling campaign for Merriweather Sportswear, currently located on the tenth and eleventh floors of the Zabin Building. Although the Merriweather account itself was fairly small by P&Q standards, the company was in the midst of a takeover action by Tantamount Enterprises, which, as you know, owns whatever Japan doesn't these days. You better believe that P&Q brass—who've been salivating over Tantamount for years—had a passing interest in the success of the campaign. And for the past three months, I'd been putting in twelve-hour days to make sure they were not disappointed.

During that time, I've gotten pretty close with the company's founder and president, Beryl Merriweather. It's not a friendship I would have predicted after my first meeting with Berry—as she is universally called. I watched the bronze arrow move slowly along the arm that marks the building's floors and thought back on that memorable occasion a year or so ago.

"YOU'RE DARN TOOTIN' I decide," I'd heard a deep, gravelly voice declare as I slid in—late as usual—to the meeting in the twentieth-floor conference room at P&Q. The speaker was an enormous blond woman, swathed head to toe in a pomegranate-red pant suit. Her many chins cascaded over the daintily laced collar of her too-tight blouse. One could easily see the buttons straining against the rising tide of her breasts. Her eyes—mere slits in the protruding flesh of her forehead and cheeks—darted resentfully around the conference table, landing finally on where I stood, uncomfortably shifting my position by the door.

"Whozzat?" the woman barked, her chins shaking as she nodded in my direction.

"That's Peg Goodenough, our head art director, Ms Merriweather," Phillip Ebert announced in his best master-of-ceremonies style. "She's won numerous awards. Goodenough. Perhaps you recognize the name?"

I always feel slightly nauseous when someone I'd like to respect slobbers all over my surname. Phillip Ebert, our group president at P&Q and my nominal boss, often gives me this reaction. Goodenough, for people who know anything about art, has the same cachet as Rauschenberg or Motherwell. A doodle of Theo's on a crumpled lunch napkin could easily fetch ten thousand dollars these days. That sort of fame unfortunately does things to people. Much to my relief, it obviously didn't do a thing for Beryl Merriweather.

"No, but I *do* recognize the fact that she's the only other female here," the obese woman shot back. "You know, I find that amazing—considering the fact that you musta known I'm a woman and that Merriweather Sportswear made its reputation in women's apparel. Boys, boys...this really doesn't bode well for a future relationship, now does it?"

If it had just been a matter of the Merriweather Sportswear account, I think Phillip Ebert would have adjourned the meeting then and there. Though well-educated and intelligent men, most of the top brass at P&Q—and for that matter up and down Madison Avenue—are closet chauvinists. Oh, they hide it well enough, promoting the requisite number of aggressive females into their ranks and addressing the lowliest secretary as "Ms." Nobody wants to be slapped with another minority suit, for heaven's sake. On the other hand, this old boy network just can't seem to accept that women are their equals. The decision about whom to invite to the initial Merriweather meeting was a perfect case in point. They pretend that women have a place in their midst... they just don't believe it. After Beryl's spiel, I counted up the bodies: there were eleven P&Q men...and me.

Yes, if it had just been a matter of Beryl and her extremely successful line of ladies' wear, I think that would have been the end of it. But Tantamount's takeover action made the account very appealing, as far as Phillip and his cronies were concerned. Satisfying Merriweather Sportswear was just the first step, the strategic thinking went, in bringing the mighty Tantamount into P&Q's fold.

"You know, you're quite right," Phillip replied in shocked tones. "How extraordinary! You're obviously not aware, Ms Merriweather, that P&Q leads the big agencies in number of female employees. What an odd coincidence, a truly startling and unfortunate one, that this majority is not better represented here today. Mark, why is that?" Phillip demanded, turning on the account supervisor of the group designated to pitch Merriweather. Mark, with whom I have waged innumerable battles, turned an unattractive green.

"I tried to get Felice Clay, but she was at some seminar," he whined. "And Marissa's on vacation. And Claire's sick. It's not my fault that—"

Beryl cut his high-pitched explanation short. "It doesn't matter now," she announced. "But it certainly will down the pike. I prefer working with women. They tend to be better organized and more detail-minded. All in all, more reliable employees. Just see that you keep that in mind in the future, gentlemen." And with those words, Beryl Merriweather, whom I quickly came to know far better and more fondly as Berry, won a large and permanent place in my heart.

THE ELEVATOR in the Zabin Building, like the lobby, had seen better days. Sun God Loves Suzie 4-Ever was scratched in huge, crude lettering across the grime-encrusted doors. Shorter and less-loving sentiments had been inscribed on the walls. As usual, it bore me upward with an inward mechanical groan, interspersed every floor or so with brief but violent episodes of shuddering. The doors finally banged open on the eleventh floor.

The reception area—usually abuzz with telephone calls, messengers, buyers and salesmen waiting for appointments—was empty. The switchboard had been closed down. The single red light of the night line—which often wasn't switched on until nine or so—glowed dully. Beyond, in the warren of offices where I'd grown accustomed to the rock-concert decibel level of Berry's executive and sales staff, silence reigned. Most of the lights were switched off, except for the blinking colored ones that had been unevenly draped around an unhealthy-looking cactus at the reception desk. And, far down the hall, neon light from one office spilled along the darkened corridor. Berry's suite. I could hear her voice clear out to the lobby and, without thinking, I started toward it.

"Yeah, I know all that," the nasal, Montanan tones of her voice reverberated. "Yeah, yeah...well, we've been over all this ground before," she continued. She sounded tired, I thought, and angry.

There was a silence for a moment, and then in a voice that suddenly dropped to a low rumble, she continued. "Is that a threat? I mean, I'd like a little clarification here. Was that a threat, buddy? Lay your cotton-picking cards on the table. I want to know what you're trying to say...."

I hesitated at the door of Berry's office. She was half sitting, half leaning on her battered worktable/desk, the phone cradled between the flesh of her chins and the swelling rise of her shoulder. She was dressed in an electric-blue caftan, one of the dozen or so garments she had specially made each year at the Hong Kong plant where Merriweather Sportswear was produced. Her bright blond hair, a mass of short, natural curls, haloed her head. She had pale blue eyes, the color of early summer skies, and the softest, most luminous skin I'd ever seen. Her features, beneath the fatty layers, were lovely, even delicate. Like many obese women, Berry looked younger than her years. Almost fifty, she could easily pass for mid-thirties. And she would be beautiful, I'd often thought, if only...

"I get the idea," she barked into the receiver. "You've painted a very detailed picture, thanks. But, guess what? It doesn't change a thing. Do your damnedest. I ain't budging.... That's right," Berry continued, her voice rising. "There's no deal. None. Over. *Fini.* Kaput."

At what point I realized that this was not a normal, friendly phone chat, I don't remember. But suddenly it occurred to me that Berry probably wouldn't be pleased by my eavesdropping. Slowly, and as quietly as possible, I slipped back into the shadows of the corridor. But I couldn't help overhearing the rest of the conversation. It was carried on at top Merriweather volume.

"It ain't gonna do any good, I tell you. I've made up my mind. No, nothing you can say... Oh, for shitsakes, okay. But I warn you, it's not gonna make a darn bit of difference. Yeah, yeah. Let's say, nine o'clock. No, make it here. We're gonna keep this businesslike, okay?" And with that Berry slammed down the phone. "Bloodsucking little—" Berry muttered, but she stopped short when she heard my timid knock on the door.

"Who the . . . ?" she cried, turning to face me. It was then I saw the tears that glistened on her cheeks, the telltale tracks of running mascara. I would have never known by her voice that the toughest, most determined woman I'd ever met...had been crying.

"How long you been hanging around?" she demanded, leaning over to rummage through her top drawer for a Kleenex. She found a crumbled tissue, wiped her eyes and then honked noisily. She looked me over suspiciously and asked again, "How long you been here, huh?"

"I, uh, just had a few last minute questions about tomorrow," I replied, hoping to change the subject. "Where is everybody? The place is like a morgue."

"Staff Christmas party," Berry replied, giving her nose another blow. She straightened, her eyes clear again. "They're all over at Donahue's tying one on."

"Shouldn't you be there, too?" I asked, impressed and a little disturbed by how quickly she recovered her equilibrium. One would never guess that moments ago this woman had been in an extremely emotional state. For the first time I realized what a good actress she could be. Iron-willed, forthright Beryl Merriweather actually hid a lot of interesting things behind those piercingly honest blue eyes.

"Nah, I just couldn't face it this year," Berry replied.

"'Bah humbug'?" I asked, taking a step into the cluttered room. Fabric samples were strewn across the floor. Sketches were tacked to the corkboard walls. Magazines and yellowing issues of *Women's Wear Daily* were piled in corners and on chairs. Two tailor dummies, one naked, the other pinned with a flowered cottony fabric, stood sentry behind Berry's desk.

"More than that," Berry replied. She frowned and looked over at me with a curious expression. Half questioning, half melancholy. "The fact of the matter is, I've decided not to sell

Merriweather to Tantamount. You know what that means, don't you?''

"Well," I replied, trying to think the thing through. "I guess it means that maybe some of those people at the Christmas party might have to go."

"Actually, no," Berry replied. "I'm hoping to keep everybody on."

"Well, if none of your people are going to lose their jobs, what is it, Berry?" I asked. There was clearly something she wanted to tell me. But it wasn't easy for her.

"It's just that—" she sighed "—you might lose *yours*."

TWO

IT WAS THREE HOURS and two glasses of cheap red Italian wine later. I was sitting across from a now florid and expansive Berry at a table in the back of the Supreme Macaroni Company. This inauspicious Ninth Avenue storefront—its windows stacked with jars of embalmed peppers and baskets of faded pasta—has a restaurant in the rear that caters to people with small pockets and large appetites. Berry falls unequivocally into the latter category. She'd already downed almost a full bottle of Chianti, a plate of antipasto and an overflowing basket of warm, homemade bread.

I, more than a little unnerved by our earlier conversation, had been nibbling tentatively on a bread stick. I'd been trying ever since we'd left her offices for what she'd termed "a quick bite" to direct Berry's attention back to the subject of my possible dismissal from P&Q. But either she was determined to ignore the issue or she had so many of her own that needed airing, she simply didn't catch my plaintive tone.

"Believe me, Peg, I'm no libber," Berry professed as she signaled the waiter to refill the breadbasket. "I'm not militant or anything like that. But, I built my business up with my bare hands. I know what work is. I know what trust is. And I tell you," she said, pouring the last inch or so of Chianti into her wineglass, "hands down, I'd hire a woman over a man every time. You know why that is?"

"Well, I've heard you say they're more reliable," I ventured, watching with awe as Berry tore into a new loaf of oven-fresh whole wheat.

Slathering butter over a slice, she responded, "Yeah, but even more important, women like details. And when it comes to creating and manufacturing clothes, details make all the difference. And," she continued, waving her butter knife in the air for emphasis, "I'm not just talking about factory work. I mean right down the line, from designers to sales staff to office managers. Well, of course, every once in a while there's going to be a bad apple or two—''

Berry broke off, sighed and stared down at her now-empty plate. Then she looked up at me, her blue gaze misted, and announced bitterly, "The bastards told me this morning that I had to cut down on my operating expenses. Told me I was way over on head count. *Head count!*" she repeated, slamming her fist on the red-checkered tablecloth. The water glasses shivered. "They mean people. *My* people. *My* girls. . . ."

"I take it that the 'they' are Tantamount?" I ventured.

"That's right," Berry replied, reaching for her wineglass and downing its contents. She ran her finger nervously around its rim and added, "You see, it's not that Merriweather isn't operating at a pretty decent profit margin. It's that those rotten, two-faced freeloaders want to put some of their own people in what they referred to today as 'key' positions. Jerks. Who do they think they're dealing with? They should've at least had the brains to wait for the ink to dry on the takeover contracts before moving in. Nor am I happy with Tantamount plans to dilute my design work. I will not have my name associated with inferior products."

"So you told them the deal's off?" I asked, thinking back to the conversation I'd overheard earlier.

"Ah . . ." Berry hesitated, looking into my eyes, then away. "I haven't officially cancelled the deal. There are still some details to be ironed out, Peg. I really shouldn't be telling you any of this, but you're a good listener."

I smiled across the table into Berry's troubled gaze. The wine had lent a permanent flush to her cheeks, oil from the antipasto a shine to her lips and chin. With her blue caftan floating tentlike around her bulk, she looked like some grotesqely oversize, aging Victorian china doll. Placid yet obstinate, generous yet iron willed. . . a massive contradiction in terms. Berry was one of the few women I'd met in my professional life who—through smarts, talent and absolute determination—was playing and winning in a man's world. She was a woman I valued as a friend . . . and would hate to have as an adversary.

"And I can be a pretty persistent interrogator, too," I replied. "For instance, though you keep avoiding the question, at some point I'm going to get you to tell me why all of this puts *my* job in jeopardy.''

Berry narrowed her gaze at the chalkboard on the wall that listed the evening's specials. ''I should have kept my flabby mouth shut about that one, but . . . I figure you got a right to know. Shall we get some dinner first, though? This isn't anything you're gonna want to hear on an empty stomach.''

She ordered eggplant *parmigiana*, a side order of spaghetti *bolognese*, an arugula and radicchio salad and another bottle of Chianti. I made do with a salad and a glass of white wine, my appetite in abeyance until I heard what Berry had to say about my future with P&Q. Or lack thereof.

You may think that any art director who'd won as many professional awards as I have would feel pretty confident about job security. That is, unless you know a little something about the advertising world. On Madison Avenue creative people are let go as regularly as fireworks at Disney World. The business is awash with incredibly talented, amazingly experienced and chronically out-of-work art directors. I've just been lucky. For nearly seven years, and on about as many accounts, I've been kept steadily and solidly employed in P&Q's art department. And what is even more unusual, I've managed to avoid unemployment without soft-pedaling my often hard-line attitudes to upper management. Among the powers that be, however, I'm not universally liked.

Mark Rollings, the account supervisor on Merriweather, is one of those powers. Thin, suave and immaculately dressed, Mark has worked his way up the account side of P&Q by sticking to one basic principle: never venture an opinion unless it's one that the client wants to hear. It's a modus operandi that spells death to any creative risk taking. It's an attitude I despise, and Mark knows it. For years, Mark and I have been thrown together on various accounts and new business ventures. And for years, in and out of meetings and pitches, conference rooms and screening halls, we've been tearing each other apart.

From the onset of our work on the Merriweather pitch, Mark has had something of an unfair advantage. I was not surprised, therefore, when Berry began her explanation regarding my job security by asking, "Did you know that Dick Byser at Tantamount and Mark Rollings went to school together?"

"How could I help but know?" I retorted. "Ever since we started working on the project, Mark has been lording his relationship with 'Dickie' over the group. The man's without shame."

"I take it," Berry answered, smiling as an enormous plate of Italian greens was placed in front of her, "that not a whole lot of love is lost between you and Mark."

"He's a spineless worm," I replied simply. "And I'm sure he thinks I have far too *much* spine. We've had it in for each other for years. Luckily, he has a way of turning most of the clients off... whereas I tend to get along with people okay."

"Yes, Peg, you do," Berry responded warmly. "That's why I was pretty shocked when Dick started to feel me out about you this morning. He implied...well, he nearly came right out and said that Mark thought you were 'difficult.'"

"Brilliant, Mark!" I cried. "We hardly have our foot in the door at Tantamount, and he's already politicking. He's that sure of Dick that he can afford to power play like that?"

"Well, up until my decision not to sell this afternoon, Dick's yea or nay could just about decide things," Berry replied, talking through mouthfuls of well-oiled lettuce. "And I don't know, maybe it's just me...but I think there's something funny going on between Dick and Mark. I mean, Peg, I don't need you to tell me that Mark Rollings is slime. He's an ass kisser of the first rank. But Dick makes like he's some kind of marketing genius or something."

"Don't you think old school loyalties account for that?" I asked.

"If Dick were equally as dim-witted, I might think so," Berry replied. "But Dick Byser, for all his faults, is one smart fella, believe me. I may not like the way he operates...but the man is effective. Look at the way he orchestrated the brand-labeling business. He's aware of every dropped stitch at Merriweather." Berry tore off a hunk of bread and swooshed it through the olive oil glistening on her empty plate. She added thoughtfully, "No, I can't believe that Mark is taking him in. Something...something else...must be involved."

"Well, Mark may not be taking Dick in," I said, sighing, "but it sure sounds like he's going to be able to take me out. Damn, and there's nothing I can do about it!"

"Well, there was something *I* could do," Berry confided to me. "I did a major sales pitch on you to Dick this morning...implying that Mark didn't know his creative ass from first base. And, you know, I got the feeling ole Dickie bought it. But, I'm warning you, honey, you've a tough battle ahead with Mark if Tantamount comes on board at P&Q. Seriously, I think it could mean your job."

"I think you're right," I told her grimly. "But thanks for what you said to Dick about me. God knows, you have enough on your mind. That was really...good of you."

"Yeah, I know," Berry said, splashing some wine on the tablecloth as she refilled her glass. The new bottle was already half-gone. "I know how you've been working your tail off over this presentation. And I've seen enough of your work to know you're damn good at what you do. But, most important—" Berry broke off as her huge, steaming plate of pasta arrived, along with my plate of tossed salad. Buoyed by Berry's kind words, I found myself digging in hungrily.

We ate in silence for a few seconds, then Berry mumbled between mouthfuls, "What was I saying...? Oh, yeah. Most important is the fact that you're good at the *details*. You've asked me questions ad nauseam about the business...from the manufacturing plants overseas to the retail chains uptown. *Details*, like I said before, make the damn difference." Berry chewed in silence for a moment, then added with sudden force, "So I told Dick that if you come through tomorrow, Tantamount should seriously consider centralizing the advertising of all its divisions at P&Q. *But* I made it clear that my positive feelings toward the agency were based on my very good developing relationship with...you."

It was one of the most generous statements I'd ever heard Berry utter...and I was very nearly dumbstruck. I took a deep breath and said, "How can I thank you? You've been far kinder than I have any right or reason to expect. The only thing I can promise in return is that I'll do my damnedest to live up to your high expectations. But, Berry..."

"Yeah?"

"Isn't our performance simply academic now? If you're not going to cut this deal with Tantamount, is there a future for the presentation, P&Q, me . . . and you, for that matter? Can you afford to go through with a campaign of this size without Tantamount's backing?"

Berry emptied her wineglass and returned it somewhat shakily to the tabletop. She picked her napkin off her lap and wiped her mouth carefully. She then gestured to the waiter, and as he hurried over, asked, "Espresso, Peg? Or a *sambuca*, perhaps? I'm going to get both. But no dessert, I think. Gotta watch the waistline, you know."

I politely declined anything more and waited patiently while the waiter cleared away our dishes . . . and Berry pulled her thoughts together. She was stalling. My question—though a rather obvious one—had thrown her, for some reason. But her composure seem to return about the same time the miniature white cup and saucer with its slice of lemon rind arrived.

"Ah, yes . . . the deal," Berry murmured, smiling vaguely as a glass of thick, transparent liqueur was placed at her elbow. "I do wish now that I hadn't told you about my decision to . . . ah . . . not go through with it."

"I won't tell anyone, Berry," I assured her.

"Oh, I know that," she responded, smacking her lips at the taste of the *sambuca*. "It's just that it would be better for you not to know anything about this right now." She glanced at me sharply and added, "I can see you're not tracking. That's fine. I don't expect you to get it. Just do yourself a favor—forget, for the time being, that we ever had this conversation."

"But won't all this come out tomorrow?" I demanded. "At the presentation? Surely there's no point in going on with the project if—"

"No, no!" Berry cried. Her tone carried the closest thing to anger that I'd ever heard her use with me. "You're going ahead with that meeting tomorrow, Peg Goodenough. It could mean hooking Tantamount, don't you see? And you listen, kid, I expect it to be the best damn presentation P&Q has ever made. I'm depending on you to shine. Got that?"

"Yes," I answered meekly, but I didn't understand. The entire body of work I was presenting tomorrow involved the new marketing strategies Tantamount had been hoping to bring to

Merriweather Sportswear—something I could now see Berry didn't want. It seemed a hopeless, tangled web of unstated motives and misunderstandings. I felt tired and let down. I tried to stifle a yawn, but I could see that Berry noticed the effort. She sat up, suddenly alert, her body rippling jellylike beneath the caftan.

"Shit! What time is it?" she cried, glancing around the room for a wall clock. I checked my watch.

"A little after nine," I told her.

"Damn!" she answered, pushing back her chair and getting noisily to her feet. "I gotta go. I got someone I have to meet." She looked disheveled and unbalanced. It occurred to me that, after two bottles of cheap red wine, she was more than a little drunk.

"Where do you have to get to?" I asked. "I'm heading uptown. Can I drop you someplace?"

"No," she replied, thrashing around for her handbag and coat. "I just gotta get out of here. Damn, I didn't know it was so late. I gotta go." And without another word, she wrestled her way into her heavy wool overcoat, hurried up to the front of the store and pushed through the heavy door to the street.

For as long as I live, I suppose I will blame myself for not getting up and making sure that Berry reached wherever she was going safely. Instead, I just sat in my chair waiting angrily for the check to arrive.

Berry was generous to a fault when it came to praise and support and just your basic human kindness. But she was downright miserly when it came to money. More times than I can count, she'd left me with the bill to pay...or shorted me on taxi fare. As I flipped through my wallet, I vowed I'd never let her stiff me again. Prescient thought.

THREE

BERYL ELEANORA MERRIWEATHER was born in Philburn, Montana, in the heart of the Rockies' rugged Bitterroot Range. A descendant of tough, pioneering stock—her father's family claimed distant yet traceable kinship to Meriwether Lewis— Beryl was raised with strict, coldhearted economy, which closely reflected the wind-whipped mountains looming over her little town. Beryl's father, a traveling snow-fence salesmen, was at home so infrequently during her childhood that when he didn't come home at all during the year of her thirteenth birthday, no one really missed him. Least of all Beryl's mother, a fervent spiritualist who ran one of the nation's first health-food stores.

There was not a big call for brown rice and bee pollen in Philburn, Montana, during the 1940s. And were it not for the munitions plant that opened nearby during the war years, gainfully employing Mrs. Merriweather and most of the other mothers in the town, Beryl and her younger brother, Wesley, would certainly have had a rougher time of it. That Beryl's childhood was far from happy had nothing to do with lack of creature comforts. If anything, her problems could be blamed on an excess of them. Beryl, who longed desperately to dress in beautiful, flowery, feminine clothes, was so fat only tent dresses would fit her properly. Weaned on her mother's whole grains, nuts and raisins, Beryl gorged her way up to a size fourteen by the time she was nine. And by then, it was simply too late. The pattern was set: the unhappier Beryl was about her appearance, the more she ate. And the fatter she got, the more she hated herself.

Beryl's self-loathing was hardly helped by the appearance of her brother, Wesley. For as Beryl grew wider, Wesley grew taller and more handsome. Blond and broad-shouldered, athletic and lovable, Wes was one of the most popular boys ever to breeze through Philburn High.

Beryl, cruelly nicknamed Berry due to her rotundity, did the only sensible thing a girl in her position could. She retreated into a world of her own creation, one fueled by the scores of fashion magazines she subscribed to, and spent most of her time plotting her escape from Philburn. And where else could a bright, physically grotesque outcast find happiness in this world? The morning after her graduation from high school, Berry cleaned out the savings account she'd built by sewing dresses for all her lovely, lithesome classmates . . . and bought a one-way train ticket to New York, New York.

I had pieced together the facts of Berry's earlier life from hints Berry herself had dropped, supplemented by various media sources, including *Women's Wear Daily* and *Vogue*. Her subsequent fashion successes—starting with her first line of "country casuals" in the early sixties—were so well documented I had no trouble compiling a fairly complete picture of her career. P&Q puts a lot of stock in these "personality profiles" when working with a new client. And Phillip Ebert had been pleased by my research when we had first started plotting our Merriweather strategy.

"Get inside the clients' heads. See the world as they do," Phillip always urged. "Discover their passions and prejudices and you're halfway home."

If the presentation to Merriweather and Tantamount could have been as simple as appealing to Berry's sensibilities and outlook, I would have had no difficulty knocking it off in several days. Because I knew, and liked, her style.

"You know how I made it in this business?" she confided to me early on in our friendship. "I did it by making one very simple observation. When it comes to clothes, women want more than anything else to be *comfortable*. When I started my first line in the early sixties, every woman in America was pussyfooting around in snug little pink two-piece suits with pillbox hats, trying to look like Jackie Kennedy. Hell, even naturally slim gals were having to squeeze into girdles just to run out to the grocery store. Talk about uncomfortable!"

The now-famous "casual" look, first introduced by Merriweather Sportswear, had been Berry's highly successful solution. Looser, more flowing in line and fabric, Berry's dresses and ensembles had been both lovely to look at . . . and to put on.

The following year, Merriweather came out with one of the country's first wash-and-wear lines, and Berry's success was assured.

"Hardly couture, mind you," Berry admitted without embarrassment. "But hey, more women in this country looked like me in 1962 than the First Lady. Halston only made fat gals look fatter, somehow. My clothes represented a kind of easy-wearing damage control. I've just always tried to make your normal, overweight American hausfrau feel better about herself. And maybe look a little better, too."

In the seventies and eighties, Berry cannily applied what she'd learned about comfort and care to a whole new army of clothes buyers: working women. Steadfastly ignoring the new pin-striped suit look, Berry brought out well-crafted separates that had enough masculine styling to stand up in the office...and enough versatility to be endlessly mixed and matched. When Berry's first business line hit the stores in August of 1978, the entire stock was sold out within a month.

It was time to expand. In a big way. In the spring of 1979, Berry took the company public. Smart investors, who knew how well Merriweather was doing off the rack, could now buy MERSPT over the counter. And they did. For more than ten years, Merriweather Sportswear kept its stockbrokers happy with juicy dividends and two separate stock splits. Then, corporate America discovered takeovers. And Tantamount Enterprises cast a covetous eye down the *M-N-O-P* listing and noticed MERSPT. And suddenly, my job wasn't so easy anymore.

"What we're looking for," Dick Byser explained at that first exploratory meeting at P&Q, "is a total merchandising program. It's going to take some time before the buy-out is finalized, but we've convinced Berry to let Tantamount steer Merriweather in new directions *now*. We feel there is a vast brand-labeling market out there that would dovetail perfectly with the Merriweather line."

"In other words," Berry explained, her expression and tone more than a little sour, "we're looking for consumer goods to stick my name on. Like, you know, perfume, linen and—"

"But, please, gentlemen," Dick cut Berry off midsentence, "don't limit your thinking to the typical brand-labeling categories. The Merriweather name stands for quality and comfort in Middle America. Whatever cross-marketing products you see coming out of that demo—well, we want to hear about them."

The P&Q "gentlemen" had all nodded thoughtfully back at Dick Byser as if already in the process of hatching brilliant brand-labeling schemes. I, on the other hand, stared at him joylessly. Not only had he rudely interrupted my new idol, but his rather offhand request for "cross-marketing products" meant that the most difficult and time-consuming part of the presentation—coming up with designs for endless boxes, tubes, packages, displays, promotions and ads—was going to fall smack on the shoulders of the art department.

Now, nearly three months and one hundred layouts later, I was standing at the back of P&Q's largest conference room— a miniauditorium, really—rearranging the order of the overhead visuals. It was a few minutes past eight on the morning after my dinner with Berry, and the Merriweather meeting was scheduled for nine.

"But the script's written with the new corporate logos coming *first*," my assistant, Ruthie, pointed out as I fiddled with the slide carousel. My senior by at least ten years, Ruthie coped poorly with anything that deviated even slightly from the P&Q employee handbook. A strict nine-to-fiver, she clearly resented having to come in early for this final run-through. With a whiny undertone, she added, "Mr. Rollings will have to be notified of the change, you know."

"Oh, damn." I sighed, realizing my mistake. Although I was usually asked to handle the entire creative part of any pitch to a new account, Mark had decided that he should be the one to present the various corporate looks I'd designed for the new Merriweather product lines.

"It's such a personal kind of thing," he had explained. "Choosing logos and such. And since I have a...uh...*personal* relationship with the prospective clients, I think I would be the best person to do this."

Unfortunately, corporate design was probably the best material we had to present...and Mark one of our worst presenters. Never a particularly relaxed individual, public speaking of any kind threw him into a state of extreme panic. His walk took on a Frankensteinian clumsiness. His voice, always on the high side, rose another octave. And his eyes glazed over, focusing either on nothing or fastening with a manic intensity on the most important person from the client side. Worst of all in my mind, though, was the fact that he was totally incapable of operating without a written script. For the sake of spontaneity, I tended to ad-lib most of my part. Mark's verbal presentations most closely resembled those of elementary school book reports.

"Damn," I muttered to myself again, reslotting the slides. "I guess we're stuck with this order."

"They're the way Mark wanted them," Ruthie replied primly, pursing her lips in a way she has when I try to buck P&Q authority. "I'm sure he wouldn't have been at all pleased with you switching them around." Ruthie believes, almost religiously, in the agency's corporate power structure. She salivates at the very sight of an interoffice envelope from the executive floor. Her voice gets breathy and girlish when taking messages for me from any of the senior V.P.'s. If given the slightest encouragement, I'm sure she would sink down and worship at the feet of Phillip Ebert. Poor Ruthie. I guess like most believers, she simply can't understand why I don't share her feelings. And she's particularly wounded by my ongoing skirmishes with Mark Rollings, whom I'm sure she feels is a paragon of corporate virtue.

"You're right," I conceded, thinking how tough it must sometimes be for her to work on my behalf. "I guess I'm just a little nervous this morning."

"Well, you haven't a thing to be worried about," she assured me, switching off the overhead projector and cloaking the slide carousel with a dustcover. Then, obviously thinking that she was imparting news, she confided, "Mr. Rollings is best friends with Dick Byser, the V.P. at Tantamount."

"Really?" I replied on my way up to the stage to check our poster boards. "And just how did you learn that?"

"Mr. Rollings told me!" Ruthie gushed, hurrying up behind me. "He told me we hadn't a thing to worry about on the Merriweather pitch. He said that it didn't matter how bad the creative presentation went . . . he knew we would win, anyway. And he said—"

"Gosh, you two must have had quite a little talk," I said, cutting Ruthie off, furious with her and Mark...and with myself for letting them get to me. "We've been so darn busy the past few months, I'm amazed you've had so much time to chat."

She knew from my tone of voice that she had said something wrong. The room fell silent, except for my rustling with the presentation boards and Ruthie's low, mindless humming. At eight forty-five she left to organize the coffee cart and pastry trays, and I was left to myself with nothing more to do but wait. And think.

Ruthie was wrong. There was plenty to worry about. Forget my encroaching showdown with Mark...and Berry's decision not to sell out. Accounts won on anything other than merit are always a problem. There are only a few lasting maxims on Madison Avenue, and probably the most important one is to never do business with friends. And to think that Mark Rollings was the friend in question...well, it simply spelled trouble.

I flipped through my note cards and considered the morning ahead without enthusiasm. Everything I'd done, each concept and design I'd created, had been with Berry in mind. Without her involvement, without her input and interest, what was the point of going through with the presentation? Mark Rollings saw the whole business as a charade, anyway. An empty exercise with a predetermined outcome.

I heard people coming down the corridor and tried to put on a happy face. Advertising is like any other sales job. You learn to lead with your smile. Except that the group that marched into the conference room that morning was hardly ready to smile back. In fact, one of them—Ruthie, carrying a tray of expensive miniature Danish—was openly weeping.

"What the hell...?" I started to ask, my first reaction one of irritation with Ruthie for spoiling at least twenty dollars in bakery goods. Then I took an inventory of the other expressions. Dick Byser's stony-faced visage. Phillip Ebert's flushed countenance. Mark Rollings's openly horrified look. A feeling of dread rushed through me. "What is it? What's happened?"

There was a long moment of awful silence, interrupted only by Ruthie's sniffing. I looked from face to face again. Then I asked, "Where's Berry?"

It was Phillip who spoke, although his voice was drained of all its usual confidence. "I'm afraid she's dead, Peg," he said brokenly.

"What?" I replied, not really taking it in. "But how? When?"

"Her marketing director found her this morning," Dick Byser reported. "In her office. She . . . she—"

"She hung herself," Mark Rollings broke in, his voice peevish with shock. "With a sample piece of the panty hose material we were going to use to launch the Merriweather hosiery line."

FOUR

THE REST OF THAT DAY was a nightmare—everything seemed to be ultrareal, hard edged, overbright. I felt I could read behind the expressions of shock and dismay that everyone seemed to be wearing. I felt I heard what people said with a kind of supersensitive intensity. For those few hours after the news of Berry's death, I actually believe I was drawing on a sixth sense, an extrasensory ability that mediums and seers purport to have. I've always looked askance at my neighbor Millie Cantwell, who thinks she can communicate with "the other side." That day I changed my mind about such claims. Because suddenly I could see things I'd never seen before. For instance, I knew without any doubt that both Mark Rollings and Dick Byser were lying.

"God, what a tragedy," Dick announced after Phillip had ushered him, Mark and myself into his executive suite. The presentation had been called off. The coffee and pastries had been wheeled into Phillip's inner office, where a "no calls" order had been issued to the executive secretary.

"Such a vibrant woman," Mark declared, selecting a cheese Danish from the doily-ringed platter. "So bright and talented. What a shame...." His heartfelt sentiments petered out as he bit hungrily into his pastry. Dick followed his example, helping himself to a pair of miniature apple turnovers and a cup of steaming-hot coffee.

"Cream?" Mark asked, holding up a little silver pitcher.

"No thanks," Dick replied, reaching for a napkin. "I prefer my coffee black."

And I, I told myself bitterly, prefer my fellow human beings with blood in their veins...rather than ice water. The two men were discussing Berry's death with less feeling than I'd heard them dispense over a football team's recent loss. Only Phillip, who sat in a troubled silence behind his massive chrome-and-glass desk, seemed to be reacting with anything that resembled real emotion.

"So strange," he murmured to himself. "I've known several suicides in my time. Berry just didn't strike me as the type, somehow...."

"Me, either," I announced abruptly, my words coming out in a harsh, dry gulp. I was trying hard not to cry in front of these corporate automatons.

"It goes to show that you just never know about people," Dick mused, licking his fingertips and reaching across the trolley for another Danish.

How could these men eat? I wondered. I felt sick and lightheaded and intensely tuned-in to the room's vibrations. Underneath their superficial protestations of sorrow, I was convinced that Dick and Mark were experiencing something very different than grief: they were feeling relieved.

"That's right," Mark replied. "From the outside, she certainly seemed to have everything to live for. This new relationship with Tantamount was going to make her a multimillionaire. But who can say what she was really feeling? It's obvious, she had her frustrations. Life couldn't be that rewarding for her...physically. Perhaps the idea of guaranteed success was just too much for her. You know, some people don't really *want* to succeed."

I listened in stunned silence to Mark's spiel, my new hypersensitive powers monitoring each intonation of his voice. And you know something? None of it rang true. Mark is not the world's most articulate guy. As I said before, he does best with rehearsed scripts. And somehow, everything he'd just said had the crafted logic and predetermined content of a written speech. I stared at him. He looked so guileless, so perfect, so vapid. And then I glanced over at Dick Byser, that dark-featured, sharp-witted, closed-book kind of a man. And I remembered something Berry had said the night before.

"Dick Byser, for all his faults, is one smart fella.... I just can't believe that Mark is taking him in. Something... something else...must be involved."

What was it? What did these two have going between them? Whatever it was, Berry's death had obviously not adversely affected it. If anything...it had helped. That final thought swept through me like a wave of nausea, and before I could stop myself, I was blurting out, "But Berry had decided *not* to sell to Tantamount."

"What?" Dick gasped, his cool facade shaken. He set down his coffee cup. "Young lady, that's preposterous!"

"It's ridiculous," Mark hastened to assure the room. "The agreement was virtually signed."

"What are you saying, Peg?" Phillip demanded. He looked tired and concerned, not a man to welcome controversy.

"I'm only repeating what she told me last night over dinner," I replied coolly, carefully monitoring the reactions of each of the men in the inner sanctum.

"She was drunk," Mark blurted out.

"How would *you* know?" I demanded, turning on him accusingly.

"I . . . I can't think of any other explanation," Mark got out haltingly. "The idea is just absurd. She must have been drunk. And we all know she drank too much."

"No need for derogatory remarks like that," Dick put in warningly. "I don't mean to question Peg's perceptions . . . or her honesty. But, quite frankly, I just don't believe Berry Merriweather ever made such a statement. Clearly, Peg misheard what she said . . . or, perhaps, misinterpreted what she heard."

"No, I didn't," I shot back, infuriated by Dick's glib tone and dismissing manner. "She was very precise and definite. She had simply decided not to sell."

"That's not true!" Mark cried.

"You're absolutely wrong, young lady," Dick added. "I don't know where you came by this nonsense."

"Let's drop the subject for now," Phillip suggested, slowly massaging his high, patrician forehead. "The fact of the matter is, we'll probably never know what Berry intended to do. She was no doubt a little irrational last night. She did take her life, after all."

"You're right!" Mark replied almost gleefully. He was eager for anything that would keep Merriweather and Tantamount a united entity. "Who knows what she might have said? She was raving."

"That's simply not true," I retorted.

"And that's enough," Phillip declared firmly. "We've other issues to discuss here. Obviously, Berry's death changes the situation between P&Q and Merriweather vis-à-vis Tantamount."

"Yes," Dick Byser confirmed, sighing deeply. "I guess it does. Until the contracts are actually signed—and mind you, that's simply a mere formality—we can't legally agree to bringing the account to you. Or to bringing all our accounts under one roof."

"May I ask," Phillip replied smoothly, "just what obstacles are in the way of signed contracts at this point?"

"Well, only one as far as I know," Dick said. "With Berry...uh, gone...the decision rests with her beneficiary and silent partner. That's her brother, Wes. I understand he's en route now from the West Coast to handle Berry's funeral arrangements. I know for a fact he's for the deal. He made that very clear early on in our discussion."

"I didn't know Wes Merriweather was involved in company business," I asserted, more than a little stunned by the news. Nowhere in my association with Merriweather had his name come up other than as Berry's ruggedly handsome younger brother. As far as I knew, Wes, his wife, Wanda, and their daughter, Star, had very little contact with Berry; they worked as fashion models out of Ford's L.A. office. Blond and beautiful, this family was currently featured in a nationwide print campaign for Cougar's Country Jeans. I know Berry had been ticked off with Wes when she learned he was, as she put it, "peddling his flesh" for one of Merriweather's direct competitors.

"I'm sure this will come as a shock to you, Peg," Mark answered snidely, "but you don't happen to know *everything* there is to know about Merriweather Sportswear."

"This is *not* the time for infighting," Phillip announced sternly, glancing coldly from Mark to myself. "We have reached a critical—and extremely sensitive—juncture in our relationship with Tantamount. Obviously," Phillip continued, leaning toward Dick Byser, "we would very much like to journey forward with you and your company. I don't believe that it is inappropriate to ask what—setting aside the tragic news of this morning—your attitude toward P&Q might be at this point. Can you comment?''

"Yes, I can," Dick replied confidently. "I've a very positive feeling toward your group. As you know, Phillip, Mark and I go back a long way. I was delighted that we were able to work as colleagues these past months, and I've been very impressed by his talents and insights. I've been assured that his staff is equally talented. And as long as I can be confident that he gets all the backup support he needs...well, I see no reason why you can't add Tantamount to your client list."

"That is, of course," Phillip pointed out, "if Wes Merriweather agrees. We all know that Tantamount won't change agencies unless it controls Merriweather Sportswear."

"Of course," Dick answered warmly. "But I hardly see Wes as a sticking point. In fact," he added, glancing at his watch, "I would be very surprised if the contracts weren't signed by the end of this evening."

Oh Lord, I thought, and Berry hardly even cold.

I'M A DEDICATED, and usually late, worker, but I left the office that afternoon a few seconds after five, taking the same elevator as Ruthie down to the lobby.

"Out to celebrate?" she asked me cheerfully.

"Pardon?"

"The account! Tantamount!" she chirped back. "Mark Rollings told me it's gonna be ours for sure. I thought you might be going out to celebrate a job well-done."

I should have realized, of course. Death, I guess especially suicide, doesn't have much of a place in our fast-track business. If it takes longer than a sixty-second spot to explain, it won't get very far on Madison Avenue. The Berry Merriweather tragedy was this morning's news. Already old. I wondered sadly how long Ruthie would keep her name on the Rolodex.

"Enjoy!" Ruthie instructed me cheerfully before pushing her way aggressively through the revolving doors. I followed more slowly, turning north up Madison Avenue and letting myself be carried along in the rush-hour sweep.

In another ten days it would be Christmas. Madison was festooned with lights and decorations, the shop windows bright with displays. At Saint Pat's I followed the crowd west, ending up with thousands of others in front of the massive Christmas tree at Rockefeller Center. A bright, angelic-looking circle of skaters swirled on the ice below. A group of carolers sang "O Holy Night" to the suddenly hushed masses. A woman leaned over her curly haired little girl and kissed her on the forehead. And alone in the festive, happy throng, I found myself crying ... and crying.

Berry's death, of course, set me off. My life, though, kept the jag going. The fact of the matter is, I just can't see a little girl or boy these days without feeling a terribly painful tug at my heart. I want one, you see. Or two. And not just any old one. I want the child of Dante Cursio. My ex-boyfriend. My always friend. The best and worst thing that ever happened to my life.

I decided to walk home. The nearly forty-block walk is a feat I would never have attempted two years ago, pre-Cursio. But, along with a number of other healthful habits—including and perhaps counterbalancing regular intakes of his highly inventive Italian-based cooking—the man got me started walking. And even though *we* had stopped ... my walking hadn't.

I don't remember what it was exactly I was thinking about. I believe I probably *felt* more than thought ... trying to let the facts of Berry's death sink in. I kept going over what I knew of the tragedy. And over it again. Berry. Distraught, disappointed, wrapping a piece of cheap nylon around her neck. *My* Berry, the woman I'd had dinner with the night before. The woman I'd laughed with. God, what we don't know about each other. What we somehow don't see....

Anyway, before I knew it, I was climbing up the front steps of my brownstone apartment on Eighty-sixth Street. Picasso, my insufferably spoiled feline, was obviously pleased by my early homecoming, but only insofar as it meant an earlier dinner. As soon as he had gobbled up his plate of food, he curled up in a fat, contented ball on the couch. Down for the night. I still wasn't thinking straight, I guess. I don't know what was really going through my head. I just kept trying to picture what had happened. I mean, Berry actually taking that piece of nylon. Wrapping it around her neck.

I dialed a number I knew by heart.

"Yeah?" the familiar, rough-grained voice answered.

"Yo, it's me," I said, trying to sound good. Up. Someone you'd want around the rest of your life. Someone you'd kinda want to marry.

"Where you been?" he asked. "I've been trying to get you since late afternoon. Since I . . . heard."

"How'd you hear?" I asked.

"Radio. It's gonna be a big story, babe. You okay?"

"Sure. Yeah. I guess. Can't believe it."

"You know why? Any idea? I mean, you two were close, right?"

"Yeah."

"You're not okay."

"No, I guess not."

"Should I come by?"

Of course, you idiot. "No. You're on duty, right?"

"Well, obviously. But it's kinda quiet. We can just keep talking. Tell me about it, Peg. Tell me what you think. I'm right here. I'll listen."

The world's greatest listener. Well, he was trained to be, after all. Yeah, by the way, the man I love . . . he's a cop. A detective. NYPD. Homicide.

"Okay, you ready?" I asked, collapsing on the couch next to my comatose cat.

"Sure."

"She didn't kill herself, Dante," I told him. At some point between the time I'd dialed his number and that moment, I'd put all the pieces together. "Somebody did it for her."

FIVE

DETECTIVE DANTE CURSIO and I had not met under the most romantic conditions. Two years ago, when my former boss, Ramsey Farnsworth, was murdered, Cursio had been the detective in charge of the investigation. We did not immediately hit it off. I found him dour and suspicious, unsympathetic and painfully blunt. And I thought his uncomfortably accurate insights into my life and problems more than a little distasteful.

During one of our very first interviews he had the nerve to declare my attempt to lead a "normal life"—despite my eccentric upbringing and infamous mother—merely a way of rebelling against Theo. He had the unbridled gall to deem my relationship with a former V.P. at P&Q—Spencer Guilden—a similar act of rebellion.

"In my book, Theodora Goodenough's daughter just is not the girl next door," he'd told me. "You want to play games with yourself, fine. But I know the score."

I despised his arrogance. I deeply resented his intelligence. I formed an instant dislike to the knowing, half-amused way he looked me over. It didn't take me long to realize that I had started to fall in love with him the moment he first walked into my apartment.

The feeling, as they say, was mutual. And for almost a year, we mutually flourished. It was bliss for me; a time filled with pleasure and security, intimacy and fun. And although, for the most part, the man could read me as easily as a crosstown bus map, he managed to miss one particularly important intersection in my character. I've always wanted to be someone's wife and somebody's mother. And the longer I hung out with Cursio, the more strongly I felt about who those somebodies should be. Unfortunately, Cursio had gone that route before. And that very unpleasant journey had ended up in divorce and the loss of his daughter when his former wife remarried and settled in England.

"Live with me or I'll come live with you," Cursio had told me. "We'll be together and that's what matters. I just can't go through this marriage business again. I've seen too many divorced cops in my time. Once is enough for me, Peg."

And no amount of persuading, cajoling or, yes, downright begging, would change his mind. And I, damn it, was not about to change mine. So that was it. Sort of. We talked a lot on the phone and saw each other for dinner from time to time. But we'd reached a stalemate, and slowly the bright, pure fire was dying. I couldn't let him sleep over anymore, because I'd start to cry and ruin things. I began to force myself to see other men, none of them worth a damn...though of course I pretended otherwise to Dante. And I still automatically turned to him in times of need.

"Peg, sweetheart, I think you're just not facing facts," Cursio replied gently when I told him I thought Berry had been murdered. "She was a good friend, a trusted colleague. It's natural for you to go through a certain amount of denial."

"Bull," I retorted, angered at the singsong "talk her down" tone he was taking. "You're not listening to me, Dante. *Now hear this,* okay? Berry had no reason in the world to kill herself. She was doing well financially. She had decided against the one thing that was really bothering her—selling her business. Maybe she didn't have much of a social life, but then she'd never really had one. She was one of those people who lived for her work. And Merriweather Sportswear has never been in better shape."

"Says who?" Cursio asked.

I could hear his ratty leather swivel chair creak as he leaned back. And I could just as easily sense his mind click into action.

"Berry, that's who," I assured him. "She told me so last night, a couple of times. She didn't *need* to sell the company. She had no reason to."

"So then why'd she even consider the offer?" he demanded.

"I don't know," I admitted. "I suppose it came with a pretty nice price tag."

"Doesn't make sense," Cursio muttered. "I mean, I'm not one of your hotshot M.B.A.'s, Peg, but I've never heard of a takeover action that didn't involve some sort of need on the part of the smaller company. Most lean, healthy businesses stay independent. It's the overextended ones that attract the sharks. They buy 'em, strip 'em down, turn a nice profit for the shareholders.''

"Well, that wasn't the case with Merriweather," I informed Cursio rather haughtily. "The company is in good shape. Berry made that very clear."

"Sounds like she went out of her way to make you believe it, anyway," Cursio observed.

"Nonsense," I snapped. "Berry was the most honest person I've ever met. She was incapable of lying. Especially to me."

"Okay." Cursio sighed. "So then why don't you tell me how your honest, financially secure, absolutely content little friend wound up with a nylon noose around her neck?"

"Someone put it there," I told him. "To make it *look* like suicide, don't you see?"

"Honestly, Peg!" Cursio burst out. "You're being totally irrational about this. Here's the scenario. A 250-pound woman is found hanging in her own office. The homemade nylon noose had been strung around an old, solid iron cross beam that someone had exposed by pushing up soundproof squares from a dropped ceiling. The chair had been pushed clear. There was no evidence of a struggle. The whole office was locked up tight from the inside. Sweetie, face it—only Mr. America would have been able to string up that kind of poundage . . . or the victim. Yes, it was murder, Peg, but she did it to herself."

"No," I said. "No. It's just all wrong. What if two people had done it, then it would have been possible, right?"

"Maybe," Cursio agreed. "But that's not what happened. Your friend committed suicide. It's hard for you to accept right now, but eventually you'll have to, Peg."

"Will there be an autopsy?" I demanded.

"I'd guess so," Cursio replied. "Standard procedure with suicide, as far as I know, unless the family objects."

"I want the report," I told him. "I want you to get me the autopsy findings."

"Forget it," Cursio retorted. "This isn't a police case, you know. No way can I get my hands on a report like that. No way.

You're just going to have to face this thing like a grown-up, Peg."

"Where'd they take her?" I asked.

"No," Cursio replied emphatically. "You're not going to go after it yourself, do you hear me?"

"She's at the morgue, right, Dante?" I asked again. "Come on, it's the least you can tell me."

"Absolutely not," Cursio was almost shouting. "I will not have you hauled in here on a B and E, hear me? Drop the idea immediately."

"I can find out on my own easily enough," I mused aloud. "I'll just contact her brother, Wes."

"You're not to do that, Peg," Cursio replied warningly. "I forbid it."

"You haven't the right, dear heart," I purred. "Sorry to bother you. Talk to you soon." And with that, I hung up.

It took less than two minutes. I picked up on the fourth ring.

"Yes?" I answered laconically.

"I'll do it," he said, his wonderfully deep voice plumbing icy new depths. "I'll let you know as soon as I have something." Before slamming down the phone, he added with a sigh, "Shit, you're something."

I guess I'm sort of hard up these days, but I took that last bit as a compliment.

BERRY'S MEMORIAL SERVICE was held in the auditorium of the Fashion Institute of Technology. The grim, drafty room was filled with the most colorful names on Seventh Avenue, including Ralph Lauren, Bill Blass, the Kleins and Donna Karan, as well as an impressive smattering of the European fashion nobility. Although Berry's middle-American designs were hardly couture, she had through the years developed close personal ties with the more glittery side of Seventh Street.

"Beryl will be missed," the owner of a major Milanese fabric company intoned, "as much for her good humor...as her good, gentle nature. Cheerful, caring..."

My mind started to wander as the well-meaning, jowly Italian prattled on. As so often happens at memorial services, the person being honored and praised seemed to bear little resemblance to the person I knew. Berry...gentle? Come on, now.

She was sharp-tongued, acerbic, tough, ironic, caustic, ornery, straightforward, demanding. At least that was the Berry I had known. But the auditorium was standing room only that afternoon. Obviously, Berry had been a lot of things to a lot of different people. And to one of them, perhaps...she had been too much.

As subtly as possible, I glanced around me. I had taken a seat next to Toni Frankel, Merriweather's marketing director, the unlucky soul who had found Berry's body three mornings ago. Berry had been extremely selective about all her staff, almost obsessively so about the executive tier. They had to be bright, aggressive, personable, ambitious—and female. Toni was all these things. Her long, successful career in retail fashion would put her somewhere in her early fifties; an age that her aggressively youthful style tried its best to deny. I found it impossible to guess what color her hair had been originally. In the months I'd known her, it had been cut, tinted and styled at least as many times. Her clothing could change radically from day to day, as well—from tight-fitting jeans and jacket to boxy, conservative suit ensembles. Although Toni always looked beautifully turned out—nails and lipstick faultless—there was an undercurrent of unrest and unhappiness to her physical presence that had always bothered me. She was, however, one of the most professional marketing people I'd ever dealt with. Despite having little in common personally, we'd developed a very good business relationship. I respected her and so, I knew, had Berry.

"I'd put Toni Frankel at the top of any list," Berry had declared at a meeting with P&Q to decide who should be privy to Merriweather's brand-labeling ideas.

"You realize how confidential this information is," Phillip had commented, trying to convince Berry to keep the circle limited to him, Dick Byser, Mark Rollings and me. "If any word of our plans were leaked to your competitors, well..."

"Read my lips, Phil," Berry had retorted, "I want Toni's input. She has more retail fashion experience than your whole staff put together. She's fast and smart...and I'd trust her with my life."

So Toni had been put on the planning committee, along with Brigitte Sonesson, Berry's top designer, and the company's sales manager, Sara Griffin. I noticed the two of them sitting together a few aisles up. Brigitte, a big-boned, earth-mother blonde, whose emotions always ran to extremes, was weeping openly. Tall, painfully thin Sara was slumped next to her, thick wings of red hair curtaining her face. Of Berry's executive staff, I knew Sara the least. I think that had as much to do with her ingrown, quiet manner as with the fact that she spent a good part of the year on the road, selling. She had managed to attend only one of the planning sessions, and even then had said maybe two words. I'd once mentioned to Berry that Sara's position as sales manager had struck me as being at odds with her character.

"Yeah?" Berry had laughed. "Well, you should hear her pitch sometime. She's really something else. It's the same syndrome as being an actress, I think. She's kind of faceless, you know, until she goes on a call... and then she could sell string bikinis to a cloistered convent."

But I'd never seen that side of Sara. And it was with the familiar, tight-lipped, dour expression that she greeted Toni and me after the service. Close friends and relatives had been invited to stay on for soft drinks and wine, which were being dispensed from a table that had been set up on the stage. I noticed that Dick Byser was already up there, pouring himself a Coke. He chugged the stuff down as if it were a much-needed whiskey before he greeted a tall, blond male with a megawatt smile and the tanned, handsome good looks of a television star.

"You never would have guessed," Brigitte said, following my gaze across the room to Wes Merriweather, "that Wes and Berry were brother and sister. It's awful hard to believe that they emerged out of the same gene pool." Brigitte, Sara, Toni and I stood together in a little clique staring at the two men. In the manner of one accustomed to being gawked at, Wes glanced over, smiled briefly, then turned his attention back to Dick. It was in the smile that I saw—despite all the obvious dissimilarities—the undeniable fact that this was Berry's brother. Wes. The high school football star. The mother's favorite. The nationally known model. And now the president and C.E.O. of Merriweather Sportswear. A man who happened to hold my future in his finely tapered hands.

Despite the fact that it was the third week of December—and a chilly, windy day to boot—Wes Merriweather was wearing a cream-colored linen suit and a lovely, pastel-colored printed ascot that was tucked casually into the whitest of silk shirts. Yes, he looked a dandy...but in a way that somehow enhanced, rather than detracted from, his masculinity. Without trying to, perhaps without meaning to, he exuded sex appeal. Even at this somber occasion, a part of him advertised satisfaction guaranteed. His kind of blatant sexuality was not something I usually responded to, yet I found myself having a hard time looking elsewhere.

"Not bad, huh?" Toni murmured, noticing my interest.

"I've seen him somewhere before," I replied, glancing around the group. Brigitte was smirking, Sara was staring at the dust-covered floor, and Toni nodded knowingly.

"I'm sure you have," she said. "His bod is currently flaunting Cougar's Country Jeans in just about every magazine in the country."

"No, I mean I've seen him somewhere before in person," I replied. "Recently, too...."

"I doubt it," Brigitte replied. "He and wifey and baby face over there have been skiing in Vail for the past three weeks. I had a hell of a time getting through to him about Berry."

A lovely blond woman and a dazzlingly beautiful teenager had joined Wes and Dick. Wanda Merriweather, though in her late thirties, had the kind of beauty that would last a lifetime: high cheekbones, luminous skin, deep hazel eyes, honey-colored hair and the lithe, graceful body of a ballerina. Yet, despite her loveliness, it was her daughter who stole the show.

Star was aptly named. She seemed otherworldly, lighted from within, a pale, alien thing who naturally drew people to her. Her skin was translucent, her mouth a miracle of curving color and unassailable innocence. Her eyes had a slightly Oriental cast, accentuated by the unexpected dark arch of her brows. She was slim, quietly dressed in a pleated wool skirt and cardigan, knee socks and loafers. Normal enough. Yet somehow she exuded an air of exoticism and mystery. She stood between her parents, but she seemed oddly detached from them, clearly not listening to the conversation that was taking place among the adults.

Suddenly, she turned in our direction. She looked at me, yet through me. And in that moment I felt a shudder of recognition. No, premonition. I don't believe in that kind of thing, as I've said before. And yet, I can't deny it. When those luminous, almond-shaped eyes met mine, when I stared back into that dark, not-quite-focused gaze . . . I knew that somehow or other I was looking straight into my future.

SIX

"HE WAS ACTUALLY *LAUGHING*—did you see that?" Brigitte cried when the four of us had reached the sidewalk. We'd lingered another fifteen minutes or so at the reception, long enough to feel our social duties properly dispensed with, and then had agreed to head elsewhere for a cup of coffee... and a chance to vent our various feelings about Berry's memorial service.

"People do that," Toni said, trying to calm her. "It's a way of relieving tension. It doesn't necessarily mean he doesn't care."

"Did you see him?" Brigitte asked, turning to me and ignoring what I considered a perfectly sensible explanation on Toni's part. "He was hardly able to control himself, he was laughing so hard. I wouldn't be surprised if he and that Dick Byser had been telling dirty jokes to each other."

It *had* been a rather alarming sight. Even I—not known for always observing the proprieties—had been embarrassed by it. Wes Merriweather, bent nearly double, chortling with glee. It had been more than a bit unsettling. Not to mention out of place. I was glad, frankly, that we'd escaped that cold, dreary room.

The wind that whipped down Seventh Avenue was hardly any warmer, but at least we were back in the land of the living. We took a taxi downtown, through streets jammed with Christmas shoppers and tourists in from the suburbs for the day. We waited fifteen minutes to get a table at Café Reggio. And we'd barely gotten our orders of cappuccino and espresso when Brigitte repeated, "I couldn't believe it! He was laughing... right there in the middle of the room! I've always known he was selfish and insensitive," she went on, "but that was downright... insulting!"

"Forget it, Brig," Toni advised her. "If you start letting him get to you at this point, what's gonna happen when we all have to start working together in the office?"

"Wes? Work?" Brigitte retorted, her full lips tightening into a nasty smile. "He doesn't know the meaning of the word."

"I, uh, take it . . . you've all met Wes Merriweather before?" I inserted quickly, hoping to diffuse the ugly atmosphere Brigitte's mood was building. "I was under the impression that he and his family lived in California . . . and didn't get to New York very often," I added brightly.

"They used to live here," Toni answered, sipping on her mug of mocha cappuccino, "until, I guess, about a year ago. They moved to L.A. about the same time Berry started talking to Tantamount Enterprises about the buy-out."

"I was kind of surprised," I added, "to learn he was a silent partner of Berry's. When he lived here, did he help her run the business?"

"Wes Merriweather wouldn't know how to run a toaster oven," Brigitte replied bitingly. "I hardly think he contributed much to the management of the company."

"That's what you *think*," Toni pointed out. "But you don't really know. None of us actually know what went on between Berry and Wes." I think as much for the other women's benefit as for mine, Toni added, "They were brother and sister, after all. Ties existed between them, deep-rooted ones, that we have no way of fathoming. Probably just his presence, his being there when she needed someone, was a comfort to her."

I was taken aback both by Brigitte's angry perspective and Toni's sympathetic one. I've always felt that Toni and Sara have a hard edge to them, a wariness that keeps me from feeling at ease in their presence. I have the definite impression that no matter how long or closely I work with Toni and Sara, my relationship with them will never break through to real friendship. From Brigitte, though, I've always felt a warmth and readiness for further intimacy. Usually so generous and open-minded, her obvious hatred of Wes came as a surprise.

Milky-skinned, azure-eyed, Brigitte looks like a Swedish blonde straight out of central casting. Though she was born and raised in Brooklyn, her voice has the soft lilt of a native Scandinavian . . . and her gentle, caring manner a decidedly un-New York genuineness. The mother of two boys—now in their teens—Brigitte and her accountant husband have managed to survive all the standard hazards of a two-income urban family. They're still together after nearly twenty years of marriage and, from all appearances, thriving. From what I gather, they've established quite a comfortable, secure nest in a renovated brownstone in Brooklyn Heights. Brigitte told me once, rather proudly, that she lives less than two blocks from the house where she was born.

"She seems hideously happy," Berry had once commented, "with her snug little world. I'd be stark raving mad with boredom. Wouldn't you?" At the time I'd somehow sidestepped Berry's question, but the fact of the matter is, I'd be delighted to have had Brigitte's life. My childhood was one long trek behind my restless, ever-experimenting mother. We never lived in one place for more than nine months. No sooner would Theo settle into some much-heralded villa on the outskirts of a little Italian hill town, than she'd declare the view too intimidating for her to work. And off we'd go again. To Copenhagen. Chicago. Cap d'Antibes. Is it any wonder that any reasonably happy, sedentary life seemed to me absolute bliss?

"Toni's right," Sara told Brigitte with a penetrating look. "Who really knows what goes on between two people? I think it's best for all of us not to judge Wes too quickly. And I think we should give him plenty of leeway. Chances are he's not going to show any more interest in Merriweather this time out than last. And we can go on as before."

"How can you say that?" Brigitte demanded, her voice tight with emotion. "How can anything be 'as before'? Berry was the life and soul of Merriweather. With her gone . . . with Wes in charge . . . I just don't know if . . ." Brigitte looked anxiously around the table. The events of the past few days had left their mark on her usually placid features. Tension creased her forehead and dragged down the corners of her mouth. And her pale blue eyes had the flat gleam of a frozen pond. It occurred to me that something other than Berry's death was weighing on her mind. Her shoulders slumped under the pressure of it.

"Pull yourself together, Brig," Toni cut in, her sharp tone surprising me. "We need to close ranks now. We all have to pull together. It's essential that we show Wes and Dick Byser and his people that we know what we're doing. We only get one chance to prove ourselves, to continue on with what Berry started. We're the company now—don't you see? It's up to us." Toni, ever the efficient and practical one, glanced sternly from Sara to Brigitte and then to me.

I felt a little uncomfortable under the penetrating force of that gaze. Although a woman and a close friend of Berry's, I had never really been one of *them*. I was a newcomer, an outsider. From time to time I'd even felt that they—perhaps primarily Toni—resented my special relationship with Berry. Sara and Toni had been with Berry for nearly ten years, Brigitte for eight. They had helped build the company to what it was today. They had lives and dreams invested in Merriweather Sportswear. For me, especially now without Berry, it was just another account. I looked away, fiddling with my coffee spoon, thinking of the best way to make a graceful exit and leave these women to carry on the discussion in private.

And then, as if reading my thoughts, Brigitte said, "We consider you one of us, Peg. Berry made it clear how much she respected and trusted you. In the end, I think she confided more in you than ... anyone else."

It wasn't said in a cutting way, yet I felt a deeper meaning in Brigitte's words. I looked across the table at her. She was smiling in that broad, all-approving way that made one want to confess one's most hidden feelings.

"Yes, we did have some long talks," I agreed. "Well, you all know how much Berry loved to talk."

"You had dinner with her the night she died, didn't you?" Toni demanded.

"Yes, I did, actually," I replied. "It wasn't planned or anything. I dropped in on her at the office with some last minute questions before the account pitch. And we got talking ... and went out from there."

"Was she..." Sara hesitated a second, then went on, "was she depressed, do you think? Did she say anything that would lead you to think she was going to, well, you know..."

"No," I answered. "Not really."

"You don't sound so sure," Toni observed sharply.

"Well, there was one thing...." I admitted, looking around at the group. "Berry told me that she had decided not to sell out to Tantamount, after all."

Instantly, I knew from their reactions—or lack of them—that they already knew this. Then I realized that the entire preceding conversation, in fact, probably the whole reason for asking me out for coffee in the first place, was to find out if I knew it, too.

"I'm stunned," Toni answered for the group.

Had this response been rehearsed? I wondered. Although Brigitte and Sara had both put on patently false-looking expressions of surprise, Toni almost managed to sound convincing.

"Did she tell you why, by any chance?"

"Not in so many words," I said. Why were they playing dumb? I wondered. What in the world could they gain by it? Or lose by admitting they knew this all along? "She did imply that Tantamount was putting pressure on her to, uh, replace some of her key people... with some of theirs." I glanced around the table at their composed faces. So this wasn't news to them, either.

"That's not very encouraging," Brigitte murmured, looking down into her empty mug. "I guess there's little doubt who those 'key' people might be."

"Don't jump to conclusions," Toni advised her. "It's important that we don't look like we're running scared. As I said before, this is our chance to show them we can carry on for Berry." Then she concluded urgently, "This is our *only* chance."

Suddenly I realized that all of Toni's admonitions about the three of them proving their worth were being uttered for my benefit. What was it that they hoped I'd do with the information? I wondered. Did they think I'd go running back to Mark, who would then pass on to Dick that Merriweather's middle management was ready and willing to take over the company? I glanced from face to face: Toni's hard, unflinching gaze; Brigitte's look of earnest, almost maternal concern; Sara's uneasy stare. I was sure that each one of them wanted to help head Merriweather; but each for her own and very different reasons.

Toni was the oldest of the group. Though attractive in her ever-changing way, it was becoming more obvious with each passing day that she was edging into the far side of middle age. Even rumored plastic surgery hadn't been able to mask the drooping chin and puckering neckline. I'd heard from someone that she lived with her aging mother in a condo-apartment in Queens. As Berry used to, she worked endlessly long hours, staying until eight or nine at night, coming in early enough to open the offices. It had been Toni, after all, who'd found Berry at a little after seven in the morning. The impression I had was that she was a tough, lonely, disappointed woman.

And talk about lonely... Sara epitomized the word. Add shy, defensive, moody and secretive to that character description for good measure. She lived alone in a walk-up not far from Café Reggio, on MacDougal. No, not quite alone; Berry had told me once that Sara had six purebred Persian cats. Long strands of exotic-colored cat hair frequently showed up on Sara's less than perfectly pressed jumpers and slacks. Hardly a front-runner for a top management job, one would think, and yet I know Berry had a lot of faith in her.

"In sales, only one thing counts," Berry had told me. "Results. And the bottom line speaks more eloquently for Sara's finer qualities than any Shakespearean sonnet could."

And finally, there was Brigitte. Certainly less desperate than the other two. Definitely more fulfilled in her personal life. Though clearly she was capable of anger and, especially recently, I'd sensed a growing need for recognition on her part. Berry automatically got the credit for every design that Merriweather produced, but, in fact, half the fall line had been originated by Brigitte.

"Oh, you like that one?" she'd asked me pointedly a month or so ago when I showed up at the offices in a rust-colored corduroy Merriweather pantsuit. "It's mine, you know. I mean, I designed it. *Vogue* called it 'the best example of Merriweather's chic new country look' in the December issue." There was pride in her voice that day...and also an undercurrent of anger. I remembered that put-upon feeling from the last few months that I'd worked under Ramsey Farnsworth. There is nothing more demeaning and frustrating than someone else taking credit for your creativity.

Toni, Sara, Brigitte. Each, quite obviously, hoping to make the most out of Berry's tragic demise. Each, in her own way, hardworking and deserving. And each, for whatever reason, holding back on me. Was it simply a practical business decision to pretend they didn't know Berry had decided to pull out of the Tantamount deal? The fact of the matter was, each had a lot more to gain long term if the company was sold...than if it wasn't.

And more to the point, it dawned on me at last as I glanced again around the table, although the stakes were now higher, each also had a lot more to gain with Berry dead.

SEVEN

THERE WERE OTHERS who stood to profit from the death of Berry Merriweather. On Sunday evening, after a long, frustrating day of last minute Christmas shopping in overcrowded department stores, I sat down with a pencil and notepad and drew up a list. With Picasso curled up on my lap to bowling-ball size—and weighing at least twice as much as one—I looked down at the blank page in my hand and tried to imagine the worst about everyone I knew.

Each of us has a kernel of evil hidden in our character. Each of us has an impatient, ambitious, dissatisfied side. But few of us allow it to grow out of control, blotting out the light of generosity and common sense, to take over the better part of our hearts. But it can happen. In people you love. Within yourself. I started to consider the various possibilities....

Dick Byser. V.P. of Tantamount, on their corporate acquisitions team, only forty-two or forty-three years old and already nearing the top of his profession. Sharp, without looking too eager. Smooth, without seeming overly manipulative. Dick is the kind of man I wouldn't mind having for a boss. He's decisive and demanding, yet he knows his stuff. The Merriweather deal could very well cinch his career with Tantamount. And the next rung up the ladder... Who knows? He's well educated, well connected.... The presidency of one of Tantamount's divisions is not out of the question. Then, unexpectedly, the deal sours. The head of Merriweather announces she's backing out. If indeed Berry had told Dick about her decision—which I wasn't sure she had—just think how much this could have damaged Dick's credibility in Tantamount's eyes! He'd be furious. Livid. Perhaps even murderous...?

Then there's Mark Rollings. A yes-man. A sycophant. A middle manager headed nowhere but sideways. Uninspired and uninspiring, Mark has gotten by at P&Q for at least fifteen years by not getting in anybody's way. He has an uncanny

ability to step out of the line of fire. He sniffs out controversy...and slinks off in the other direction. He's the same age
as Dick Byser, but not half as smart...or as successful. Mark's
had the same job—account supervisor—for nearly ten years.
Most of the other senior account people make V.P. a year or
two into their tour of duty. But Mark hasn't. What a dim picture. What a mediocre future!

And then out of the blue comes Dick—old frat brother—su-
perachiever and Tantamount honcho. Tantamount, an account the agency's been hyperventilating over for years. What
a piece of luck for Mark! Suddenly his star is on the rise. He's
lunching out weekly with Phillip Ebert. He's headed for V.P.
at last...and probably higher. And then the deal falters. This
Merriweather woman decides to back out. How maddening! If
not for her, the takeover would have gone ahead—and Mark
would have gotten ahead. If he knew, he must have felt like
killing himself. Or did he turn his frustrations on somebody
else...?

Then, of course, there's the question of Dick, quite a savvy
guy, pretending to think Mark Rollings is a marketing genius.
Who's going to deny a potential major client its little whims?
Still, I've heard Phillip Ebert privately refer to Mark in less-
promising times as "that wimp." The entire creative department calls him, and frequently to his face, "cipher." What was
going on between Dick and Mark? I wondered. Was it really
just an old college bond...or were more sinister forces at work?
Blackmail, maybe? Was Dick's sponsorship of Mark by way of
some sort of payoff? Perhaps Berry stumbled onto the
scheme...and one of them decided she had to be shut up.
Permanently.

I yawned and scratched Picasso's slightly balding head. Then
I wrote down two more names. Wes and Wanda Merriweather. I yawned again, trying to imagine their lives, their expectations, their motivations. A few minutes later I shook
myself awake.

"C'mon, dummy," I told Picasso, gently nudging him off
my lap. "Some of us are heading into bed." He bounded off
me, landing on the floor with such a resounding thump that my
neighbors below no doubt thought the roof was about to cave
in. A sweet, elderly couple, the Lefkons have taken me aside on

several occasions and expressed concern over my tendency to move heavy things at odd times during the day and night.

"Surely some nice young man could lend you a hand?" Mrs. Lefkon has suggested. I know neither believes me when I tell them that the reverberating thuds they hear overhead are actually caused by a cat disembarking from various pieces of furniture.

Picasso stretched lengthily, then tiptoed into the bedroom. I was about to follow when I glanced down at the list again. On impulse, I picked up the pencil and quickly made a final note. Silly, I knew. Ridiculous, I thought. But something made me add one last name to the list: Star.

I WAS TO GAIN more insight into the lives of the surviving Merriweathers the very next day. At nine-thirty, just as I was trying to warm my system up to the idea of a new week with the bribe of a second cup of coffee, my intercom buzzed.

"Mr. Rollings on line four," Ruthie confided breathlessly.

"Tell him I'm not in yet," I replied, deciding it was too damn early on Monday morning to deal with ciphers. "I'll call him back later."

"But ... but he says it's important," Ruthie protested. "There's some sort of emergency meeting about to start in the tenth-floor conference room."

"Damn," I muttered, picking up my phone.

"Peg! Thank God you're in early for once!" Mark cried, his voice cracking like an adolescent's from nervousness or excitement. With Mark, it's often hard to tell which. "Wes and Wanda Merriweather are here. They want to see the whole group right away. In the tenth-floor conference room. *Pronto.*"

"Whoa," I said, realizing he was about to hang up on me. "What's all this about? An agency review? Should I bring the presentation materials with me?"

"I don't know!" Mark snapped peevishly. "I can't get through to Dick ... and Phillip's in London for the international board meeting. I ... I have absolutely no idea what they want. Please just *hurry*."

Our tenth-floor conference room can comfortably seat around thirty people. The oval teak table was built in proportions befitting King Arthur's crowd. The black leather swivel chairs, recessed ceiling and track lighting lend the room a portentous aura. Nubbly, inch-thick crimson carpet and Motherwell lithographs provide the requisite corporate finish. This is where the executive board holds its weekly meetings. This is the agency's holy of holies.

"And here's my better half...." I could hear the deep bass as soon as I got off the elevator. The famous Merriweather voice. I followed it to the end of the corridor as it went on, "Ain't she a peach? And this is our little baby, Star. Say hello to everybody, Star, honey."

I stepped into the room...and into the middle of an awkward silence. Four people from P&Q were assembled at one end of the table, with notepads and pencils in front of them. Clustered around Mark Rollings were Felice Clay, our media director, Peter Hendrick from the promotion department, and Larry Milner, one of my favorite writers. At the other end of the table—nearly ten feet away—sat the Merriweather family. Wes was seated at the foot of the table, his beautiful womenfolk on either side. At that moment everyone's gaze seemed to be fastened on Star, who, despite her father's admonition, sat staring in front of her at nothing in particular, her lovely, pouting lips pressed unhappily together.

"Hon?" Wanda said, reaching across the table and nudging Star's shoulder. "Say hi to these people, okay? We're all going to be working closely together from now on."

A collective, silent sigh of relief was released at the P&Q end of the table. Mark glanced at me and smiled weakly. I nodded back. So we'd be working closely together. At least that indicated they intended to stay. I took a seat next to Larry.

"And this is Peg Goodenough," Mark announced, his high voice quavering. "She's been working with...uh, your people, developing the new campaign. We were all ready to present it the day that...that... Well, anyway, as soon as you'd like to see what we've done, just let us know."

I felt like leaping across the table and strangling the man, or, perhaps more humiliating for Mark, mussing the blown-dry hair he'd carefully trained over his bald spot. In any case, I wanted to scream. What a botched way of telling a new client that there are months of wonderfully creative work at their disposal! And how asinine to act as though the mention of Berry's name was forbidden. I glared at Mark, then turning on my brightest smile, leaned down the table and said, "Mark forgot to mention that I'm the creative director for your account. With a lot of input from Berry, I think we've come up with a truly innovative way to launch Merriweather's new product lines. And I think—"

"Now honey—" Wes cut me dead in midsentence, "—I'm sure you did a real nice job. But like I was saying to Mark and the group here before you came in…it's a whole new ball game now. From this moment on, you're gonna have to think of Merriweather Sportswear as being under new management." Wes turned his megawatt smile on me and, nodding first to Wanda, then Star, added, "And we're it."

"Well, that's just great," Mark warbled, flashing his expensive capping job at the Merriweathers. "We're all—and I know I speak for upper management when I say this—just delighted to have you at the helm. We want you to think of all of us as part of your company. We're behind you day and night. An extensive support system..."

I'd heard Phillip Ebert deliver this welcoming-in speech dozens of times. And somehow he'd always managed to make the unctuous-sounding sentiments seem boyishly heartfelt. The same words from Mark's lips rang with insincerity. I felt Larry squirming next to me and glanced cautiously down the table to see if our newest clients were exhibiting any signs of nausea. But Wes and Wanda beamed back at us with the faked expressions of the high-priced models they were. Star remained lost in her own thoughts, her gaze trained blankly over my right shoulder.

"In other words," Mark said, beginning to wind down, "think of us as your refuge. Your home away from home."

Your doormat, I concluded for myself.

"Well, now, that's real generous of you all," Wes replied, grinning warmly.

His teeth—dazzling white against the rugged tan of his face— were worthy of a network toothpaste campaign. I could easily see why art directors cast him. Although exceptionally handsome, he generated a certain modesty, a kind of "aw shucks, who me?" aura that didn't alienate your average-looking con-

sumer. Housewives would fantasize about him as a lover...
while their husbands imagined him a friend. He turned his
smile on me suddenly, and I felt the full force of its impact. My
limbs felt airy, my skin tingly, my lips soft and ready. I tried to
inhale deeply to get my bearings, but my breath escaped me in
quick, ragged gasps. Damn the man, I thought, glancing away.

I frowned purposefully at my notepad, looked up again and
asked in a level tone, "So, when and how do we start? I'd love
the opportunity to show you our work to date. I think it will
give you a good sense of where we're coming from—and where
we might go together from here. If you like, I'll run down to my
office and—"

"Now, sweet thing, you just listen to me for a sec, okay?"
Wes cut in, his voice and eyes full of an intimacy that made me
flush with embarrassment. I glanced quickly at Wanda, who
seemed oblivious to her husband's inviting tone. Star remained locked in her own closed world. "I—or should I say
we—are not interested in whatever damn fool thing you put
together for Berry. We have our own ideas, understand? We
have a brand-new agenda."

My blush deepened to burn as I returned Wes's faintly
amused, definitely provocative grin with an outraged glare. The
man's quasi-cracker-barrel charm had suddenly lost all of its
appeal. Mark, sensing my anger, broke in before I could respond.

"Why, of course you have your own ideas! Of course you
have your own needs. Why don't you, well...why not tell us
exactly what you have in mind? We'd love to hear...."

"Well, we've just been waiting for someone to ask," Wanda
answered laconically, flicking her honey-colored hair off her
shoulders with an irritated shake of the head. "Though,
frankly, I'd think it might be obvious." She smiled toothily
down the table at us, the perfect all-American cookie-cutter
wife and mother. Despite her whiny tone, Wanda managed to
come across as a contemporary June Cleaver. At the same time,
she generated all the intelligence and charm of the cardboard
characters she stood for. I had absolutely no idea what she was
really thinking...or what she might want.

"Uh ... I'm afraid you're going to have to spell it out a little more clearly for us," Mark interjected sweetly, adding with an encouraging smile, "if you don't mind?"

"We feel," Wes responded for his wife, letting his voice drop a few authoritative tones, "that what Merriweather Sportswear needs desperately right now is a unifying theme. A character. A constant, recognizable look that consumers will immediately identify with the line. Whether it's our standard ladies' leisure wear ... or the new brand lines of hosiery, shoes or lingerie. We need *something*," Wes began, underscoring the word by lowering his voice a few more decibels, "to bring the whole kit and caboodle together."

I looked from Wes to Wanda, then back to Wes again. Suddenly, I had it all worked out. "Let me guess," I said. "You want Wanda to be that 'unifying' force, right?" Some of the worst advertising the world has been forced to witness was created by clients insisting they be in their own commercials. Even a professional model like Wanda couldn't counterbalance the inherent hokeyness of the idea. I thought longingly back on the lively, informed conversations Berry and I used to have about creative strategies and marketing positions. Obviously Wes was from a very different school ... and hardly a postgraduate one.

And then for a few brief seconds, I thought that I'd somehow misread the situation, because Wes said, "Heck no, folks. It wasn't Wanda we were thinking of."

"Me?" Wanda laughed throatily. "Oh, no, hon. Sweet of you to suggest it, though. But I know my limits. No, you see, we were thinking of..."

"Star," Wes finished for her, smiling around the table, his eyes falling at last on his daughter. "Star will be the new Merriweather model. Our spokesperson. Our emblem. Our...Star."

"But she's just a ..." I started to say "baby" before Mark cut me off.

"She's perfect!" he cried, beaming down the table at the silent, glassy-eyed girl. Slim and tall for her age, which couldn't be any more than fifteen or sixteen, Star's face had not yet ripened into full maturity. Delicate bones lay beneath translucent skin waiting to draw cheeks and nose, jawline and forehead into what would undoubtedly be the lovely proportions of womanhood. For now, though, her face was a bud: all expectancy, all promise, all innocence.

I'd seen what the professional modeling world would do to a face like that—the layers of foundation makeup and mascara, the hours of primping and styling—to turn it into an adult facsimile. Makeup artists and photographers often prefer working with extremely young models because they are more pliant, less formed. Their faces, like Star's, are clean palates on which to paint a nation's vision of beauty...all individual character and spirit sculpted away.

"Star," Wes prompted her. "Star, honey, say something, will you?"

"Star, sweetie," Wanda chimed in when their only child refused to budge. "Wouldn't you like to say something to these nice people? Wouldn't you, hon?"

The almond-shaped eyes flickered briefly, then settled with a focused urgency on Mark.

"Yes, Star?" Mark asked, leaning toward her, his smile at full wattage. "Yes?"

"Where's the bathroom, please?" Star murmured under her breath. "I gotta pee."

EIGHT

"I DON'T LIKE IT at all, Mark," I announced when we'd regrouped in my office later that morning after the Merriweathers' departure. Larry and Peter lounged in the swivel chairs facing my desk, while Mark paced the sunny, cluttered room. Already late for another meeting, Felice had begged off what she called "the Merriweather postmortem." But as far as I was concerned, the Star issue was hardly a dead one yet. To a person, we all hated the idea of casting a child as the signature model for a middle-American line of women's wear. Though, of course, I wasn't including Mark Rollings in the category of person.

"I beg to differ," Mark replied, digging his hands deeply into the subtly striped pockets of his suit. "I think it's an excellent notion."

"In what possible way?" I demanded. "Every shred of market research we've compiled supports the fact that Merriweather clothes are purchased primarily by overweight women, thirty and older. Star gives off totally the wrong signals to that market segment. And you know it. You *know* it's all wrong! I can't believe you didn't have the guts to say so!"

"Calm thyself," Larry instructed me gently. Balding and handsome in a portly, rather British manner, Larry Milner is not only a top-notch copy writer, he's also a reasonable, mediating force in the creative department. "And come off it, Mark," Larry continued with an audible sigh, "we all know Peg's right. Including you, chum. I hardly think this is going to fly with the senior command. Do you honestly think Dick Byser and Phillip Ebert are going to look fondly on a nymphet prancing around in girdles and such?"

"Yes," Mark shot back nastily, "I think they'll go with whatever Wes and Wanda want. You guys don't quite get the picture yet, do you?"

"I guess not, Mark," Peter replied wearily. One of P&Q's lifers, Peter Hendrick has been a stalwart of the promotion department for nearly twenty years. His chapped, puffy skin attests to a weakness for supplier-financed lunch-hour vodkas. And though somewhat testy in the mornings and overly voluble in the afternoons, he still manages to turn out some of the most professional and effective brochure and catalog work on Madison Avenue. "Why don't you sketch it in for us?"

"Okay, okay," Mark snapped, "be like that! You all think you're so smart. But, let me tell you.... You better start treating me with a little more respect." He turned to face each of us in turn, his pale blue eyes bright with anger. "This is *my* account, get it? And what I say, goes."

"Certainly, sir," Larry responded plummily. "But no one doubts your authority. It's your judgment, or shall we say lack thereof, that we're bringing into question."

"I don't have to stand for this!" Mark cried, striding to the door. "I'll let you rethink your attitudes a little. Phillip's flying back from London tonight. And I'm going to bring your disobedience up with him when we have lunch tomorrow at the club." With that, he slammed the door so hard on the way out that one of my framed CLIO awards crashed to the floor.

"Lord, I hope that's not an omen," Larry said, leaning over to pick up the shards of glass. " 'Disobedience'! Did you ever hear such drivel? One can only pray the man's wrong. Peg, do you honestly think Phillip might side with him on this?"

"Of course not!" I responded vehemently. "Phillip always puts the agency's interests first. He'll know perfectly well that using Star as the Merriweather model would turn us into a laughingstock. He'll pop Mark's silly little balloon fast enough. You can bet on it."

But just to hedge that investment a little bit, I arranged to see Phillip privately the next day—before his lunch engagement with Mark.

AT TEN-THIRTY the following morning, Phillip's executive secretary ushered me into his huge corner office. Always the perfect gentleman, he stood when I came in, took off his half glasses and gestured with them to the leather chair facing his desk.

"Coffee, Peg?" he asked, sitting down again with a sigh. The man looked tired—and worried. His usually pale features were ashen, his eyes shadowy with fatigue.

"No, thanks," I answered quickly, knowing that he was obliged to serve the drip variety produced by one of our leading clients. It tasted like pencil grindings in warm liquid form. "But you go ahead."

"That's okay," he said. "I think I'll pass it up, too." Only the newest P&Q employees, or unsuspecting visitors, ever actually drank the awful concoction.

Phillip sat back in his leather swivel chair, steepled his hands together under his chin and gave me a long, fatherly look. In my seven plus years at P&Q, I had learned to respect Phillip Ebert as a man—and as a manager. Though I didn't always agree with him, he was consistent in his judgments, undeviating in his philosophy. Phillip Ebert was a true believer in the great corporate god of Peabody & Quinlan. He was a proselytizer of its virtue, a defender of its name. The two of us got on because, despite my often rebellious stances, I believed in the importance of good, honest advertising. And though not as strict a religion as Phillip's, it was one he could appreciate and respect.

"So, young lady," he said, "what can I do for you? A raise, I assume. Now, when was your last review? I'd say you're about due." He smiled encouragement at me, and some of the shadows around his eyes started to clear.

"Actually, no, this isn't about me, Phillip," I answered. "It has to do with Mark Rollings and the Merriweather Sportswear account."

"Oh?" Phillip responded sharply. He sat up, his high forehead creasing with concern. "I understand Wes and Wanda dropped by yesterday. I just read Mark's call report. It said the meeting went quite well."

"Did he happen to mention their idea for the new campaign?" I demanded.

"Uh, no...." Phillip answered, reaching for a folder in his Out box. "It just says that creative, promotion and media met with the Merriweathers and the account seemed definitely green light. Is there something else I should know?"

"I'd say so. The Merriweathers want Star, their daughter, to act as the signature model for the entire new line of products."

"Oh that," Phillip answered. "Yes, yes...I know about that. Mark and I discussed it before I went to London. Cute idea, don't you think?"

"You *discussed* it already?" I cried. "You think it's *cute*? Phillip, have you ever met this girl? She's a child. She's simply a very lovely girl. In other words, she's all wrong for the Merriweather Sportswear role. You've got to take a look at her before you agree to this!"

"I've met Star," Phillip answered firmly. "Yes, she's a bit young. But with the right stylist and photographer, I'm sure she'll be just fine. Merriweather could stand a slightly younger image, anyway."

"I can't believe that you're saying this!" I retorted. "I can't believe you're giving in to them. Mark Rollings, I understand. But you! You *know* better than this. You know it's wrong. It's sleazy. It's corrupting."

"It's what the client wants," Phillip added quietly.

"Since when did that make it right?" I demanded. "Since when did we start giving in to clients' whims?"

"In this case," Phillip answered evenly, "I'd say roughly since the moment we learned Tantamount was trying to buy our client out. That deal has not closed, and if we want to hold on to Merriweather, and therefore strengthen our position with Tantamount, we had better let the Merriweathers have their way on this particular issue."

"But it's all wrong for the product line," I cried. "It's strategically wrong. And morally wrong. And creatively wrong. All of which adds up to bad advertising."

"I don't necessarily disagree, Peg," Phillip conceded. "But it's right in one very fundamental way that you're simply not considering. It's right in that it means we keep Merriweather and therefore Tantamount in the future of P&Q." Phillip's god had won.

"I don't want anything to do with it," I announced bravely.

"You don't have much of a choice, I'm afraid," Phillip answered. "That is, of course, if you intend to stay on here. And in case you haven't heard, Peg, this isn't the greatest time in the world to be dragging your portfolio around town. Between the major mergers and the repercussions of the stock market crash...well, it's pretty much a buyer's market. You know how many top-notch creative directors I have knocking at the door right now? Did you know that Jack Butterfield was let go from DDD&O last week? He called me up, literally weeping. He has a new wife, two ex-wives, three children and a co-op to keep up. The man was pretty desperate for a job. I could see him working out very nicely on the Merriweather account, couldn't you?''

"That won't be necessary, Phillip," I answered quietly. He had me and he knew it. Jack Butterfield was one of the great names on Madison Avenue. It was a sad day for us all when Jack went begging for employment. "I'm sure that I'll eventually be able to warm up to the idea."

"Now, there's my girl," Phillip said fondly. "I knew you'd come around. And, Peg, about that raise...I think we can work something out."

"Thanks, Phillip," I answered, standing to go. "But it's really not necessary. What I was hoping to gain by coming in here...well, money won't make up for."

"Don't go casting the first stone, Peg," Phillip replied gravely. "Principles are a luxury we would all like to be able to afford. But the longer you stay in this business...the more costly they become."

He was right, of course. If I had had the courage of my convictions, I would have resigned then and there. Gotten out of advertising. Taken up nursing or teaching or social work. But convictions were such pure, simple things. And already, I knew the situation was too murky and complicated to be solved by applying the usual moral standards. Berry's life had been taken. Star's innocence was about to go. It was not the moment to split hairs over ideals. It was time to get down in the trenches. At least that was what I told myself that morning. The truth of the matter might very well have been what Phillip had warned: my principles had already been priced right out of the market.

NINE

As ALMOST EVERYONE who follows modern painting knows, my mother, Theo, fell in love with the Florida Keys two years ago. It was about the same time she fell in love with Calvin Hotchner, the legendary Olympic gold medalist diver, and the combination of the subtropics and Cal did things to both her pallette and her personality that I, and the rest of the world, are still recovering from. Tangerine oranges, azure blues, vermilion reds, parakeet greens...suddenly her wall-size canvases were awash with the most dazzling—and often discordant—colors imaginable. What drama! What life! The critics and the collectors fell all over themselves to praise her. An art critic in the *Times* put it best: "the preeminent abstract expressionist painter of our day." Gone, at last, was that double-edged qualifier "female."

And gone, too, was the fierce independence, the demanding aloneness, the driven spirit. Theo, one of America's most radical feminists, had found her man. Yes, Cal is a good twenty years her junior. Yes, even her closest friends gave the relationship six months on the outside. Because, yes, my own dear mother has a tendency to go through handsome men the way most women go through panty hose. But Cal, I sensed from the onset, was different. For one thing, Theo—the most opinionated woman I'd ever met—had suddenly taken to repeating all of Cal's opinions.

"Calvin thinks I should buy a boat," she announced brusquely a few months after they'd met. "A little yacht or something we could use in the Keys... big enough for a studio for me, of course. Calvin knows all about boats, you know." And that was another dead giveaway that the man was going to be a fixture and not just another of Theo's passing fancies. I had never heard Theo discussing anyone of the masculine gender in boastful terms. But there was plenty of pride in her voice whenever Cal was mentioned and, as time went on, I could also hear that there was plenty of love.

"We're going to be in Miami for the holidays, darling," Theo had informed me when I spoke to her at the end of November. She had been calling from London, where a new show of Goodenough lithographs had just opened. There was no question anymore who the "we" was. She and Cal lived together now, in whatever far-flung spot on the globe Theo decided to call home next.

Despite the fact that I was weaned on it from an early age, I had never managed to get used to Theo's nomadic way of life. Although we lived everywhere from an ancient castle in Scotland to a towering lighthouse above San Francisco to a sprawling château on the Loire, I longed only for a settled, ordinary little house in some quiet suburb. I fantasized endlessly that I was a cute, middle-class surferette whose mother, blessedly, had died. It took me years to realize that my inability to adjust to my mother's flamboyant living arrangements was as upsetting to Theo as it was to me.

"What say we hop over to Paris for the weekend?" I remember Theo proposing jubilantly one Christmas Eve when I was thirteen or so and we had just rented a drafty town house in Boston. I recall that I'd been asked out to a sleepover the day after Christmas by one of the girls in the private school in which Theo had just enrolled me. At that point, already a world-weary traveler, the prospect of Paris was nothing compared to the bliss of a bunch of potential girlfriends giggling in their pajamas. But when I tried to explain that to Theo, she just looked down at me in bewilderment.

"What's going to become of you, Peggy?" she asked sadly. "Before I know it, you'll be marrying some investment banker and raising your requisite 2.5 children in Scarsdale." I'm sure Theo could not imagine a worse fate for her only child. But for me, at that time, it seemed an ideal future. And that my cherished dream has not come true is more a matter of accident and misjudgment than any change of heart. All my life I've longed to plunge my hands into the warm, yeasty dough of married life. It's only recently—okay, since Dante Cursio walked through my front door—that I've finally realized that marital happiness depends absolutely on one's choice of mate. Ironically enough it's Theo, who never really wanted it, who has managed to obtain domestic harmony. While I still wake up beside my wheezing feline shorthaired domesticus.

"We'll be in Miami till the twenty-sixth, then sailing down to the Keys for New Year's," Theo had told me during her call from London, "and we'd love to have you join us for the weekend."

"I'm afraid I can't make it, Theo," I'd told her at the time. It was during the height of my frenzied work on the Tantamount creative, I explained, and the prospect of traveling farther than Midtown and back seemed humanly impossible. Well, that was part of it. The other part was that I didn't yet know Cursio's plans for the holidays. He might, after all, midst the spirit of the seasons, à la Jimmy Stewart in *It's a Wonderful Life*, have his eyes opened to the joys of home and hearth. Christmas is a great time for sentiment and self-revelation— look at Scrooge, for heaven's sake—a hopeful time for pining potential brides. I just didn't think I should risk being out of proposal range.

"Well, damn it all, Peg," Theo had retorted, "can't you tear yourself away from that job of yours for even a day or two? I honestly can't believe that—" At this point I heard some muffled argument on the other end of the transatlantic line, and Cal got on the phone.

"What Theo's trying to tell you, dummy," Cal explained in the warm, reasonable tones that had already done so much for mother-daughter relations, "is that we miss you. We haven't seen you since...when? July, right? And, to be a little bit parental for a minute, we're worried about you. You work too hard. You play too little. Now, we're going to be having one hell of a party on the boat at Christmas—with all sorts of fascinating single men—and we want you there. Do you read me, Peg?"

"Really, Cal, I'm so busy," I demurred. "And incredibly tired. I think it's best if I just kind of hang around here and—"

"What?" Cal interrupted. "Wait for the phone to ring?"

"I don't know what you're trying to say, Cal," I replied haughtily. "But my reasons for not coming have absolutely nothing to do with anyone but *my*self and *my* needs."

"Sure, Peg," Cal answered with a sigh. "Whatever you say. Just don't wait too long, understand? And, remember, you can always change your mind and fly down. We'll keep your cabin free."

Needless to say, Calvin and Theo simply cannot understand why I am so set on living with Cursio in a state of holy wedded matrimony—or not at all. Theo, who has tried all her life to inculcate in me the notion that marriage is an outdated, chauvinistic form of male domination, was positively livid when she heard that Dante and I had broken up over the issue. Cal, in his gentler, more reasonable way, was hardly less upset.

"Damn," Cal had said when I told Theo and him the news. "He's become a friend. And a damn good tennis partner. Are you sure it's worth it? I mean, Theo and I have been ridiculously happy for nearly two years—without benefit of clergy. I don't know, Peg, I can't help but side with Theo on this. I think you're making a bit of a mistake."

Theo's quite verbal opinion had actually been that I was set on the most god-awful, stupid, pigheaded, disastrous course of a lifetime. It was one of the reasons we'd seen so little of each other in recent months. Whenever we did meet, Dante's name inevitably cropped up...followed quickly by emotional squalls. Unlike Theo, I don't make a habit of brandishing my beliefs like swords, provoking battle with everyone who doesn't see life exactly my way. My mother, at the slightest hint from a talk-show programmer, will march in front of a television camera and proclaim her feelings about everything from gun-control reform to saving the Antarctic seal population. My beliefs, though as deeply felt as hers, are not as easy to articulate or defend. The fact of the matter is, despite—or even perhaps because of—the way I was raised, I believe that marriage and family are the basic building units of civilization.

"It's a great theory," Theo had informed me the last time we skirmished over the issue. "But I've learned from experience that theories make lousy dinner companions."

In that sense, Theo was right. And there's nothing quite like the holidays to make one take emotional inventory. In the last few days before the agency closed down for the four-day break, I worked frantically on ideas for recasting the Merriweather brand-labeling campaign around Star. Keeping my mind active seemed as good a way as any to distract it from what was going on in one of my other vital organs: my heart. Because the closer we got to the beginning of the holidays, and the more carols I heard, and the more smiling, happy dads and moms and kiddies I saw…the more my right and left ventricles seemed to ache.

I slugged through the brightly lighted streets and department stores checking off my long shopping list for friends and family. And all the time, I kept thinking about my short list for husbands. On Thursday afternoon, the day before the holidays officially kicked off, I put down my Pentel, pushed aside my sketch pad and dialed a friend of mine who repped advertising space for a major airline's in-flight magazine. I reminded her casually how I'd recommended the magazine to Felice Clay, our media director, for a major P&Q luggage account. Within seconds I had confirmed round-trip seats to Miami International Airport.

"But you gotta be at La Guardia by nine tonight," the rep warned me. "So if I were you, Peggy, considering the outbound traffic situation, I'd get a move on right now."

My seventy-nine-year-old psychic-cum-fairy-godmother neighbor, Millie, was delighted to take Picasso for the holidays. "Carlos and Pepe will be so pleased we're having a houseguest!" Millie exclaimed, referring to her two pedigreed Persians. "And, of course, I'll get your mail for you. Are you, um, traveling alone, dear?" If anyone was more dashed by my parting with Cursio than me, it was Millie. From the moment she laid eyes on him—the night he came to investigate a break-in at my apartment that was later tied to the death of my former boss—Millie knew he was "that major Virgo influence you've been waiting for, dear." In other words, she, too, saw him as prime marriage material. Our breakup had irked her.

"It's not natural," she informed me severely one night after I had confided the news to her. She'd been peering suspiciously into my palm, her glasses perched on the bridge of her nose. "Everything here says you two belong together. It's wrong for you to separate. Absolutely against all that I know. Well, one thing's for sure, you'll be back together in no time!" The longer, in fact, Cursio and I stayed apart, the more upset

Millie became. I think she took it as a personal affront to her psychic abilities.

"No, I'm flying down alone," I told her, and was sorry to see her expectant smile fade. "Just for a few days to spend some time on Theo's boat. I'll be back Sunday night."

As I threw my most presentable lightweight summer things into my leather carryall, I switched on my answering machine to check my messages. There were the usual hang ups and short "call me later" requests from friends, and then, just as I thought the tape had wound to an end, the following: "I need you. Desperately. Call me at work as soon as you can. It's important." There was an urgency in the voice of the person I loved . . . and also a tone bordering on fear. With trembling fingers I dialed the switchboard at One Police Plaza and asked for Detective Dante Cursio.

"In reference to what, please?" the nasal Brooklyn operator demanded.

"I'm not sure," I answered, though I had allowed a ray of hope to beam into my heart of hearts. "I'm returning his call."

"No answer," I was told. "Try again later, please." Click.

I called twice more before finally dragging myself out the door. And I tried again from the airport. Minutes before the plane was due to take off, in fact just at the moment they started to board "those in need of assistance and families with small children," I heard the police switchboard transfer me through to his direct line.

"Homicide," he said. "Cursio speaking."

"Hi, it's me," I replied, trying for a light and breezy tone. "I got a message that you, uh, needed me. 'Desperately,' I believe was the word."

"Peg! Oh, great! Where are you?" There was something equally light and casual about his response. Not, I had to admit as I watched the passengers with tickets for rows eight to twenty-four jockey for position in line, what I had been hoping for.

"At the airport. I'm flying down to Florida to spend Christmas with Theo."

"Of course," he muttered, and happily I could detect a definite note of disappointment in the words. "For the whole weekend, huh?"

"Yes," I answered. "In fact, they're calling my seat now for boarding. What desperate thing was it that you wanted?"

"Eva's coming from England for Christmas," he said.

"Eva?" I demanded.

"My daughter, remember?" he explained. "I told you that Gwen was pregnant again and that I had agreed to take Eva when the time came. Well . . ."

"Time's here, huh?" I finished for him.

"Right. And . . . and I was hoping that you . . ."

Well, you would have laughed out loud, too, if you could have heard his hopeless, helpless tone of voice!

"Peg, this isn't funny," he retorted. "I don't know how to entertain an eight-year-old girl. I haven't even seen her for three years! How am I to cope? What should I do? When in hell will you be back?"

"Well, gosh, I'm just not sure," I answered slowly, as if thinking it over. "Sometime Sunday, I suppose."

"Listen, the first thing you do, the very first thing, is call me. Okay?"

"Sure," I told him. "But right now I've really got to run before they peddle my seat to the standbys."

"Okay," he said with some regret. "Give my love to Theo and Cal and . . . and everyone."

Though we boarded on time and taxied out for takeoff, the plane didn't actually leave the ground for another hour due to, as our pilot obliquely put it, "traffic delays." I stared morosely out the window at the bright red, blue and green runway lights and tried not to listen to the piped-in Christmas carol music. I also tried not to question whether or not I'd just blown my one big opportunity for proving the quality of my wifeliness to Cursio. But my mind kept gnawing at the issue.

To the slogging Mantovani-like strings of "Have Yourself a Merry Little Christmas," I pictured myself rustling up a batch of my famous oatmeal-raisin cookies—the secret is massive amounts of pecan pieces—and impressing the daylights out of little Eva Cursio-Pickford. To the tinny horns of "The Little Drummer Boy," I imagined myself curled up under Cursio's Christmas tree, a glass of champagne at the ready, opening up his gift to me: an inch-square, velvet-lined box containing a tasteful gold band. I was making ready to unhitch my seat belt and tell the stewardess I'd changed my mind when the plane suddenly turned a sharp corner, started to roar and within seconds ascended into the heavily congested New York-Miami corridor.

Oh, well, I told myself as we arced above the deceptively dazzling lights of Midtown, the decision had been wrenched out of my hands. I sighed and sat back to admire the mirage of beauty and promise with which nightfall always cloaks the city. The bridges, linking the outer boroughs to Manhattan, gleamed like lustrous pearl necklaces. The fabulous canyons of glass and chrome crowned by the Empire State Building—itself lighted red and green for the holidays—glowed in the city's heart like the embers of some mythical volcanic fire.

Always, for a minute, when I fly above Manhattan, I remember the city as I saw it when Theo first brought me here as a young child: a place of endless noise and motion, of mystery and delight. And then, in the blink of an eye, I see it again for what it's become to me: a well-known warren of concrete and glass, exhaust fumes and taxi horns, experience and memory. A place where people I love are living . . . where people I love have died. A city that has etched along its streets and parks, its museums and office buildings, the path of nearly a decade of my life. A place that undoubtedly carries within its granite core the unmarked chart of my future.

It was with a sigh of relief that I closed my eyes, pushed my seat back to a reclining position and considered that for the next few days, at least, I wouldn't have to worry about what that future might be.

TEN

THEO AND CAL have a way of referring to *The Argo* as "the boat," as if she were some ten-foot Fiberglass dinghy. Built in 1910 by a master Danish shipbuilder, this hundred-foot Baltic trader, with her fluid lines and massive rigging, hauled cargo for the first sixty years of her life. In the mid-seventies *The Argo* was converted into a private yacht with a teak-paneled main saloon and inlaid fireplaces, four sumptuous private staterooms, a dining room and gaming parlor, not to mention gleaming decks and generous servants' quarters. When Theo purchased *The Argo* two years ago, she converted the maids' rooms into a large artist's studio, complete with built-in mahogany settees, storage cabinets and skylights opening to the aft deck. Though not a typical racing yacht, Theo's "boat" is generally considered one of the more charming and comfortable pleasure crafts in the world.

I woke two mornings later to the sound of gulls and sea traffic—the gurgle of motors and the metallic whine of pulleys—and the warm Florida sun pouring in my half-open porthole. Above, I could hear Theo's deckhands getting under way. The crew consisted of Captain Carlos and five men, each of whom could double as cooks, stewards, waiters or sommeliers—whatever the occasion required. All small, wiry, darkly tanned Cubans, the crew seemed to me happy and self-sufficient, proud of their craft and in awe of the eccentric mistress of their good fortune.

"Pedro, I'll want coffee and orange juice in my studio," I heard the gravelly voice of the woman in question saying somewhere overhead. "And maybe one of your wonderful omelets a little later. Ring me around ten in the studio and I'll let me know. Otherwise, I don't want to be disturbed."

I smiled and turned my face toward the porthole, where I could watch the gleaming new jumble of Miami Harbor slide past as we picked up speed. In another twenty minutes or so we'd be in ocean water, find the Gulf Stream and drift through the afternoon. Cal and I would spend the day sunbathing and fishing and helping Carlos and his men get ready for the big party back in the harbor that night. Theo, despite the fact that it was Christmas Eve, would spend the day painting.

"She's as impossible as always," Cal had declared with affection the night before at dinner. As we would today, we had spent my first day sailing out of Miami Harbor, to return to the safety and convenience of the city around sunset. Theo had holed up that day as well in her studio, emerging only after we'd anchored, looking as fresh and relaxed as if she'd spent the day at Elizabeth Arden. "Work, work, work. And, damn it, it only seems to make her look younger—and more beautiful."

"Why the third person, Cal, darling?" Theo had responded dryly, though you could tell by the look she gave him that she was pleased by what he'd said. "I am right here, you see, and as far as I know, with all my faculties still intact."

Oh, yes, they definitely were. I have spent most of my life struggling against the tidal force of Theo's personality. A whirlpool of opinions, talent and energy, she has a way of sucking people into her swirling sphere. I've seen the weaker and more susceptible of these victims spend the rest of their days gravitating around Theo like lost moons around Jupiter. It's taken me years to realize that she hates the influence she has over people, that she longs for equally powerful forces to pull her out of herself and keep her on course. That's what Cal does for her, I realize now. And perhaps, that's what I do sometimes, as well.

I had smiled across the candlelit table at Theo. Though nearly sixty, her tanned face was aglow with health and the nearest I've ever seen her be to happiness. Her long black hair, with its lightning streak of white flashing downward from her widow's peak, was pulled back in a thick ponytail. She has a face that is too intelligent and daunting to be thought beautiful, until she laughs or smiles, and then she seems to exemplify the eternal beauty of one of Picasso's neoclassical paintings.

"We're glad you could make it," Theo told me brusquely when she saw my smile.

It has taken us both so many years to come to terms with each other as mother and daughter. I think we each remain a little afraid of our hard-won truce . . . leery of the intimacy and understanding that's now within our grasp.

"I'm glad I could get away," I answered. "It's been a madhouse at work."

"Oh, you Goodenough women," Cal interjected. "You thrive on madhouses—and work."

"Not in this case," I told him. "One of my main clients, a woman I'd actually gotten pretty close to, well . . . she died."

"Darling, how awful!" Theo exclaimed. "What in the world happened?"

What could I say? I, and I alone in the world, believed Berry had been murdered. Though I could identify about half a dozen possible suspects and at least twice as many motives, I had no evidence. The police refused to consider foul play. The family had accepted—or used as a cover—the ruling that she had committed suicide. All I had going for me—or against me—was my dogged refusal to believe Berry would take her own life. Not enough, as Cursio had quite rightly pointed out, to build a case on.

"She killed herself," I replied finally, and then with obvious alacrity, I changed the subject.

What with espresso and brandy and a stroll on the deck to see the stars, we didn't get to bed until after one o'clock. And though Cal and Theo were up with the sun, I didn't actually make it aboveboard until we'd cleared the long breakwater of South Miami Beach and were headed into the azure blue of the Gulf Stream.

I found Cal on the aft deck, a breakfast table in front of him and a copy of the *Miami Herald* resting on his lap. He had on a faded blue work shirt, worn khaki shorts, balding sandals and what might once have been a souvenir cap from a Miami Dolphins game. Despite his pedestrian attire, you only needed one look at Calvin Hotchner to surmise that he could be a movie star. Or a model. Or an Olympic athlete. And after taking a second look at this hulking bronze god of a man, I don't think anyone would have been surprised to learn that, at one time or another in his life, he had been all three. Cal is the last person in the world, however, to throw any light on his illustrious past. And Theo, with her usual vagueness, has given me only sketchy information about the man she so obviously adores. It's not that either of them is embarrassed by the fact that Cal has spent most of his adult life in the public eye; it's that they no longer think it important. Cal is a private person now; Theo's manager and man. In the same way, the multitude of men who've passed through Theo's life are all but forgotten in Cal's mind. Theo is his. They are together. Only in odd snatches of conversation do they imply that they've ever been apart. But I've been able, over time, and with the help of Theo's and Cal's multitude of friends, to piece together the facts of Cal's pre-Theo existence.

He had been America's Olympic gold medalist diving champion in the early seventies. Then, through the next decade and a half, he lent himself to the country's two most voracious star-mongering enterprises: advertising and Hollywood. Surely you remember him—the gold medal gleaming against his beautiful bare chest—diving off the box front of a major national brand of cereal? And though a few people purport to recall his three-year stint on the television sitcom *Anchors Away*, where he played the part of the sought-after but altogether stupid ensign, almost no one I've met admits to seeing any of the four films in which he performed to varying degrees of ignominy. I know Cal prefers it that way. If selling out to Madison Avenue had made his life unhappy, his experiences in Los Angeles apparently had made his existence unbearable. Theo and he met after he'd abandoned Tinseltown and returned to his first love: diving. He was giving swimming lessons in a resort on the Côte d'Azur, where Theo had taken up residence temporarily. It wasn't long before she had taken up Cal—permanently.

"Coffee, sleepybones?" Cal asked, looking up at me from under the shade of his ratty visor. "Or would you like some fresh orange juice? Carlos has already squeezed about an orchard of the stuff for screwdrivers tonight."

"A little of both, I think," I replied, collapsing in the royal-blue director's chair beside him. Next to his perfectly toned, bronzed biceps, my arms looked the color of mushrooms that had been left in the icebox too long. The day before he had insisted that I slather my doughy body with ultraforce sunscreen. It had done its job, all right, I decided ruefully. I looked as though I'd just emerged from two weeks vacation on the IRT. I yawned and reached for a section of the paper.

"What's the news?" I asked, flipping through the Living Today section.

"The usual mayhem," Cal answered, lowering the front page. "Let's forget about world events for a second and concentrate on you."

"All right," I said a bit warily as Carlos set up a tray in front of me. My wants had obviously been anticipated—along with thick black coffee and fresh orange juice, he'd arranged a colorful display of strawberries, cantaloupe and kiwi. Croissant, butter and jam completed the delectable picture. "What do you want to know?"

"How's Dante, for starters?" Cal suggested. "Unless that's classified information. You haven't uttered his name once since you've been here."

"You know, Cal, you sound exactly like a typical mother would sound," I answered, taking a swallow of freshly squeezed citrus, " *if* I had one."

"And if I weren't in such happy spirits," Cal retorted, "I would consider that remark, first, a slam at Theo, and second, a typical Peg Goodenough evasive maneuver. Instead, I'll just pass on to my next question. How *are* you? I've a feeling something's bothering you."

"That's very incisive of you, dear," I replied, slipping on my sunglasses against the fierce morning sun as well as Cal's scrutinizing gaze. "Actually, there's more than one thing."

"Well, the way I see it," Cal answered, leaning back and cupping his hands behind his head, "we have most of the morning to mull over your troubles...and then all of the afternoon to come up with some solutions. Where would you like to start?"

They don't grow men like Cal and Dante anymore, I have begun to realize. Since splitting up with the latter, I've tried to make the usual rounds. But even though the specimens out there look and talk like men, I've come to think that New York City has actually been invaded by a race of alien beings: serious, hardworking dullards with absolutely no sense of humor, who are intent only on getting ahead in banking or brokerage or whatever "career ladder" they've decided to scale. In other words, most of the male human beings I've been seeing don't seem to me very human at all. That's probably why I opened up to Cal the way I did. I've desperately missed talking to a full-bodied, broad-minded *man*. Poor Cal. He probably wished he'd stuck with the news.

"But you two keep tabs on each other, right?" Cal asked after I'd droned on about Dante for a good twenty minutes or so. "I mean, you're the first person he calls when he has a problem, like this business with Eva."

"Yeah, but he just wanted *help*, Cal," I responded. "Not me. I don't want to just be there for him as a person. I want to be there as a wife. I know you and Theo think I'm crazy. I know you think I'm being obstinate...and stupid...and—"

"Actually, you might be surprised," Cal interrupted, "how much we do understand."

"Well, say," I replied, sitting up and smiling across at him. "That's darn nice to hear. Since when have I earned your sympathy, may I ask?"

"Oh, I don't know," Cal answered cryptically. "Time has a way of changing things. But, listen...there was something else I wanted to know, since I'm prying anyway. Tell me about this woman, this client and friend of yours, who...died."

"Berry," I replied. "Berry Merriweather. One of the smartest, toughest women I've ever known. Besides Theo, of course."

"Merriweather.... The name rings a bell for some reason," Cal said.

"You've probably heard of Merriweather Sportswear," I told him. "It's one of the biggest, most successful womenswear lines in the country. Berry founded it."

"Merriweather...Merriweather...." Cal repeated to himself. I wasn't sure he'd even heard what I'd just told him, he seemed so lost in his own thoughts. "Now, I remember!" he cried. "I knew a fashion model once, back in the days when I was peddling my flesh, Wanda Welsh, who married a guy called Merriweather."

"Wes?" I asked.

"Yep. A handsome blond dude with a smile as big as Texas. Nice enough guy, I thought. Felt kinda bad when I heard he'd teamed up with Wanda."

"Why?" I demanded. "I met Wanda recently. She seems like the perfect wife for him. They look terrific together."

"Looks are mighty deceiving, sweetie," Cal answered, stretching and standing up. He tipped his cap back on his head and stared out toward the shimmering horizon as he leaned his strong, tanned arms on the teak railing. "You want to hear about Wanda Welsh? When I knew her, oh, back about fifteen years or so, she looked like Miss All-American-Girl-Next-Door."

"She still does," I told him. "Though now it's more like Mrs. Girl-Next-Door. Honey-blond and slim. She has the face of an angel."

"A very fallen angel, Peggy, dear," Cal answered sadly. "Wanda Welsh was one of the biggest heads in the business back in the mid-seventies. Man, she took anything—speed, cocaine, Quaaludes—you name it. She lived on dope. Some people claim she even lived off it—dealing, I mean."

"Good God, I don't believe it!" I replied, jumping up. "You're sure about this, Cal? We are talking about the same woman, aren't we?"

"I'm afraid so, Peg," Cal answered. "But, say, we've gotten way off the subject. This doesn't have anything to do with his sister, right?"

At the time, I said no, of course not. But then, as the afternoon drifted by in a warm glow of sun and conversation, I thought back again and again to what Cal had said about Wanda. It could very well be that her addictions were behind her, that marriage to Wes had steadied her, that she had rebuilt her life to be exactly what she seemed in her commercials—a pretty, happy wife and mother.

On the other hand, if she hadn't recovered, what kind of life would the Merriweathers be leading? Addiction tears at the fabric of any family, burning lasting scars in the emotional lives of the children, warping the love of married partners. Dependence breeds counterdependence as families try to hide the ugly problem from the rest of the world. If Wanda was still an addict, then nothing about the Merriweather family would be what it seemed. Behind those perfect smiles and clear blue eyes that we see in their advertisements, a complicated pattern of lies and unhappiness would be at work. As Cal said, looks could be deceiving. And if they were in this case, I wondered, just how far did that deception go?

ELEVEN

THEO'S PARTIES are famous throughout the art world—and among the big-money benefactors who keep our culture afloat. My earliest memories involve the chatter and tinkle of some party or other heard from my bedroom as a nurse or baby-sitter tried desperately to read me to sleep. I remember how much I longed to be downstairs—in this case, I believe the house in question was the drafty sixteenth-century Scottish castle—with the laughter and lights...and Theo. Because, as in most things in her life, Theo is always the magical center of whatever party she's hosting. That night on *The Argo* was no exception.

The boat had been decked with thousands of lights, soaring up the towering masthead and stretching from bow to stern, giving it the appearance of an enormous floating Christmas tree. A lavish buffet was set up in the main saloon. Draped in red linen, the twenty-foot table labored under the weight of local delicacies: platters of stone crab claws, baskets of conch fritters, bowls of chilled bonito and Maui-Maui salad, heaping tiers of freshly steamed gulf shrimp, a spicy mélange of grilled lobster and avocado, all surrounded by a lush garden of sculpted pineapple and oranges, mangoes and grapefruit. The deck crew, transformed into elegant waiters with the help of white tie and tails, circled the rooms and decks with silver trays of brimming champagne flutes. A band, imported from South Miami, held sway on the aft deck, doing things to "White Christmas" that Irving Berlin wouldn't dream possible.

But far more interesting than Theo's selection of food or music was her eclectic choice of guests. She knew just about everyone worth knowing in the plastic and performing arts. And Cal's wide range of acquaintances included international sports figures, top-ranked models and some of Hollywood's hottest young stars. Tonight, because *The Argo* could accommodate only about fifty people comfortably, they had invited just their closest, oldest friends. It was a fascinating crossbreeding of glamour and culture, talent and pizzazz, radiant youth and well-preserved age.

As I made my way across the jam-packed saloon, I did a quick tabulation of the luminaries in the room: two novelists, three actors—including England's current leading Shakespearean thespian—a Broadway musical composer, two international financiers, the female lead in TV's top-ranked sitcom accompanied by her tennis-champion husband, France's favorite avant-garde choreographer and two of Theo's most ardent collectors. I waved to Nattie Zellerman, Theo's diminutive agent, whose beeswaxed Dali-style mustachio arched in a smile when he saw me. He held out his arms.

"Can this be little Peggy?" he cried as he kissed the air beneath my chin. Nattie is just under five feet. And though I loomed above him in my high-heeled sandals, I knew he still saw me as the wild-eyed, wayward little girl I was for him for so many years. "Good heavens, how you've grown, young lady! You look positively smashing. The image of Theo when I first knew her."

I smiled down at Nattie and gave him a hug. For him, as for so many of the men who have surrounded my mother all her life, Theo has become the ultimate barometer of beauty and style. I suppose they couldn't imagine a higher compliment than to hold my candle up to hers. But I am no fool. Even though I've inherited my mother's dark gypsy eyes and curving brows, though I have her full-lipped smile and slightly cleft chin, though I seem to have that "certain something" that makes the male of the species offer me his seat in crowded subways, my beauty is a mere table lamp next to Theo's blazing candelabra. I remember once when Theo and I were shopping for gloves in Harrods, a beautifully dressed middle-aged man walked up to her and announced in clipped British tones, "You are the sexiest woman I have ever seen." He then turned on his heel and disappeared into the crowd. That's what Theo can do to men.

But then, a few moments later, when I saw Felix Northfield swaying toward me across the crowded saloon, I recognized the dark side of Theo's powerful thrall.

"Peggy, Peggy," Felix said with a sigh, smacking me damply on the check. He emitted that sad, sweet smell—a mixture of cigarette smoke, bourbon and despair—that implicates the most careful drunk. A music critic of international renown, Felix had had an affair with Theo a quarter of a century ago. She threw him over after a few months with her usual callousness, and poor Felix has followed her around ever since. He's been one of the few fixtures in my life. And although he usually put an acerbic, superior, often slightly pickled face on the fact of his hopeless infatuation, in the past few years I had noticed that his ironic veneer had been wearing thin. "What's going to become of us?" he demanded heavily, his bleary gaze staring off across the crowded room. "What shall we do, Peggy, dear?"

"Why don't we get some coffee, for starters?" I suggested gently, taking his elbow. I was alarmed to discover that his arm, in fact his entire body, was trembling slightly.

"Don't you dare attempt to sober me up!" Felix announced, shaking off my grip. "I have just managed to leverage myself into this state of unfettered intoxication. It's taken me most of the day. I won't have all my fine work destroyed by a well-meaning busybody."

He was clearly drunk, so I tried not to take offense. Still, it couldn't help but hurt to have him—the closest I'd ever come to an uncle—turn on me. Just then one of the deckhands glided by with a fresh tray of champagne, and Felix reached out and grabbed two glasses. It took me a few seconds to realize that he intended to keep them both for himself. He gulped one greedily as his eyes lighted and held on the doorway. I followed his gaze and saw Theo and Cal sweep into the room.

"Darling, how good of you to come!" Theo cried, embracing Nattie. "Oh, and dearest," Theo went on, turning to a diva of international reputation and nearly mythical proportions, "you look just divine!" Together, Cal and Theo made their way around the room, greeting guests and redefining the epicenter of the party. I felt Felix start to drift away as Theo glanced in our direction. As subtly as possible, I caught Theo's eye and mimed someone tipping a glass, nodded at Felix, then followed him as he made his way unsteadily up the winding steps to the upper deck. It was a lovely night, the exotic jumble of flashy new downtown Miami behind us, the inky, ancient darkness of the ocean in front, and a sky glittering with stars overhead. The air was soft and warm, pungent with the fishy smells of the bay.

"Hmm . . . it's nice out here, isn't it?" I murmured.

"I came out here for a little solitude," Felix retorted as he worked clumsily at his cigarette lighter. He got it going finally and managed after several unsuccessful passes to get a cigarette properly lit. He inhaled deeply and then coughed.

"What's the matter, Felix?" I asked. "I don't think I've ever seen you like this before. Is there anything I can do?"

"Yes, damn it," he snapped. "I thought I'd already told you. Leave me the hell alone."

"If that's what you want," I retorted, "then fine. Good night—and good riddance."

I started to back down the steps when I heard a strangulated voice cry, "Damn, I'm sorry, Peggy. Please come back. . . ."

He slumped into one of the deck chairs, and I leaned against the railing. "Okay, chum," I said, patting his shoulder, "why don't you tell me what's up."

"Oh, Peggy, I'm afraid it's rather obvious." Felix sighed, trying to recover himself. "It's Theo, of course. It's always been Theo, damn it. All these long, long years. You see, Peggy, I've always hoped. I've always thought that someday, when she got tired of all those silly little boys, she'd look up and see faithful old Felix waiting for her. She'd come to her senses."

"And now?" I asked, my heart going out to him.

"She's found a silly little boy she's not going to get tired of," Felix replied.

"They're happy together, you know," I told him gently. "I've never seen Theo this happy before."

"I know, damn it," Felix replied. "Don't you think I see that? Why else would I be so upset? She's found someone who's good for her. Better than me. She's found someone who's right for her . . . and now I'll never be able—"

"Peg! Peg!" I heard Cal calling my name below.

"Yes?" I called back.

"Telephone for you, sweetie," he replied. "Take it in our stateroom so you can hear yourself talk."

I patted Felix's shoulder again and hurried down the steps. People had started dancing on the aft deck, and in the main saloon what had once been conversation was now babble. Cigarette smoke and perfume filled the corridors. As I closed the door to Theo's stateroom behind me, I heard the Broadway composer break into a rousing rendition of his most recent hit song.

"Yes?" I said, picking up the phone as I sat down on the queen-size bed.

"Peg? Is that you?" I heard Cursio cry from what seemed like miles underwater. "I can hardly hear you!"

"I can't hear you, either!" I yelled back. "Must be a bad connection. Why don't you call me back?"

"No, I had a hell of a time getting through as it is," he started to say before a piercing whine muffled his words. "Are you there? Peg? Can you hear me?"

"Yes, but this is hardly the most pleasant telephone conversation I've ever had. Is there something specific you wanted to say? I've a feeling we could be cut off at any moment."

"I know..." Cursio began before a storm of static intervened. "You still there? Good. Okay, I'd better hurry. Listen, I wanted to tell you that... you were right."

"Right?" I demanded, my heart kicking over. "Right about what?"

"About what you said when..." This time an ear-shattering beep interrupted us. I waited, hardly breathing, until it abruptly stopped. "Did you hear what I said?" Cursio demanded.

"No," I said. "Please hurry. What was I right about?" But I knew, damn it! I knew! It was Christmas Eve. He was sitting alone in his big old Brooklyn brownstone with his daughter asleep upstairs. He had been sitting alone, thinking of me, dreaming of us, and all of a sudden his eyes and heart had been opened, and he knew, yes, he knew, I had been right about...

"Berry."

"What?"

"Berry. You were right. The M.E.'s office has finally released the autopsy report. They'd been dragging their feet, as you know, for days. And finally, yesterday, a reporter from *New York* magazine pulled a number on us—said he had some evidence indicating Berry's death had been a homicide and that the NYPD was obstructing justice unless we went public with what we had. And, well, you were right. She didn't selfasphyxiate. The mechanics of that were apparently impossible."

"Then how did she die?" I asked, dying a little myself. This was hardly the subject I wanted to be right about on Christmas Eve. "Were you able to figure that out?"

"Yeah. I'm afraid she was strangled, Peg."

"Oh, Lord," I murmured before the siren wail cut me off from him again.

"Peg? Are you there? Can you hear me?"

"Just barely," I replied. "What are we going to do about this?"

"If you mean about Berry, it's not a question of 'we' anymore. This is a police matter now, Peg. You've done what you had to. Now it's in our hands. We'll take care of it."

"But—"

"I gotta go, Peg," Cursio interrupted. "My three minutes is almost up. We'll talk about this when you get back."

Cheap bastard, I thought, gripping the phone receiver to keep myself from saying what I was thinking. Instead, I replied, "Okay, we'll do that. Merry Christmas, Dante. Thanks for calling," and with that I hung up.

Damn him, I thought as I collapsed onto the bed. I stared sightlessly at Theo's beautiful, beamed ceiling. Damn him, and damn the police department. And damn the whole, rotten world. Hot tears streamed from the corners of my eyes, ran along my temples and curved with irritating warmth down my neck to soak Theo's white chenille spread.

"For they are jolly good fellows... for they are jolly good fellows..." I heard the carrying tenor of the Broadway composer above a rousing chorus of Theo's guests. Why the hell were they singing that? I wondered as I snuffled back some tears. Damn Christmas, I thought. And damn parties. I got up and found some tissue on Theo's dressing table.

"For they are jolly good fell-ell-ows..." I blew my nose and then made my way out into the hall. "Which nobody can deny!" Suddenly, there was loud cheering and catcalling all over the boat.

"What's going on?" I asked Nattie, who happened to be the first person I ran into in the corridor.

"Oh, there you are!" he cried, his eyes bright with excitement. "We were looking all over for you!"

"Why?" I demanded. "What's happening?" The party seemed to have dissolved into absolute chaos. The Shakespearean star had stripped naked to the waist and was dancing a tango with a New York prima ballerina, a rose clasped between his teeth. Shouts and laughter echoed up and down the halls. I noticed Pedro and Carlos toasting each other with glasses of champagne.

"You haven't heard, then?" Nattie asked, searching my face. "Come I'll let Theo and Calvin tell you." He took my hand and led me through the noise and hilarity to where a tight knot of people surrounded my mother and Cal.

"Here she is!" Nattie piped. "I found her for you!" He thrust me at Theo, who—and this was rare for her—drew me warmly into her arms.

"What's going on?" I demanded when she let me go. She held me at arm's length and gave me a deep, searching look. If she noticed that my eyes were red rimmed, she didn't say anything. Instead, she said something I was absolutely positive I'd never hear her say.

"Peg, darling," my mother announced quietly, "Cal and I are going to get married."

So what did I do? I burst into tears all over again.

TWELVE

THREE DAYS LATER. Manhattan Island. Windchill factor somewhere in the minus double digits. I was pushing my way against a stiff wall of frigid air on Canal Street. It was noon, and the merciless winter sun highlighted every grimy window and patched awning, each tacky storefront and filthy alleyway in Chinatown. As I turned north up Mulberry, the onrushing wind forced my mouth into a rictuslike smile.

But I was far from happy. I had managed to come back from Florida with a second-degree sunburn and a first-degree head cold. The combination had turned my nose as red as Rudolph's and kept my sinuses in a constant "flush" position. It wasn't just that I felt like hell; I looked like hell warmed-over. And in the next few minutes I'd be coming face-to-face with Dante Cursio for the first time in months. Ah . . . choo!

Never mind that I remained furious at the man for his miserly treatment of me on the phone Christmas Eve. I still wanted to look my best when I was around him so that he could see what he was missing when I wasn't. Hoping to salvage the situation, I'd left work around ten o'clock that morning for an emergency session at Tumzi's Hair and Makeup Salon. But I think even Tumzi sensed his valiant efforts with scissors, foundation and blush had made matters worse. My eyes water when I sneeze, which is something Tumzi didn't take into account when he applied the midnight-blue mascara. Now dark smudges circled my eyes with racoon-like intensity. And every time I blew my nose, the Kleenex came away smeared a frightening orangy beige. Luckily, I was well acquainted with the layout of China Delight Garden, Cursio's favorite Chinese eatery, and knew that I could probably duck into the tiny rest room for a repair job before meeting him.

Then I saw the bane of my existence waiting for me in front of the shuttered restaurant, stamping his feet to keep warm. Never the world's snappiest dresser, he had on a dark green hooded parka several sizes too large and military-looking boots, veterans, obviously, of several wars. Into these, familiar faded jeans had been haphazardly tucked. A black turtleneck and sunglasses completed what even the least fashion-minded person would have to agree was a pretty pedestrian get up. He had the pallor of a man who spent too much time under fluorescent lights, and his dark hair was in serious need of a cut. And yet, when Cursio turned and saw me, when he started to smile, I was struck by the unfairness of the fact that good-looking men required such little upkeep.

"'On pleasure journey,'" Cursio said, nodding to an oblong of cardboard that had been taped to the door. "I forgot that Mr. Chin takes a winter vacation. Damn." It was only then that he leaned over and brushed his cold, hard lips against my unevenly powdered and peeling cheek.

Since our denouement, we'd both been uncomfortable with greetings and partings. After all, we had been passionate, happy lovers once. It's something the body doesn't easily forget, despite what the mind dictates. I found myself listing hungrily toward the green parka, breathing in the warm, animal scent of masculinity. I had to yank myself back into an upright position.

"So." I sighed, meeting his dark eyes. God, how I'd missed those eyes! "What do we do now? Whatever it is, we'd better hurry before I lose all circulation in my extremities."

We ended up at Hunan Palace, the huge, echoing dim sum restaurant just off Canal, which could easily double as an airplane hangar. Because it was Wednesday, and in the middle of a slow holiday week, the place was fairly empty. We were quickly led to a large round table at the back of the restaurant, an area reserved for English-speaking Occidentals, who could be expected to slow up the regular flow of the dim sum carts.

"Not everyone knows me here," Cursio apologized. One Police Plaza is in the demarcation zone between city hall and Chinatown. In the fifteen or so years Cursio has worked in the neighborhood, he's managed to pick up more than a smattering of Cantonese along with a pretty fair appreciation of Chinese cuisine. Most of the better restaurant owners know him now and, flattered by his patronage, bring out their more exotic delicacies for him to sample. During the heady days of our relationship, I, too, had tried to work up some enthusiasm for the boiled chicken claws and coagulated duck's blood that Cursio cherished. And I had learned the hard way that love, though a conqueror of many things, is basically useless when it comes to a squeamish stomach.

No doubt remembering a few of our less-than-successful culinary experiments, Cursio procured a bowl of wonton soup for me along with a small steamer tray of shrimp balls. After a rapid-fire exchange in Cantonese, a plate of blackened strips of something with eyes was placed with a flourish in front of him.

"Ah...." he murmured, picking up a strip with his fingers. It crackled when he bit into it, and I had to turn my face away.

"How's Eva?" I asked, hoping conversation would ease the strain between us. Because it was there again—that ripple of tension, the prickle up the spine, the shortness of breath—whatever it was that now always kept us from relaxing in each other's presence. Oh, we're fine on the phone; then it's easy to play at being friends. But up close, when a face you have kissed a hundred times is only a place-setting away, it's hard to shut out the memories. Intimacy is a dangerous thing; it leaves a scar, as deep as anger or hatred. It never entirely heals.

"Great, fine," Cursio replied, biting into another black, greasy piece. "Though I have a feeling she's kind of lonely. Eleanor's coming in every day now to take care of her. But I don't think they have a whole lot in common." I wouldn't think so, I silently agreed. Cursio's housekeeper is a television addict; she carries a little portable set with her from room to room when she's cleaning his place. She can watch the thing with slackened mouth and glazed-over eyes for hours on end.

"And how's Gwen? Any word?"

As always, Cursio frowned at the mention of his ex-wife, but this time there was something more there than the usual old disappointments and regrets. Cursio has the rugged, closed-in face of someone used to looking at a far horizon—a sailor or a lineman. Perhaps because he's become so adept at observing others, he's able to keep his own expressions almost unreadable. Only unexpected pleasures—a favorite song on the radio, the sight of someone he loves—light up the shadows that hover around his eyes. He's a homicide detective, after all, and life's most sordid back streets are his regular beat. But it's a job that has made him sensitive rather than cynical...cautious rather than hard. And it's because of those distinctions, the humane way that he's dealt with an endless round of senseless murders, that I love him. Hope and pride are difficult things to sustain when you spend your days dealing with those who have lost them.

"She's overdue," he said finally, wiping his fingers on the worn nylon napkin and signaling to the purveyor of a cartful of steamed baby clams. He tucked into the gray mountain of half-open shells with a relish that seemed to me totally out of line with their muddy-looking appearance. Then he added, "By almost two weeks."

"Is that a lot?" I asked stupidly, realizing too late that this was information I was probably supposed to know. "I mean, it's not serious, is it?"

"In most instances, no," Cursio agreed. "But Gwen didn't have an easy time of it when Eva was born...and now she's nearly nine years older. There's some talk of them inducing the baby if things don't start happening pretty soon. But, well, you know Gwen, she's determined that the whole thing be absolutely natural."

I'd never met Gwen in the flesh, but I felt I knew her in spirit. I had gleaned from numerous things Cursio had said during our relationship that she was one of the most organized, rational, determined, detail-minded, clearheaded and responsible people in the world. A dark, unexplored part of me was convinced that it was my lack of these fine qualities that had decided Cursio against me matrimonially. Forget what he said about being driven crazy by her perfectionist tendencies—men marry women who know how to darn sock heels and make bread from scratch. The most practical thing Theo ever taught me was how to open a beer bottle on the door handle of a car.

"I'm sure there's nothing to worry about," I volunteered in my most womanly tones. I almost reached over and patted his arm, but added instead, "She's going to be just fine."

"Gwen?" Cursio asked with a short, hard laugh. "Of course *Gwen* will be fine! It's Eva I'm worried about. She was only supposed to stay with me over the Christmas holidays. Now it looks as though she'll be around at least through January. And that will mean finding her a school temporarily. Buying her some new clothes. I . . . I don't know where to begin."

"Well . . . if you want, I could help," I suggested uncertainly. "I . . . I know a lot of people with school-age kids. I could ask around. And I could take her shopping, I suppose. . . ." This was my chance, I thought with a sudden, leaping joy.

"Would you?" he asked eagerly. "You really wouldn't mind?"

"Of course not," I replied without thinking. "How about late Friday? I could take her to Macy's after work."

So, within minutes of sitting down, I found myself on the threshold of a new intimacy with Cursio, one that revolved around the very issue that had torn us apart: family. He had said he was through with marriage and children. He had asserted that domesticity and the NYPD were two totally incompatible concepts. Was I kidding myself? Or was there an undercurrent of hopefulness to his plea for help with Eva? Was I being used as a temporary replacement for Eva's mother . . . or was this an audition for a more permanent position? I glanced across at his hard, chiseled face, but it was like trying to read a rock.

It wasn't until Cursio had worked his way through a plate of what looked to be seared lawn hose—he claimed it was grilled eel—a bowl of glutenous-looking coconut pudding and about a gallon of tepid tea that he finally found his way around to the supposed subject of our lunch.

"Tomorrow morning," he said, as if in passing, "we're releasing a statement to the papers along the lines that Berry Merriweather did not, as was originally stated, commit suicide. And that a full-scale investigation is under way."

"It's funny," I replied. "I really don't know whether to be happy or sad. I mean, I feel vindicated . . . but I also feel just awful. Who would have done it? Why?"

"Any thoughts of your own?" he asked casually. "You probably know all the possible players as well as anyone."

"Well, sure . . . I have some ideas," I told him, and then I gave him the list I'd been mentally compiling: Toni, Sara, Dick, Mark, Wes and Wanda. I was flattered to see him taking notes on a smudged-looking pocket-size pad. He stopped when I did and studied what he had written.

"What about other people at Merriweather?" he demanded. "That Brigitte what's-her-name, the designer."

"Sure, she's a possible," I conceded. "But my gut feeling is she's the sanest of the lot over there. Both Toni's and Sara's lives are limited in certain ways—both have invested too much emotionally in Merriweather. I could see either one of them flying off the handle when they heard that Berry was backing out of the deal. I'm sure they hoped Tantamount would offer them big money—and promotions—to stay with the company. Brigitte has other investments—her family, her talent . . ."

"I'm putting her down anyway," Cursio told me, scrawling her name across the page. "Anyone at all close should be considered. That means Star, too."

"Oh, for heaven's sake, Dante!" I retorted. "She's just a kid. . . ."

"Age is not the issue," he answered decisively. "And there's one other person, as well. . . ."

"Yes?"

"I'm heading up the investigation, Peg," he replied, not answering my question. "You realize that I have to cover every base. Consider each possibility. Be as thoroughly objective and diplomatic as is humanely—"

"Cut to the chase scene, okay?" I interrupted. "What are you trying to say?"

"You and Berry were close," he answered slowly.

"Yes."

"The account was important to you . . . and had the possibility of growing even more so, *if* Tantamount came on board."

"True."

"Berry's decision to back out would have hurt your career. And you knew she was planning on it. You were with her that night. Your fingerprints are all over her office."

"Are you actually saying that you think I . . . ?"

"Of course not, Peg," he answered. "I'm just laying down an argument for putting you on this list. I can't let it look like I'm playing favorites."

"But Dante," I argued, "it was me who insisted you look into Berry's death. I was the one who kept saying something was wrong. I've been onto this from the very beginning. You idiots have just started."

"Actually, sweetheart, that's another little area we'd better try to clear up," Cursio said.

"What exactly does that mean?"

"We've known it was murder from day one."

"What?" I cried. "I don't believe it! But you kept telling me that I was being ridiculous, not facing up to the facts."

"Well, that was for your own good," Cursio replied. "We could tell from the first go-round at the M.E.'s lab that she'd been strangled. But the chief and I agreed that it would be better to keep the details quiet with the hope of solving the whole business quickly. Damn that reporter from *New York* magazine!"

"I can't believe you've been lying to me like this!" I cried. His dark, deep-set gaze met mine head-on.

"It wasn't a lie," he told me piously. "It was a nontruth. One that's obviously backfired, if it makes you any happier. Now, instead of a speedy solution, we're facing a bogged-down investigation. And we look like dim-witted fools, to boot."

"Oh . . . what a pity," I said, pulling out my compact and examining my patchy red nose. My fury at Cursio was equaled only by my anger at myself. Somehow, in the upset of Berry's death and in my inner turmoil over my nonrelationship with the man beside me, I'd forgotten just how thoroughly and ruthlessly he was dedicated to his job. I should have known better, I realized now. I should have sensed he was playing me along, that his quick, suspicious mind would have leaped to the same conclusions I did about Berry's demise. How could I have let myself forget that Dante Cursio's first priority was his job? Mere human relationships finished a very poor second. I snapped my compact shut. I started to stand up.

"Please, Peg . . ." Cursio said, pulling me back down to my seat. "Please, don't be mad at me about all this. What real choice did I have? I couldn't involve you—I couldn't tell you. On paper, at least, you're a suspect—and the whole purpose of the operation was secrecy and speed. I just couldn't bring you in on it."

"Bull," I said roughly, trying to pull my hands away. "Baloney," I added for good measure, trying to stand up again. God, I'm articulate when I'm angry.

"Peg ... please...." Cursio said. I could tell by his low, intimate tone of voice that he was trying to get me to look him in the eye. But I knew that once my gaze was caught there, he could pretty well do with me what he wanted. With a pained, sainted expression, I trained my gaze just over his left shoulder.

"Would you mind letting me go, please?" I asked blankly. "I've already taken far too much time for lunch. And obviously *you're* very busy with your little investigation."

"Peg ... I ..." Cursio muttered, exasperation clear in his voice. "Be reasonable, please...."

"I'm being held hostage," I replied evenly, "by the police department. What does one do? Dial 911?"

"Okay!" he cried, releasing my hands. "Think what you like. But one of these days you'll realize that I did this for your own good."

"Spare me, Detective, please!" I retorted, standing up and pulling on my overcoat. "You know what your problem is?" I added as I swung my purse over my shoulder.

"Do tell," Cursio replied evenly, watching me with an odd expression. What was it? Sadness? Regret?

"You want to be in charge of everything," I said. "In absolute control. So you can't trust anyone, you can't listen to anyone. You can't, damn it, *feel* anything."

"Please," Cursio said, his eyes darkening with anger, "don't turn this into a personal thing. I'm just trying to do my job."

"Living is your job, too," I retorted. "Or have you decided not to take your life too personally, either?" It was a good exit line, I thought, so I acted on it.

Outside, the day had turned overcast, the cloud cover low and pregnant with snow. I caught a cab and bounced roughly on the broken springs of the back seat as we headed uptown. I should have felt badly, I know. I should have been angry and let down. Old wounds had been freshly opened. Banked arguments newly sparked. Instead, my heart and my mind raced ahead as we idled in traffic. For months now I'd been letting my life drift, hoping it would be swept up once again in Dante Cursio's strong, sure current. I'd been waiting and hoping. I'd been a fool.

There was only one way, I realized now, that I was going to get him to see what I saw so clearly: that we belonged together as man and wife. He was far too complicated a person to be moved by the niceties of affection. Or the stormy thralls of passion. The center of his world was his work, after all, and it was that core that I needed to penetrate. I had to meet him on his own ground, convince him on his own terms.

I knew suddenly what I had to do. It was so simple, I started to laugh. The cab driver gave me a sharp look in the rearview mirror as we pulled up to the curb in front of the P&Q building. I gave him a handsome tip and my best smile. I was going to solve the murder. Before Cursio did.

THIRTEEN

IT WAS ON THE FRONT PAGE of *Women's Wear Daily* and in column one of the Metropolitan section of the *New York Times*. The local TV stations carried it as a lead story on the evening news, and the *New York* magazine reporter who had pushed the police to go public had to scramble to complete his article in time for the next issue's closing. The news that Berry Merriweather's death had been suspicious had all the right elements: a glamour industry, a high-profile personality, violence and mystery. During the first week of January, you couldn't open up a newspaper without seeing Berry's smiling, jowly face.

"It's not doing us any harm," Toni confessed at the start of a meeting I'd requested at the Merriweather office at the end of the first Friday of the new year. "We have new buyers climbing in the windows. It's amazing."

"And sickening," Sara added bitterly. "They're nothing but a bunch of ambulance chasers. Thrill seekers. One-time buyers at best. Mark my words." Sara chewed nervously on her lower lip as she spoke, a mannerism that I could see had become a bad habit: her lips were chapped and red. And I noticed other indications of inner tension: fingernails bitten to the quick, a bleeding cuticle.

Toni, on the other hand, was the picture of composure. She was sporting yet another new hairstyle: a short, feathery cut with frosted highlights. A broad-shouldered, big-checked jacket over a black sweater dress gave her an air of authority. She sat at the head of the table in the small, airless conference room on the tenth floor of the Zabin Building, Sara and I on either side.

"Well," Toni announced, folding her hands in front of her on the table, "shall we get started, Peg? I've a lot of work ahead of me today." It was nearly four o'clock, the close of the workday for most. But Toni Frankel's hours were some of the longest and most grueling I'd ever known. She frequently stayed until ten at night and often came in on Saturdays. I looked across at her, wondering what that kind of dedication did to one's soul, especially if one discovered it might all be for nothing.

"I was hoping we could wait until Wes got here," I told her. "And Brigitte."

"Wes?" Sara snorted. "Wes Merriweather? Here? After three-thirty on a Friday afternoon? Surely you must be joking—"

"Mr. Merriweather has gone," Toni cut her off abruptly. "And I'm afraid Brigitte had to leave early—some function at her sons' school. But we'll be happy to pass on your ideas to both of them. Why don't you just begin, Peg?"

With a small pang of guilt, I pulled the new sketches for the Merriweather brand-labeling campaign out of my portfolio. This meeting, actually, was a hoax. Although it was nice of me to show the Merriweather contingent our ideas before presenting them at the joint meeting with Tantamount, it was hardly necessary. But it had seemed as good an excuse as any to discover how the company was taking the news of Berry's homicide. Toni seemed to be taking it in stride. Sara, a more inhibited and nervous person anyway, seemed to be having a rougher time of it.

"Oh, God, do we really have to use that little girl?" Sara demanded as soon as she saw the first sketch, which, like the rest, featured Star. "It's so silly... and demeaning for everyone concerned."

"Come on, Sara," Toni replied sharply, "we've already discussed this at length privately. You know perfectly well that was Peg's assignment. Now is hardly the moment to start challenging the validity of the issue." Toni's long, perfectly polished right index finger traced the delicate profile of Star that I'd sketched on the layout. "Please proceed, Peg," Toni added with a sigh, "or we'll be here all night."

"Well, you can see it was quite a challenge to have a teenage model work in all instances," I went on, fanning out the sketches on the conference table. "The women's lingerie and panty hose, for instance, gave us particular headaches. These are just rough layouts by the way. Finished, full-color comps will be presented at the Tantamount meeting next week."

"Wanda, at least, is going to be delighted," Sara predicted spitefully. "This is just what she wanted."

"You think so?" I asked eagerly, pretending not to hear the bitterness in her tone. "I'd sure feel better knowing we were on the right track."

"How can you go wrong with that damned brat in every frame?" Sara retorted.

"Sara, *please*," Toni cut in warningly. "You're being both rude and indiscreet. Whatever problems we may have with the premise of this work, I think we best keep it to ourselves. Considering the, uh, difficult circumstances under which Peg and her people had to operate, I think they did an excellent job. Yes, Peg, a very nice solution." Toni went on, patting the work in front of her.

"To a perfectly ridiculous problem!" Sara added angrily. "I mean, it's not as if we don't have enough crises to cope with right now! First we lose Berry, then we have to deal with Wes. Plus we have Tantamount breathing down our necks. But to be saddled with a positively inane advertising campaign . . ."

"I'm sorry," I said in hurt tones. "I thought we did a rather good job."

"You did," Toni asserted. "Sara's just in a self-pitying mood. We're both under a lot of pressure just now. But that's no reason to lash out indiscriminately. Come on, apologize, Sara. Peg's a friend . . . and we need all of them we can get."

"Well, shit," Sara retorted, flicking frizzy red hair back off her forehead, "would I be so honest if I didn't think Peg was on our side?"

"The fact of the matter is, Peg," Toni confided with a sigh while dropping some of her standoffish professional manner, "we're being watched very carefully at the moment. As you know, Wes is definitely selling out to Tantamount—the papers should be signed within the next few weeks. For some unknown reason he's just taking his sweet time about signing. And, well, Sara, Brigitte and I are part of what Tantamount's buying. Unfortunately, the expendable part."

"Surely Wes is making some provisions for you," I replied. "Some kind of employee contract clause? Isn't that just S.O.P. in buy-out situations like this?"

"I doubt it," Toni said. "Wes doesn't give much of a damn about Merriweather Sportswear, to be quite frank."

"He just wants to take the money and run," Sara added gloomily.

"You're being awfully hard on him," I observed. "The time we all met him at P&Q to discuss the marketing campaign, I thought he seemed very involved with Merriweather's direction. He seemed to know precisely what he wanted."

"Yeah," Sara replied darkly, "he wanted to showcase his daughter. Tell me, honestly, Peg, does that make good advertising sense? I somehow doubt you jumped up and down for joy when the Merriweathers told you their plans."

"Well . . ." I mumbled, stalling for time and thinking of my confrontation with Phillip Ebert over the very issue. "Sometimes, clients' personal needs do get a little bit in the way of their better judgment. Still," I added, gesturing at the layouts in front of us, "I don't think these are anything to be ashamed of."

"Okay, okay," Sara answered, nodding. "Let's say this campaign works fine for now. But what happens next year when the family Merriweather has split with their pot of gold? I mean, here we'll be with an ex-owner's daughter featured in every goddamned one of our ads! We'll have to redo the whole thing, and we'll look like fools in the process."

"You really think Wes is going to walk away from the company?" I demanded, looking from Sara to Toni. "He gave me the impression that he was looking forward to the challenge of running Merriweather."

"The man is terrific at impressions, huh, Toni?" Sara retorted with a tight little smile.

Toni shot Sara a hard glance of warning and added, "Well, I'm afraid it's true. Wes tends to come across like gangbusters. All enthusiasm and drive. You have to remember, though, that he's a model. Appearances are everything for him."

"And underneath the good looks and glamour?" I asked softly. "Just what is Wes Merriweather like?"

"A boy," Toni replied immediately, with a gaze looking inward. "A handsome, charming, spoiled little boy."

" 'Spoiled' is the operative word," Sara added dryly. "He's gotten everything he's wanted in life, just by asking. I mean, he's so great looking, so big, like a cowboy, a hero. It would seem almost unpatriotic to refuse something to a man who looked like that. Wouldn't it?" Though Sara's tone of voice was still brittle with sarcasm, a note of self-reproach had crept in. Somewhere along the way, I guessed, Sara had awakened to Wes's childishness the hard way. I remembered my own bitterness when I discovered that my former boss, Ramsey Farnsworth, whom I adored, actually had feet of clay. There's nothing more devastating than being disillusioned about an idol.

"And Berry knew this about him?" I asked.

"Oh, sure," Toni responded. "Better than anybody. They grew up together, after all."

"Yes, but one hardly needs to be Wes's sister to realize how irresponsible he is," Sara added.

"True," Toni conceded. "Especially in this damned business, where you need to hustle and wrangle. You've got to cover every angle, follow every lead."

"I'm surprised Berry kept him on as a silent partner," I observed casually. "Knowing what she did, isn't it odd that she left the company to him?"

"Who else did she have?" Toni replied. "Their mother died years ago, and God knows where their father is. Oh, Berry realized that Wes was something of a bad penny. Lord, I'll never forget how furious she was the day she ordered him out of here!"

"You mean when the family went to California?" I asked.

"Yes," Toni responded. "It was about a year ago. I really thought they were going to come to blows."

"What was that about?" I asked as casually as possible, pulling together my layouts.

"I still don't know," Toni answered thoughtfully. "Do you, Sara?"

"No, I was on the road at the time," Sara replied. "I heard about the fight secondhand. They said you could hear Berry's voice clear over to the Jacob Javits Convention Center. But as far as I'm concerned, she should have chucked him out ages before then. He was useless."

"What," I asked, the thought occurring to me for the first time, "did he do here, exactly?"

"The accounts," Toni replied. "He kept the books up...or, I suppose more to the point, let them run down."

I left soon afterward, not wanting to push my luck. Absorbed in their own problems, neither of the women seemed to pick up on the fact that I had been pumping them. Or, if they had, they had been skillful at feeding me answers that took suspicion off of them...and laid it rather heavily on the shoulders of Wes Merriweather. The handsome, charming, lazy and—to me at least—increasingly fascinating younger brother.

As I walked south through the gathering darkness toward Macy's, I tried to imagine just what it was Wes had done that would cause Berry to throw him out. Something to do with the accounts? I wondered. It was easy enough, I would guess, in a business as fast paced as retail fashion, to finesse the figures a bit. Money....

"It's behind about 90 percent of the homicides I've handled," Cursio confided to me once. "That is, if you count all the drug hits. But, since most dealers want to make fast bucks, I put them in the money column."

"And what about love?" I'd demanded, disappointed. "What about all those crimes of passion?"

"The other 10 percent," Cursio had replied. "And in many ways, the trickier slice. Money, you know, is easy to trace. You just have to be persistent, dogged and careful as hell. Love, though, babe, now that's a challenge. It ain't fun sorting through the messy drawers of somebody else's heart."

I longed to ask him which way he was playing this new investigation. He always operated, I knew, from some visceral, unarticulated series of impressions about motives and suspects. And somehow this amorphous guiding principle grew into the deductive conclusions that made him one of the most successful detectives on the force. I longed to know what he was thinking now, but I wasn't going to ask. I didn't intend to owe the guy any favors, even though he was about to owe me one.

I'd agreed, despite our falling out, to take little Eva shopping for school clothes at Macy's. It couldn't hurt, I decided, to have the kid grow attached to me. After all, she needed some female figure right now to look up to. To emulate. To admire. And for some reason, which would later totally escape me, I'd decided that I was just the person for the job.

FOURTEEN

I'VE ALWAYS CONSIDERED myself a reasonably funky dresser. Open-minded, experimental, ahead of the usual fashion trends. I got a lot of my clothes sense from Theo, one of the most eclectic and emulated stylists in the world. Theo assembles her wardrobe the way she puts together her famous collages. Her fine eye is capable of taking risks few others would dare: mixing hot-pink viscose with mustard-yellow wool, Scotch plaid with houndstooth check.

The afternoon I met Cursio and Eva at Macy's main entrance, I was wearing my favorite brown leather bomber jacket—a wonderfully weathered specimen on which I'd sewn a dozen or so medals and patches—my snugly, close-fitting black wool tights, an over-size, crazy-quilt Kamali sweater and my favorite of Theo's Christmas gifts: two-tone, black lizard and green suede Maude Frizon ankle-high boots. Not exactly your typical corporate female uniform. But, hey, advertising art directors are *supposed* to look a little wild and crazy, right?

As far as I could tell, Cursio had adjusted easily enough to my slightly left of left fashion statements. During our last months of intimacy, I don't believe he ever commented on what I was wearing—unless it happened to be nothing at all. And I'm not usually in the least self-conscious about my clothes; being gawked at on the street is the price you have to pay for being a little different. Like most artists, Theo holds originality and self-expression sacred. And I've gone along with her on that. It's one part of my character that seems at odds with other parts.

"Peg!" Cursio cried, waving to me as I arrived, breathless and ten minutes late—hardly a record for me—at Macy's bustling Seventh Avenue entrance. As I hurried over, a dark-haired, pale-cheeked girl glanced from me to Cursio and back to me again. Large black pools of intensity looked me up and down unbelievingly. Her tailored, dark blue wool overcoat and

well-buffed black riding boots seemed a cool affront to my
offhanded snazziness. She was very slim and delicate, with
neatly trimmed bangs and a pale pink Cupid's bow of a mouth.
Her forehead was wide and intelligent, her brows serious,
straight lines, her nostrils slightly flared, like those of a young
colt. I felt very large suddenly, out of proportion to the rest of
world, loud and brash and gaudy. I felt recently marked down.

"Hi!" I chirped inanely. "You must be Eva."

"How do you do?" Eva sniffed, holding out five cold, very
stiff fingers, which were withdrawn almost before I had a
chance to squeeze them. Her voice was pure upper-middle-class
British disapproval.

"Well," Cursio said helpfully, "here we are."

"Yep," I agreed, looking down and trying to smile at the
perfect-looking eight-year-old before me. She stared back
coldly. It was not a look that invited fast friendship. My hopes
for easy conquest of Eva, my daydreams about enlisting her in
my campaign to win over her father, crumbled and turned to
dust in a single instant. "Here we are, all right."

"So, where do you want to start?" Cursio asked. "What all
do you need, sweetheart?" He draped his arm easily around
Eva's shoulders and gave her arm a little squeeze.

Eva looked up at him and, through lashes that would shat-
ter hearts one day, replied, "I know precisely what I want,
Daddy. I have a list right here," she patted an expensive-
looking navy handbag. "But it's perfectly ridiculous having you
tag along. Why don't we meet you back here at eight-thirty?"
It was the voice of a mature woman speaking. Self-contained.
In charge. The voice of her mother, no doubt. It made my
blood run cold.

"Okay, fine," Cursio said. He smiled over Eva's head at me
uncertainly. "You two will be all right together?"

"Right as rain," I replied quickly, realizing as soon as I'd
said it just how apt the analogy was. Rain, after all, was wet.
Often cold. Hardly pleasant.

When I was Eva's age, or was it a few years older, few things
were as important to me, or as eagerly anticipated, as shopping for clothes. Theo and I used to make a day of it once a
season, slam-banging our way through the most expensive department stores of whatever city we were then inhabiting. We

shopped creatively, excitedly, instinctively—trying on whatever took our fancy. We rarely had more than the vaguest sense of what we really needed.

"Keep your mind open and your eye alert," Theo had instructed me the day we scoured London for the dress I needed for my prep-school graduation. We eventually found it, but not in any of the acceptable stores. I emerged from Miss Longsworth's Girls' Academy in a nineteenth-century wedding dress made of Belgian lace, train removed, redyed the palest of peaches. Theo had glowed proudly over the fact that three different Longsworth's mothers, the most proper and privileged matrons in London, asked her which dressmaker we'd gone to for my gown.

Before meeting Eva, I had imagined the two of us embarking on a similar kind of acquisitory adventure. I saw us riding gaily up and down escalators, poking experimentally among sales racks, even venturing into the toy department. But as soon as she set off at a brisk pace for the elevator banks, I knew I was in for a different sort of shopping experience.

"Where are we going first?" I asked, hurrying after her. "Perhaps we should stop at the information counter and find out what floors things are on. Macy's is a pretty big store, you know."

"I'm well aware of the size of this building," Eva retorted over her shoulder. "And I've already visited the information booth. They were extremely helpful. See, I've written it all down." She flashed a neatly inscribed index card under my chin. As she pressed the Up elevator button, she added, "I had plenty of time to prepare, as you were so late."

"Ten minutes, tops!" I replied indignantly. Eva is an eight-year-old going on forty, I thought. "But not to worry, I'm sure we'll make that up in no time flat if we follow your little flow-chart there."

Without a sound, Eva stepped into the opening car and in quick succession pressed number three and Close, nearly cutting off my arm as the doors started to shut.

"Hey," I snapped, rubbing my elbow. "Show a few manners, why don't you? I'm giving up my Friday evening to help you shop, you know."

"Well, you asked for it," Eva replied haughtily. "Daddy told me this was your big idea."

"That's true," I answered evenly. "But that was before I met you, remember? Now that I've made your acquaintance, I've got to say that trailing behind your highness in Macy's is hardly my idea of a great weekend opener."

"I shall tell Daddy you said that!" Eva cried, her pale face flushing as she stepped off at the third floor.

"You do that, smarty-pants," I retorted, all too aware that my future as Mrs. Dante Cursio was wobbling horribly in the balance. Which was worse: being unmarried . . . or being untruthful? Unfortunately for me, I have this chronic need to speak my mind. I know, I know. I'm going to end up one hell of an honest old maid.

Eva looked me over haughtily. "Who exactly are you?" she asked, her words escaping in short, angry breaths. "I mean . . . are you actually *dating* Daddy?"

"What does he say?" I asked in reply.

"As little as possible," Eva said with a laugh, looking for the first time not altogether sure of herself. "He . . . he told me you were very, very good friends. But, well . . . *you* aren't married, correct?"

"I thought we were clothes shopping here," I replied briskly, and started to walk toward a large jeans display. I stared at the cutout promotional unit blindly, trying to steel myself against the wave of sympathy welling up in me for Cursio's insufferable daughter. Clearly, she had been brought up to be a pompous, self-righteous little snit. But was it her fault that she had the personality of a stale saltine: dry and hard to swallow? Of course not. It was her mother and stepfather's doing. What a different girl she would be if Cursio and—well, I couldn't help but imagine it—I had raised her. A rush of maternal longing flooded me, and I had to blink back tears when an approaching saleswoman asked, "Would your daughter like to try on the jean jacket? It's Cougar's latest design and quite the rage right now."

Cougar's Country Jeans. The international brand that Wes, Wanda and Star modeled for. I looked up with newly opened eyes at the life-size cutout display; the wholesome, handsome faces of the Merriweather family smiled down at me.

"What's her size, hon?" the saleswoman asked, misinterpreting my interest in the jackets.

"Oh...I'm not sure," I replied, then quickly improvised, "She's been growing so fast this year." I glanced across the floor to see Eva fingering long flannel nightgowns in the sleepwear department. As I started toward her, I promised the saleswoman at the jeans counter that we'd come back later to try on one of the jackets.

"You're going to get *that*?" I demanded as I followed Eva to a checkout counter. She had a long, red-checked flannel nightgown tucked primly under her arm. It had green piping across the chest and lace-fringed neck and sleeves. To me it looked frumpy and old-fashioned, the kind of nightgown grandmothers wore. I glanced around at the various displays: huge polka-dotted pajamas in bright primary colors; lacy, glamorous nighties in romantic shades of peach and aqua, skintight ones printed in wild patterns....

"Yes," Eva replied evenly. "It's just like the one I have at home. Besides, it's nice and warm."

"Whatever you say." I sighed, fingering a pair of black stretch pajamas trimmed with red lace that were displayed near the checkout counter. Madonna would have been proud of these, I decided. Too bad they didn't come in my size.

"I suppose you think I should want something like that?" Eva demanded, nodding to the pair I was looking at.

"There are no 'shoulds' when it comes to clothes," I responded, repeating one of Theo's early lessons. "You buy what's right for you, that's all. I only think that...well, if it's exactly the same nightie as you have at home, why not try something new?"

Eva didn't respond, and I waited in silence as she paid for her purchase. We didn't have much to say to each other for the next hour as I followed Eva on her rather predictable tour of Macy's pre-teens floor. I could tell, even before Eva singled it out, which skirt—the knee-length pleated one—and dress—the dark green corduroy jumper—and pair of pants—navy-blue wool ones with a permanent-press crease—she was going to buy. I watched her move with calm precision through the crowded, colorful racks, selecting the clothes her mother would have chosen for her. She obviously had her mind made up about what she was going to get before she even came into the store. I thought of what Cursio told me once about why his marriage to Gwen had failed. "I just wasn't fitting into Gwen's grand schemes." No doubt Gwen already had her daughter's life pretty well worked out in the same way that she had her wardrobe established.

"We still have half an hour to kill before meeting your dad," I said when Eva had announced that her shopping was completed. "What do you want to do?"

"Nothing in particular," Eva sniffed. "I've got everything I need."

"Well then, let's just wander," I suggested, taking a few of her packages. "Maybe you'll see something you like—just on impulse." If you have any impulses left, I added to myself.

We strolled slowly back through socks and shoes, lingerie and sleepwear, skirts and dresses, until the Cougar's Country Jeans display loomed above us over the sportswear department.

"Isn't that Star Merriweather?" Eva said with a sigh, looking up at the three smiling faces. "She's just about my favorite model in the world."

"Is that right?" I asked. I saw Eva reach out and caress the sleeve of one of the jean jackets. "Why don't you try one of those on?" I suggested. "I bet you'd look great in it...just like Star."

"No...you think so?" Eva asked, slowly unbuttoning her tailored blue overcoat. "I'm afraid it's just not me."

"Oh, come off it, Eva," I snapped, taking her coat and other packages as she slipped the jacket on. "At your age, who knows what *you* really is? You're changing every day."

The stone-washed gray denim accentuated the pale softness of Eva's complexion, the dark arch of her brows, the sweeping wings of auburn hair. She looked both older—and more vulnerable. I helped her adjust the collar so that it sat up, brushing her cheekbones, and then I turned her to the mirror.

"There you go," I said, watching her stare at her reflection. "Now just look at you! As pretty as Star Merriweather, if you ask me."

"No," Eva replied vehemently, but she turned her right profile to the mirror and struck a pose. "She's the most beautiful teenager in the world. Ten times better than Brooke Shields ever was, I think."

"She's okay," I agreed. "But you're just as pretty in person as she is."

"How would you know?" Eva demanded, staring at her reflection in the mirror.

"Didn't your Daddy tell you?" I replied innocently, though I knew he hadn't thought to. "I'm an art director. I'm working on a campaign for Merriweather right now…and Star is the featured model."

"No!" Eva squealed, whirling around and facing me. Her eyes were bright with excitement. "You're kidding! You really mean it? You know Star Merriweather? You work with her? You *direct* her?"

Of course, I had wanted Eva to like me for myself. I had hoped that she would cast me as a role model, a new and different kind of mother figure. But, well, you have to learn to grab what you can in life. Seize the moment. Improvise. By the time we hooked back up with Cursio, Eva had dropped all traces of hostility. She was smiling up at me. We were laughing. From all outside appearances, it looked indeed as if I had won her over completely. But, I knew better.

It wasn't me she liked. If anything, she disapproved and distrusted me as much as when we had first met. No, it was what I had promised. As I watched one young girl excitedly embrace her father, I thought of another, far less happy, girl.

I saw Star's bright, blank public smile. I thought of her monosyllabic responses at our last meeting. Her dazed, faraway look as the table of adults dickered about how best to use her for their gain. As adults had no doubt been doing since she was born. As I had just done.

FIFTEEN

"SHE'S OUT like a light," Cursio told me as he came down the stairs. I was sitting in a well-worn leather chair by the fire, watching the flames leap behind the iron mesh fireguard. As with everything else in his Brooklyn brownstone, the fireplace was arranged with aesthetics taking a back seat to safety. The lovely French windows that looked out on the back garden were obscured by thick iron gridwork. A fire extinguisher hung with ominous prominence on the wall of his bright, high-ceilinged kitchen. Watch Your Step and No Smoking signs dotted the basement. When we had decided to call the whole thing off, I had given him back his keys with something bordering relief. Four different locks had to be negotiated before making it through his front door.

"She was half-asleep at the table," I observed, prodding the fire with a wrought-iron tong. A crumbling log spat sparks through the mesh.

"Hey, watch it!" Cursio cried, crouching and examining the rug. He ran his hand along the carpet, then reached over and took the tongs. "You've got to be more careful, Peg. You could set the place on fire."

"Not with Mr. Safety on the premises," I replied with a tired laugh. We'd had discussions like this too many times in the past. And I wasn't in the mood to consider all the little things that tended to separate us. The big ones were bad enough. The firelight threw Cursio's features into stark relief, highlighting his cheekbones and underscoring the hard, fine curve of his lips. His eyes were shadows.

"I don't want to argue," he replied softly, putting the tong back in its rest. He stepped back into his favorite leather chair; its armrests were worn right through to the stuffing. "I want to thank you for taking care of Eva this evening."

"Oh, I just trailed along behind her," I told him honestly. "There wasn't much I could take care of, really."

"Well she came back happy," Cursio countered. "Happier than I've seen her since she got here. I've got to attribute that to something, Peg."

"Try Star Merriweather," I replied sourly. "I promised that I'd introduce Eva to her sometime soon. Seems Star is a big hit in England. And Eva adores her. It was as simple as that."

"You sound angry about it, for some reason," Cursio observed.

"I am," I replied shortly. "It's...it's hard to explain, but as soon as I told Eva I'd fix her up to meet Star, I felt like...
I don't know. I felt like I was taking advantage of that poor kid. Everybody seems to want a piece of her."

"But isn't that simply the price you pay," Cursio replied, "for being a child star? The public eye is hardly a loving one."

"I just wish I felt like *she* wanted it all more," I told him, turning over in my mind just what it was about Star's attitude that bothered me so. "I mean, there Wes and Wanda and everyone sits working on strategies to push her popularity quotient through the roof, and Star just stares out into space. What does *she* want, Dante? I'd sure feel a lot better about all this if I knew."

"What did you want at that age? Do you remember?" Cursio asked.

"Oh sure! I wanted to be just like everybody else. I longed for a boring, normal mother who'd bake cookies and sit on the board of the PTA."

"Maybe Star wants the same thing," Cursio mused. Then he added, as if as an afterthought, "We discovered something that may make that hope just a little more distant for her."

"Yes?" I asked, sitting up. This was typical Cursio; make like you're about to light a match while you're actually getting ready to drop the A-bomb.

"We did a phone check of all calls to and from the Merriweathers' L.A. residence," Cursio replied, picking absently at the loose fabric on his armrest, "since they moved there from New York. Thirteen and a half months."

"Well?" I demanded. "What did you find? Who had Wes been calling?"

"Not Wes," Cursio replied slowly. "Wanda. She and your little friend Mark Rollings talked to each other on the phone at least once a week for more than a year."

"Mark?" I gasped. "And . . . Wanda?"

"Yep," Cursio replied. "Care to hazard a guess why?"

"No. . . ." I mumbled, trying to fit these strange new pieces together. Mark Rollings and Wanda Merriweather. Both appeared to be so one-dimensional. It seemed impossible to me, but could their superficial sameness have inspired love?

"Do you think they were . . . involved?" I asked him.

"God knows, Peg," Cursio said. "What else could it mean? We can't seem to make any other connection. When did P&Q start handling the account?"

"A year or so ago," I replied, seeing his point. "Mark and Wanda could have met through business dealings although Wanda and Wes had already moved to California. Do you think this has anything to do with Berry's death?"

"I don't know," Cursio said. "All I can say is that it's the one obvious anomaly we've come across so far in the investigation. We're going to question both of them again. And I've a tail on each of them now. I don't want to scare anyone off, though. It's the only lead we've got so far."

A small trickle of guilt circled my heart. Should I tell Cursio what I'd learned about Wes from Sara and Toni? How irresponsible he was? How it was probably his mishandling of the Merriweather accounts that had prompted Berry to banish him to L.A.? Surely this was information Cursio would find relevant. Enlightening. And, I thought coldly, surely it was something he should be able to find out for himself.

After all, I reasoned with myself, I hadn't asked for this new lead about Wanda and Mark; Cursio had volunteered it to me. On the other hand, I had to admit, the poor man had no idea what I was up to. He was confiding in me as a friend . . . and I was stealing his confidence as a rival. I looked over at his dark head, bowed in thought, his left hand cradling his chin. Perhaps if he had looked less attractive, less unobtainable at that moment, I would have reacted differently. But I decided he was a man worth fighting for—even if that meant fighting against him.

"I'm boring you with all this," Cursio said a few minutes later, looking over at me and smiling. "How about a brandy before you head back?"

"Sure," I said, and we sat together by the fire for another half hour, cradling snifters and talking softly about inconsequential things. It felt so comfortable, so right when Cursio's hand grazed mine. It seemed just natural that he should pull me onto his lap a moment or two later. Oh, what a joy it is to kiss a man you love when his lips are sweet with brandy!

"God, you smell good," he murmured, kissing my neck and that particularly responsive spot just below my left ear. He knew what he was doing. I shivered. "I've missed you, Peg," he went on when he sensed I was not about to break into tears as I usually did at this juncture in our postrelationship lovemaking.

"Hmm," I said, enjoying each delicious second.

"This is stupid, you know," Cursio went on, his breath coming a bit faster against my skin. Ah, he was working his way downward to one of his favorite nestling spots. Well, two of them. "Why don't you stay tonight? I'll tell Eva you slept on the couch. She's too young to know the difference."

"But," I murmured, pulling away, "I'm not."

"Please," Cursio said, his voice rough with longing.

I knew the feeling, but I wasn't about to give in. Not now. "Sorry," I answered brightly. "Big day tomorrow. Saturday, you know. Laundry to do. Grocery shopping. Hep, hep."

"Damn," he muttered, pulling himself together. "I'll call you a cab."

I KNOCKED for a second time, and waited. Then I pushed the door, which was already slightly ajar, and stepped into the room.

"Mrs. Merriweather?" I called, searching the large, sun-filled hotel suite for any sign of female life. The silence seemed odd to me; when I'd arranged the appointment the day before, she had made a point of telling me to be punctual. Heavily curtained, richly carpeted, spectacularly furnished, the Merriweathers' luxury accommodations at The Carlyle were among the most expensive in the city. I breathed in the mingled scents of fresh flowers and furniture polish and, a little more loudly this time, called her name.

As with Toni and Sarah, I had asked to see Wanda with the excuse that I wanted her approval on my new creative strategy for the campaign. But my secret agenda for this meeting was even more complicated—and possibly more critical—than the one at the Merriweather offices. I had begun to draw it up in the taxi on my way back from Cursio's Friday night. Just what was the connection between Wanda and Mark? If it was love, I thought I knew how to find out.

"Excuse me?" I called again as I wandered across the main salon. Sharp winter sunlight streamed in the huge windows overlooking Madison Avenue, highlighting the rich, dark patterns in the large Oriental carpet. "Anybody home?"

A hotel room-service cart sat in the corner beside the love seat. I strolled over and glanced down at the ruins of a half-eaten lunch for one: smoked salmon, pumpernickel toast, tossed salad. A bottle of Kalin Cuvee Sonoma Chardonnay had been nearly drained. A small prescription bottle sat on its side next to the water glass. I picked it up and looked at the label. It was Valium, made out to Wanda Merriweather. Between the wine and the tranquilizers, I decided, advertising's answer to June Cleaver had had a pretty potent lunch.

I made my way across the living room, through a foyer and down a short hall to the master bedroom. I heard, before I saw, Wanda Merriweather. An indelicate, uneven snoring filled the hallway. I pushed open the door to find her sprawled, **fully** clothed and sound asleep, across the perfectly made-up king-size bed.

SIXTEEN

"PERHAPS YOU'D LIKE some coffee?" I suggested to a tousled, bleary-eyed Wanda Merriweather ten minutes later as we sat side by side on the couch. I had decided not to wake her and had been tiptoeing out of the bedroom when she sat bolt upright in bed, stunned and disoriented, as if waking from a bad dream. It had taken me several minutes to explain who I was and what I was doing there, then she had followed me zombie-like into the living room. "I could call room service for you."

"No," Wanda answered sadly, shaking her head and looking helplessly down at the hands resting in her lap. "It will only make me jumpy. I'll be fine, really." Her practised composure had entirely fallen away, revealing a pale, jittery blonde whose once luminous, youthful beauty was quickly hardening into middle age. Her usually placid blue gaze was trained with a troubling fixity on her clenched fists. "Damn," she muttered to herself.

"I could come back another time," I suggested, "if you don't feel up to it today." I patted the big leather portfolio resting on the couch, which contained the new layouts. "You can see these at the formal presentation next week, if you prefer to wait."

"No," Wanda muttered in a small voice, unclenching her hands and running long, beautifully tapered fingers through her hair. She sat up, straightening her shoulders. "I'd rather see them now. I...I've been so looking forward to this," she added girlishly. I glanced at her to see if she was putting me on, but she wasn't. She smiled back at me as best she could, her left cheek still creased with sleep marks. What is it about people in trouble? I found myself liking this messed-up, hung over, private version of Wanda about ten times better than the glamorous public rendition.

I started to present the new work systematically, beginning with a short explanation of the difficulties inherent in using a young model, but Wanda interrupted me.

"Forget the advertising gobbledygook," she cried excitedly. "Just show me what you've done for her. Please."

Within minutes, Wanda had spread all the new layouts I'd given her over the carpet and was going through them with the uncontrollable joy of a four-year-old opening up Christmas presents.

"These are wonderful!" she cried. "They're perfect."

"Well, they're not finished yet," I reminded her modestly. "We're working on the final comps now for the presentation to Tantamount."

"Who cares what *they* think?" Wanda replied gaily. "I say these are terrific. And when it comes to Star, what I say goes."

"Well, that's good news then," I answered, and started to stack up the layouts to put back in my case.

"Oh, no, leave them out, please," Wanda begged. "Just for a while longer? Stay and have something to drink, okay? I just want to look them all over again.... You can't know how much this means to me."

She quickly ordered soft drinks and pretzels from room service, then turned her attention back to the work spread out on the carpet. I've dealt with happy clients before, but Wanda's reaction to the new layouts went far beyond the usual enthusiasm. She smiled hungrily at the rough sketches, like a person lost at sea who spots a distant shoreline.

"I hope Star will be pleased," I said. "Is she around? Maybe she'd like a little preview, too."

"Oh, no," Wanda answered, sighing, "my baby's at school. Dalton, you know. She started back on Monday. God, how I miss her!"

Is that why you were passed out at one-thirty on a Wednesday afternoon? I wondered. As we waited for the snacks to arrive, I watched Wanda sort through the layouts yet again and remembered what Cal had told me about Wanda's problems with drugs and alcohol. They were problems that, despite her image as the perfect little homemaker, clearly hadn't gone away.

The drinks came, and she poured me a ginger ale, herself a Coke. She sipped the soda through a straw with the innocence of someone who had never tasted anything stronger than cooking sherry in her life. To me, it was just one more thing about the Merriweather household that didn't add up.

Why, for instance, were they staying at one of the most expensive hotels in the city? Surely it would make more sense—and take a lot less money—for them to sublet an apartment. And how were they financing their extravagant life-style? I knew what the top-ranked models made. Though a comfortable living, it wasn't enough to underwrite the costs of Wanda's and Wes's elaborate wardrobes, this luxury suite, Star's exclusive prep school and God knew what else. Berry had told me once that her younger brother had no sense of what things cost. I could see that. What I wanted to know was how, exactly, did he get things paid for? And, for that matter, what did Wes do all day? According to Sara and Toni, he put in only token appearances at the Merriweather offices. Seeing Wanda's relaxed and satisfied expression, I decided it was time to get down to some of my real reasons for being there.

"I can't tell you how glad I am," I began, "that you're pleased with what we've done. All of us at P&Q put a lot of work into the project."

"I can see that," Wanda said warmly.

"Mark Rollings, especially," I went on, lying a little in the hope that it would help me get at the truth. "He kept at us night and day. Your account is obviously a special one for him."

"Oh, I doubt he cares all that much about Merriweather," Wanda observed, sucking on her straw. "Anyone can see he has his eye on Tantamount."

"I don't know about that," I mused. "I can't remember when I've seen him so involved, so wrapped up in all the details of a presentation."

"That's nice," Wanda answered, smiling down at the clutter of layouts. She was not taking the bait.

"He's a very . . . special kind of person," I observed. The untruth caught in my throat and came out at top volume.

"Who?" Wanda asked, startled, looking up and over at me. "Mark Rollings, you mean?"

"Yes," I said, "don't you think?"

"Oh, honey," Wanda said with a sad smile. "I'm afraid I don't think any man is particularly special anymore. But, you're still young. It's best to find these things out for yourself."

"But surely with Wes...I mean, your husband...?"

"Oh, Lord, don't tell me he has you hoodwinked, too." Wanda sighed. She looked me over objectively and shook her head. "Well, at least his taste is starting to improve."

"I beg your pardon?" I replied huffily. "There is nothing between your husband and myself...if that's what you're trying to imply."

"Then that makes you something of an exception," she said with a bitter laugh, "for a single woman working in the fashion industry."

"Mrs. Merriweather," I replied, wondering suddenly if she had managed to spike her Coke with something stronger, "do you know what you're saying?"

"Of course," Wanda answered evenly. "My dear, handsome husband has screwed his way up and down Seventh Avenue for the past twenty years. He knew a good thing when he saw it. It's an industry chock-full of stylish, pretty women... and hardly one straight man in the lot. Let alone such a big, good-looking one. Oh, heavens, yes, he knew a good thing. So he cut a wide swath through the lovely ladies...then the not-so-lovely ladies. If they have skirts on that he can pull down, that's just about the only thing that matters. And maybe that's what hurts the most."

"What?" I breathed, stunned by what I was hearing.

"That he doesn't even care if they're pretty anymore," Wanda answered. "I mean, I think I'd really feel better about the whole thing if he made it only with beautiful women. But when I found out about those two losers down at that dreary little office, well, I just gave up on him. How could I have any pride left after hearing about that?"

"I...I'm sorry," I replied, trying to recover from the shock and at the same time process the information she had just given me. "Whom do you mean by 'losers'? Are you telling me that someone in the Merriweather office had an affair with your husband?"

"Frankly, honey, I'd be pretty surprised if someone in the office hadn't."

"But specifically?" I demanded. "You know for sure?"

"You sure he's not making it with you, too?" Wanda asked. "You sound all wrought up about this."

"Oh," I replied, reining in my curiosity. "No, of course not. I'm just shocked, that's all. Upset for you. And Star."

"Well, thanks anyway, but we don't need your sympathy," Wanda replied proudly. She stood up, made her way rather regally across the room and rummaged around in the top drawer of a desk. She lit a cigarette from the crumpled pack she'd found and inhaled with the quick, deep breath of a practiced smoker. "At one time, I could have used it, but not now."

"How long have you known?" I asked, wondering how I could decently get back around to asking who the "two lovers" might be.

"Over a year, now," Wanda replied, exhaling slowly. "Though I figure he's been on the make almost since we got married. But, I don't want to make him out a complete slob. In the beginning, you know, maybe ten years ago or so, Wes had his reasons."

"Yes?" I asked, thinking of what Cursio would probably give to be sitting in my seat right now. A woman will easily confide things to another woman that she'd never dream of telling a man. "What were they?"

"You see, I had a few problems," Wanda replied, pacing in front of the window. "Drugs, stuff like that. I was a party girl, you know? And even after Wes and I got married, well, I just couldn't seem to pick up a knack for domestic life. And, see, Wes wanted the big, happy family scene. I guess...well, I must have been something of a disappointment for him."

"Did he realize what was going on?" I asked. "Did he know you were in trouble with drugs?"

"Oh, he knew, but he didn't know," Wanda tried to explain, looking out the window but staring into the past. "He was such a together kind of guy. I mean, he was hardly your Mr. Nine-to-Five, or anything. But in his own way he was pretty conservative about things. At parties he'd like to say, 'Okay, that's my limit,' stuff like that."

"You're speaking of all this in the past tense," I observed. "Has he changed?"

"About booze and pills, no," she answered quickly. "But there are other addictions in this world, you know. Worse ones, if you ask me."

"Women," I said. It was a statement, one she didn't dispute.

"The sad thing is," Wanda went on, "the real shame of it is, just when I got my act together, I found out that Wes had let his all hang out."

"You're saying you kicked drugs?" I asked, for good reason not particularly convinced.

"The hard stuff," Wanda replied, turning and looking me straight in the eye. She stubbed out her cigarette in a heavy cut-glass ashtray and walked back over to the couch. "The bad news stuff, yes. I'm off it. I'm clean. Have been for over a year now."

"So what was that business when I first came in?" I asked. "You would hardly have passed a breath test, you know."

"We all slip now and then," Wanda replied defensively. "I've been pretty damned good for the most part. I have to be. You see, as soon as I can swing it, I'm getting Star and myself out of this hole."

I looked around the spacious, beautifully appointed room. It took me a second to realize she meant the psychological one she and Wes had built together in lieu of a marriage. "You mean, you're going to leave your husband?"

"You got it," Wanda replied triumphantly. She then gestured to my layouts on the carpets. "And this is how we're going to do it! I'm going to build Star up into one of the biggest models in the industry. And I won't let her fall into any of the traps I did. I'm going to help her save her money. We'll have a real clean, careful kind of life. We're going to start all over again, Star and me."

"You're pinning some mighty heavy hopes on a pretty young girl," I observed coolly.

"You don't believe me," Wanda cried, turning to face me angrily. "You don't think we can do it."

"I didn't say that," I replied, reaching down to gather up the layouts. This time Wanda didn't try to stop me. "I think you can do anything if you want to badly enough. But there's always a price, always something you've got to give up if you want to succeed. And, if you ask me, all the give-backs in your scheme are going to come out of Star's life—her freedom, her youth, her individuality.''

Wanda didn't ask me to linger after that, and I can't say that I blamed her. It was easy enough for me to cast judgments; I had nothing to lose. But Wanda's future was hanging by a thread or, more exactly, by the tissue layouts in my portfolio. I felt badly for the woman and also a lot more warmly toward her than I had before. Behind the superficially glamorous life lurked problems no one in this world would envy.

I'd gone there thinking I'd ferret out a little love affair between Mark and her...and had come away with the major news of Wes's insatiable appetites. I hadn't asked again who Wanda suspected Wes had been involved with at the office. The more I thought about it, the more convinced I became that it was Sara and Toni. Both so needy, so willing. And there had been all those strange undercurrents in their discussion of him. Had each discovered the other's affair with Wes? Were they united against him in love...or in bitterness? How much did Brigitte know? What exactly had Berry suspected? Did Star have any idea what her mother was planning?

I took a taxi back to the office, my thoughts tangled in a thickening web of speculation. Everywhere I looked there seemed to be traces of passion, jealousy, greed, longing. Understandable need. Life-affirming emotions. Yes, there was pettiness and deceit. But something was missing. Nowhere did I sense amidst these natural rhythms of the human heart the irregular beat of hatred and murder.

SEVENTEEN

IT WAS ONE of those grim, snow-laden, mid-January days when evening seemed to settle in shortly after noontime. The raucous good feelings of the holidays had dissipated, almost as if they had never been, and the next possible thing to look forward to was the long weekend over Washington's Birthday. Light-years away. The P&Q offices felt overheated and drafty, overlighted and yet somehow dreary. The Christmas decorations had finally been taken down, leaving one with the sense of something newly missing in the corridors and reception areas. If the spiritual tide of the P&Q offices were ever mapped, that day would have marked its lowest ebb.

Even Ruthie, our model of corporate bonhomie, looked glum and listless. A woman who has spent most of her adult life waging a private, agonizing war against carbohydrates, Ruthie had since the beginning of the new year looked both overfed and undernourished. She had the pallor of one who had recently devoured a full bag of Oreos in the light of an open refrigerator door.

And none of this was good news. Because at three-thirty that afternoon, Peabody & Quinlan was scheduled to present its new creative and marketing concepts to the executive staffs of Tantamount Enterprises and its newest subsidiary, Merriweather Sportswear. As Toni had predicted, Wes had finally signed over the ownership of the company. Just where that left Merriweather in terms of leadership, however, was still very much up in the air. But I had a feeling that the afternoon meeting would answer a lot of the unresolved questions. Issues that demanded decisions—such as ad layouts and media plans—had a way of illuminating even the vaguest chains of command.

The new business team for Tantamount, which was comprised of Phillip, Mark, Larry the copywriter, Felice Clay, who was our media director, and myself, had held three run-throughs of the presentation materials. The creative work was as strong as it could be. The media planning was sound. Our brand-labeling strategies were based on the latest research data and buying-trend analyses. And yet I felt restless and uncertain. Forty minutes before the meeting was scheduled to begin, I decided to stop pretending I was going to get any other work done. I told Ruthie to hold my calls and headed down to the conference room to go through my part again.

I hadn't been in the large, semicircular auditorium since the morning of Berry's death. About a month ago now. I switched on the overhead lights as the door swooshed shut behind me, and I started down the carpeted ramp to the stage area. I was halfway up the steps when a small, flat voice said, "Um . . . excuse me?"

I whirled around. Star Merriweather sat in the front row, dressed in her school clothes, a winter coat folded on top of a pile of books in the seat next to her. "Wanda told me to meet her here. A secretary showed me where to come. I hope it's okay?"

"Well, sure," I replied, smiling down at her. She looked so young in the conservative, pleated skirt and navy blazer. And she looked more nervous than I recalled from our first meeting; her dark brows formed a questioning arc on her forehead. "You're a little early, though," I added.

"I know," Star said. "I'm sorry. I promise to be quiet and not bother you. Now that the lights are on, I could study my algebra."

I wondered how long she had been sitting alone in the dark and what adolescent fear had kept her from turning on the lights herself. I remembered suddenly how odd and treacherous the world seemed when I was in my early teens. I grew up, as Star was growing up, surrounded by adults. No longer a child, not yet a grown-up, I remember feeling that I belonged nowhere in particular . . . and that I was never going to fit in.

"God, I hated algebra," I replied, walking across the stage to the large easel. It was to be a multimedia presentation: slides, video, concept boards. I flipped through the boards; everything was in order. I walked back down the steps to the rear of the room, where the slide carousel was set up. "Hey," I called down to Star. "You want a private screening?"

"You mean of the stuff I might be doing?" she asked, turning around in her seat. Her perfect, heart-shaped face, usually so pale, flushed suddenly. "Is that...legal? I mean...you won't get in any trouble or anything, will you?"

"Oh, probably," I answered, laughing, wondering what Star's laugh would sound like. I couldn't remember ever seeing her smile. "But then I'm usually in hot water around here. Come on back. I'm not going to turn on the projector. I'll just go through the slides with you."

"Thank you," Star said formally, walking back and slipping into the seat next to mine. She held out her hand as I picked up the first slide.

"Now hold it up to the light," I told her. "That's right."

"It looks just like me!" she cried, staring up at the inch-square chrome of the finished comp. "But the dress is too big."

"It's supposed to be," I told her, taking the slide back and handing her another. "You see, the point of the campaign is that you *are* too young for all the clothes you'll be wearing. You are the age you actually are—a young girl—daydreaming about what you're going to look like when you grow up."

"Oh," Star answered slowly, holding up the new chrome. It was a scene of the French Riviera, perhaps along the promenade des Anglais in Nice. Star, dressed in an oversize sun hat and beach robe, lounged in a deck chair. I had worked for an air of innocence and fairyland fantasy throughout the campaign. I glanced over at Star as she studied the comp and thought that if the photographer could capture the expression on her face at that very minute, we would have just the look I was shooting for.

"This is Venice, right?" Star asked me eagerly after she'd studied the next slide. Dressed in one of Merriweather's new formal evening dresses—a red velveteen affair with a bustline hedged with fabric roses—Star was being poled across the Grand Canal in a gondola. "Would we get to go to the different places to shoot these?"

"I sure in hell hope so," I told her, handing her a new chrome. "Why do you think I went to so much trouble to sketch out exotic backgrounds? I try to use my head, you know."

"I can see that," Star told me earnestly. "These are very good. And I can't tell you how happy I am that...I won't have to pretend about my age. I've been trying to practice looking older, but it's not easy."

"I bet," I answered, smiling across at her. A pair of mist-shrouded blue eyes met mine, uncompromising in their seriousness. And I concluded that even though Star looked younger than her fifteen years, emotionally she was much older. I sensed that she had been born old, that she'd somehow skipped the wonderful silliness of childhood. Like all adolescents, I'd been difficult and troubled, but my problems in the end had added up to the usual growing pains. There was a sadness, a knowingness to Star that made my heart go out to her. At the same time, I sensed she would resent any signs of sympathy.

"This will be the first time I've worked alone, you know," Star told me, handing back a chrome and staring out across the rows of empty seats. "I've always had Wes and Wanda around for moral support before."

"You'll be fine," I told her, wondering what it meant psychologically when parents, mine included, wanted to be called by their first names. Did they hope to be thought of as equals? Or did it absolve them from certain parental responsibilities? "Besides, I'm sure they'll be around when we're shooting."

"Yes," Star answered without conviction. "I'm sure."

As if on cue, the right-side door to the conference room swung open and Wanda Merriweather swept in, followed at a more regal pace by Wes. Both were impeccably dressed. Wanda's tall, stylishly thin frame was draped in one of Armani's latest triumphs: a caramel-colored cowl-necked woolen jacket with matching pleated trousers. Her hair was pulled back off her face and clipped at the nape with an oversize black velvet bow. Wes, affecting a country gentleman look, sported a Harris tweed jacket with leather patches, a cashmere sweater-vest and a pair of perfectly buffed riding boots. All he needed was a pipe and a pair of golden retrievers to pass as landed gentry.

"Darling!" Wanda drawled, hurrying over to Star and kissing her dramatically on the forehead. "Darling, I was so worried! But you got here safely? You took a cab like I said?"

"Actually, no," Star replied, stepping out of her mother's embrace to look her over carefully. The wide azure eyes searched her mother's face, looking for... what? I wondered. Signs of drinking? Pills? "It was really just as easy to take the Fifth Avenue bus. And a lot less expensive."

"For heaven's sake, hon," Wes said with a laugh, his voice booming around the room, "you are the miserliest little gal I know. You're gonna give this lovely lady here," he added, flashing me a smile, "the impression we don't got two sticks to rub together."

The door had opened again as Wes was talking, and Dick Byser, Mark and Phillip strolled in.

"We all know you have a hell of a lot more than two sticks these days," Dick called out as he approached. When he reached our group, he held out both hands to Wanda and murmured as he kissed her cheek, "Stunning, my dear."

In the next fifteen minutes, the conference room filled. Toni, Sara and Brigitte, along with half a dozen other Merriweather employees, sat together in the back of the room. The family Merriweather, Dick Byser and three expensively dressed gentlemen I took to be Tantamount brass took positions up front. As usual, P&Q had rounded up every available secretary and clerk to stock empty seats and give our prospective clients the not-altogether-accurate impression that legions of people were waiting breathlessly to serve on their account. Those of us on the new business team took our places, and Phillip moved center stage to deliver his prepared speech. But, as with all effective speakers, when Phillip began to talk, it was with the ease and sincerity of a husband greeting his wife after a long day.

"Hello," he started, his smile managing to take in the whole room. "Thanks for coming by. We've been looking forward to this day for a long time. We've been preparing for it, too. And what you'll be seeing in the next couple of hours reflects that hard work. It also reflects something that, I think, separates a good agency from a great one. What you're going to see shows our *thinking*."

As Phillip spoke, he started slowly down the steps. He continued now up one aisle, down the other, his hands in his pockets, his voice and expression reflective. "You see, I think that any agency worth its salt can pull together some nice creative layouts, a coherent media plan, sensible marketing ideas.

So why go with one agency over another, if they can all do pretty much the same thing? Well, every once in a while an agency will find itself with a group of people that has the experience and brainpower to do more than solve marketing problems for a particular client. They can actually provide you with business solutions. It happens that for Merriweather and, even further, for Tantamount, Peabody & Quinlan is lucky enough to have those people. Friends,'' Phillip concluded, walking back up the steps, ''what you are about to hear and see are not just *ideas* for Merriweather Sportswear. What we have here are *solutions* to a range of very difficult and pressing needs. Enough said by me,'' he added, taking his seat at the end of the dais. ''Mark, why don't you begin?''

I don't remember exactly when I knew that everything was going to work out, but it was shortly after Mark Rollings launched into his opening remarks. To my amazement, the very worst public speaker on our team had managed to find a new, authoritative voice that afternoon. Mark spoke forcefully. He projected confidence. He made me want to listen. He even smiled a few times—something he'd never had the presence of mind to manage before during a new business presentation—in the general direction, I noticed, of Wanda Merriweather.

I wasn't the only one to observe Mark's transformation. A few minutes into his speech, Larry Milner, seated to my left, nudged me and whispered, ''Heavens, Peg, what's come over Rollings? He actually sounds like a human being!''

And an intelligent, savvy one at that. I scanned the faces in the crowd, from Dick to Brigitte to Star. Every eye was on Mark. I even saw one of the Tantamount honchos nod in agreement with something he said. It was happening. The big ball of approval was bouncing in our direction. All the rest of us had to do now was keep the momentum going. And we did. Felice Clay with her meticulously planned media proposal. Larry with his very funny reading of the copy lines. Me with the graphics. After we got rolling with the creative presentation, after hearing the first laughs and grunts of approval, it was easy. It was just like performing on any stage. It was fun. And it was over way too soon.

''Well, thank you,'' Dick Byser said, rising as Phillip ended his closing remarks. ''Congratulations one and all for a first-rate presentation. It's not often that one gets the opportunity to accuse an ad man of understatement." There was a hardy round of laughter at this juncture. "But," Dick went on, "I just want to tell you, Phillip, that what I saw here today was more than just sound thinking. It was brilliant strategizing. The kind of input both Merriweather and Tantamount hope to continue to get from you and your people in the future."

And that was that. I couldn't quite believe it. And neither, I realized, could Phillip. For one of the first times in memory, he seemed to have lost his bearings.

"Um, you mean," he stuttered, standing up abruptly at the dais and knocking over a full glass of water, "we have the account?"

"Yes," Dick replied simply, standing again, as well. The rest of the room shuffled to its feet, gathering briefcases and overcoats.

Phillip, still stunned, asked again, "You mean we have the *Tantamount* account?"

"Well, yes, Phillip," Dick said, "I thought that was clear. You do want it, don't you?"

Recovering himself, Phillip answered, "Oh, yes, Dick." He righted the glass. "Yes, indeed."

It is not every day that an agency gets a new client the size of Tantamount. An hour and forty-five minutes after we started the presentation, we had managed to add to P&Q's billings by nearly 10 percent. New staff would be needed. Another floor leased. Phillip would now no doubt be elevated to the board. Mark, too, would receive a major promotion. Bonuses would float down like so many bright balloons on Felice, Larry, myself and others of us lucky enough to have been involved with the pitch. For that's what this always came down to: luck.

I don't care what Phillip and Dick said about thinking. Most agencies win accounts on totally emotional grounds. It's all chemistry, as far as I'm concerned, not logic.

Later, after Phillip had invited the interested parties up to the executive dining room for a celebratory toast, I was able to analyze the various chemical reactions and interactions more closely.

Mark, sipping his Perrier-Jouët and chatting with Toni Frankel, could not take his eyes off Wanda, who, gulping her second glass of champagne, listened to what appeared to be quite a lengthy monologue by a very intense Dick Byser. Dick and Wanda? I mulled over the idea. Had Cursio's tidbit about the phone calls been misleading? Had it been Dick all along with, perhaps, poor Mark as a lovesick go-between?

Wes, on the other hand, seemed uncomfortable in the corner where Sara had trapped him. He kept glancing around the room, obviously looking for some means of escape. I could only imagine what Sara, a woman scorned, would have to say to her ex-lover. I saw the look of pure relief that swept across Wes's face when Brigitte came up, her plump face dimpled with a smile, her infectious laugh lightening even the worried expression that Star was wearing.

I watched as Star kept glancing over at her mother and Dick. Wanda lit a cigarette and waved the waiter over for another flute of champagne. I would be upset, too, if I were Star, especially if I knew that Wanda planned to leave Wes as soon as Star's career was established. And speaking of Wes . . .

"Hallo, there, honey chile," the rich base rumbled behind me. I could feel his breath on the back of my neck. "You know something, dark eyes, I've been watching you. Real hard. The way you move. How you speak. And, you know, I've come to the overwhelming conclusion that you are dynamite—I mean pure TNT when it comes to—"

"Oh, excuse me," I mumbled, turning away. But I heard him whisper after me, all softly seductive . . .

"Lay . . . outs."

The Tantamount contingent, led by an obviously self satisfied Dick Byser, left a few minutes later. Phillip drifted off to his executive suite. Larry and Felice made their excuses. The room started to empty until, around seven o'clock or so, found myself alone with Mark, Wanda and Star.

"Where's whozzits?" Wanda demanded thickly, turning around and looking at the door.

"If you mean Wes," Star replied calmly, "he told me he had some calls to make and that he'd meet us back at the hotel."

"Calls my ass," Wanda muttered. Then she turned to Mark and asked with a giggle, "Where's the bubbly, bub?"

"Umm, it's . . ." Mark began, but I cut in.

"It's all gone, Wanda. And so is just about everyone. I'd say it's about time the rest of us headed home."

"Party pooper!" Wanda cried petulantly.

"Come on, Wanda," Star interjected. "She's right. It's time to go."

"Husband grabber!" Wanda hissed, her tone turning suddenly nasty. "I saw the two of you in the corner! God, I hate a liar!"

"I don't know what you're—"

"Wanda, come on," Star broke in again. "I'm tired. And I've got a ton of homework. Let's go now, please?"

"Okay, honey, okay," Wanda answered wearily, allowing Mark to help her into her ankle-length beaver. Mark tried to take her arm, but she shook him off. "I'm fine, damn it! Perfectly fine." At the door she whirled around and, fixing me with a blurred, angry look, announced, "I know him one hell of a lot better than you do, hon. I know what he wants sometimes even before he does. And what my Wesley wants . . . he gets."

It wasn't her anger that unnerved me. It wasn't even the weird, sad tone of pride. But after I heard the elevator door close behind them, I looked down at the half-empty glass in my hand and realized it was shaking. As were my hands. And my knees. I collapsed into the nearest chair and drained the glass of lukewarm champagne. No, it was her sense of certainty that made me feel so edgy. It had become clear to me during the past couple of weeks that I was not going to solve the mystery of Berry's death without somehow unraveling the truth about her younger brother. I had been avoiding him, I realized now. I had been circling around him with my visits to Sara, Toni and Wanda. I had been purposely keeping clear of Wes Merriweather. And for good reason.

Even now I could feel his breath, warm and caressing, on the back of my neck.

EIGHTEEN

WINNING THE TANTAMOUNT ACCOUNT turned out to be just the
lucky break that P&Q needed. I hadn't realized how bad a need
there had been until Phillip Ebert called me in for a private
conference two days after our remarkable conquest.

"Oh, yes, my dear," Phillip confided. "There was even talk
of disbanding the board. We just managed to make our fourth-
quarter projections by carrying over all sorts of expenses into
this fiscal year. God knows, only a miracle could have saved us
this quarter. And, by God, we have achieved that miracle!"
Our usually sober, cautious leader seemed downright gleeful
that morning. He couldn't stop smiling to himself.

"Just as well that I didn't know all this the other day," I told
him. "I would have been scared stiff if I had realized how much
was riding on the show."

"Nonsense, Peg," Phillip replied forcefully, leaning back in
his black leather swivel chair. "You would have been splendid
whatever the circumstances. All of us are very pleased with
your work, my dear. You have not only stepped into Ramsey
Farnsworth's shoes, you have more than filled them." Phillip
smiled benevolently across the table at me as I tried to think of
the right thing to say. But all that came to mind was a mental
picture of a pair of Ramsey's size twelve alligator loafers.
Ramsey Farnsworth had loved beautiful things and intelligent
people, and he probably would have groaned aloud at Phillip's clichéd compliment. I managed to curb my own impulse
in that direction and at last got out a humble "thank you" to
the president of the division. As it turned out, it was definitely
the right thing to do.

"Yes," Phillip repeated again with relish, "we have been
pleased. By 'we' I'm referring, of course, to the board of directors." For some reason he seemed intent on belaboring the
point. I glanced sharply across at his beaming countenance,
realizing at last what he was trying to tell me.

"You made the board!" I cried.

"Right you are," Phillip answered. "A yellow memo will be posted this afternoon." Yellow paper was reserved for the very highest level of executive announcements. "A blue one will be circulating, as well," Phillip added. Blue was the next level down in terms of importance.

"Well, congratulations," I told him. "You deserve it, Phillip. I just hope this won't lift you so far up in the P&Q stratosphere that I won't get to see you anymore."

"I'll only be dealing directly with vice presidents," Phillip answered soberly, "from here on out."

"Oh," I said, saddened, but not really surprised. P&Q, like so many other major corporations, was run like the armed forces. You didn't survive long unless you appreciated the deeply stratified chain of command. As head of a department, I could challenge another department head—Felice Clay, for instance. But I would always have to defer to the judgment of a V.P., no matter how junior. "Well, it's been nice knowing you, then," I added with a weak smile as I got up to leave.

"Sit *down*, young lady," Phillip commanded. "Good," he added, nodding, after I'd plunked myself back in the chair again. "Since you've studiously avoided picking up any of the hints I've dropped, I'm just going to have to come out and say it. The blue memorandum today will announce your promotion to vice president, creative director."

"Me?" I demanded, automatically sitting up straighter in the chair.

"Yes, you," Phillip said, beaming. "You, Mark and Felice. You're all being made V.P.'s. But, Peg, I've got to tell you that I'm particularly pleased at your appointment. You're the youngest V.P. in creative we've ever named. And I guess I like to flatter myself into thinking that the congeniality, the closeness between the two of us has helped your growth here."

"You're right," I answered quickly, hardly about to tell the man that I had Ramsey to thank for just about everything I knew. But I added graciously, "I don't quite know how to pay you back for all your help and advice over the years."

"Well, I do," Phillip replied, a bit too quickly for my taste. "There's a small, and I think not too unpleasant, favor you can do for us."

"Yes?" I asked. I was beginning to regret that I had just admitted I owed Phillip anything.

"You were planning to shoot the Merriweather ads on location, right?"

"Well, yes," I replied. "I was hoping to. But if there are budget restrictions, I understand. We could always opt for a studio, I guess." I thought it over for a few seconds. "Sure, I suppose I could manage to produce it all in the city, if that's what you want."

"Not at all, my dear," Phillip responded. "We want you to shoot in Europe, just as you had intended. And we want you to start scouting locations as soon as you can get away." I stared at the newest member of the board of directors; he was full of surprises today, all right.

"Well . . . that's very generous of you," I replied cautiously. "What's the hitch?"

"No hitch, Peg," Phillip told me with a warm smile. "No big deal at all. We just want you to take your featured model along with you when you go."

"Star?" I asked incredulously. "But why?"

"Yes, Star. And Wanda, too," Phillip replied. "We thought it would make a nice diversion for them."

"What do you mean 'diversion'?" I demanded. "And who is 'we'?"

"Peg, please," Phillip responded, throwing up his hands. "Why so suspicious? What's the problem? Good Lord, anyone else would be jumping at this assignment. Three weeks in Europe, expenses paid, yet?"

"But what am I supposed to be doing there, Phillip?" I asked querulously. "Baby-sitting? Chaperoning? God knows, it doesn't take three people and two weeks to locate a nice piece of coastline on the Côte d'Azur."

"I don't like your attitude, young lady," Phillip told me stonily. "If you'd rather pass on the project, just let me know. Although I'm afraid that resigning from Merriweather at this juncture would put your new promotion in jeopardy."

"I see," I said slowly. "Well, I guess that doesn't leave me much choice. What does one wear in Cannes during the off-season, I wonder?"

"I knew you'd come through for us," Phillip told me as I stood up to leave. "That's my girl."

And whose girl, I wondered throughout the rest of the day, was Wanda Merriweather? Someone with enough clout to arrange this little European holiday for her. Mark? I doubted it. Even his new V.P. status didn't bring him that kind of weight. Wes? I wouldn't think so. Except for the necessary public appearances, I got the impression the two adult Merriweathers had as little to do with each other as possible. So that left Dick Byser. Dick, who had just handed P&Q one hell of a lucrative account. Dick, who could demand just about anything he wanted from an all-too-anxious-to-please Phillip Ebert.

But why, if Dick had a thing for Wanda, did he want her out of the country? Did he see, as I certainly did, that her drinking was starting to get the better of her? Was it concern for her health...or fear that Wanda's breakdown would bring to light things Dick would prefer hidden?

It occurred to me, as I spent the afternoon making travel arrangements, that being in close contact with Wanda and Star for three weeks might just be the biggest break I'd had yet in my private investigation of Berry's murder. It didn't surprise me that the head of the public investigation into the case came to exactly the same conclusion.

"You're going away for three weeks with them?" Cursio cried when I called him that night at police headquarters to tell him my plans. "I can barely get my foot in the door for a five-minute interview. I shouldn't allow it, you know. I should put some kind of restraining order on them."

"I take it things aren't going so well," I replied gently.

"Damn it, no," Cursio barked. "The few times I've gotten in to see that damn Merriweather woman, she's half-crocked. The great and benevolent Mr. Merriweather, though sober, is about as talkative on the subject of his sister as the mayor is on housing for the homeless. In other words, no. Things are not going well."

"Anything I can do?" I asked sweetly, pleased with Cursio's bad news. At least I was beginning to see the various pieces in this muddled jigsaw puzzle; I had the feeling that Cursio hadn't even gotten the box open yet.

"Yes," Cursio told me. "Come down here and rub my neck. No, better yet, come down here and rub—"

"Dante, please," I interrupted him. "Is that any way to talk to a vice president of creative services?"

"A what?" he demanded. "You said what?"

"It'll be in the papers tomorrow," I told him. "But Ebert gave me the word today. I'm the youngest in P&Q's history."

"Hey, way to go," he said proudly. "That's great. Really, Peg. I just wish we could celebrate before you had to leave. I just wish..." His words trailed off, but a wonderful tenor of longing came through in the sigh that followed.

"When I get back," I told him, promising more in my tone of voice than the words said. We talked for a while longer, and he agreed to stop in at my apartment once or twice to see that Millie, Picasso and my various houseplants were all getting along together. And I promised him I'd get in touch with Brigitte, who had two school-age boys in Brooklyn, to ask if she could recommend a temporary school for Eva. Perhaps the one the boys went to at Eva's age.

I called Brigitte directly after I hung up from speaking to Cursio. A soft-spoken man answered the phone, though in the background I heard a confused racket of rock music and adolescent voices. Brigitte came on the line, her voice as sweetly tempered as her husband's. She was happy to help Cursio out, to the extent of insisting that she call her sons' school the very next day to see how soon they could take Eva on.

"It's a fine place," Brigitte told me. "Well run and disciplined—God knows it has to be with my two boys to contend with."

When I started to explain to Brigitte that I'd be away for a while, she broke in excitedly.

"When did you say you'd be in Venice?"

"The week after next," I replied. "We'll be flying there from Nice."

"Well, that's great! What a coincidence! I'm in Italy myself that week, Milano mostly, shopping for fabric for Merriweather's new line. But, hey, I could easily swoop down to the old Veneto for a night. Could we all have dinner together, you think?"

"I'd love to, Brigitte," I told her warmly, and together we made plans to meet in Venice in twelve days. I called Theo down on *The Argo* after that and heard from both her and Cal, who was on an extension phone, about their plans, matrimonially speaking.

"We're thinking about a big bash on the Fourth of July," Theo enthused. "Up on the island in Maine. Don't you think it fitting irony, darling, to tie the knot on Independence Day?" They were thrilled to hear about my promotion, though I sensed that Theo, whose life represented the antithesis of corporate culture, didn't quite understand that I wasn't yet running the company single-handed.

They wished me bon voyage and a safe journey, and I hung up the phone feeling more content with my life than I had for many months. My future was becoming brighter. The storm clouds that had gathered around my hopes with Cursio seemed to be slowly breaking up. The fog surrounding Berry's death was lifting as well, it seemed to me, though I couldn't make much out of the half-shrouded facts.

I treated myself to a carton of chicken with cashews from the Chinese take-out down the block, which I shared with a ravenous Picasso, along with a bottle of Tsingtao, which I did not share despite a lot of whining and carrying on. While Picasso looked on with growing suspicion, I packed my battered but still dignified Vuittons with enough clothes to keep me going in Europe for decades. And then, catching Picasso off guard in a semidoze, I grabbed him and ran next door to Millie's.

"Here we go," I told Millie after she'd opened the door. Though I'd called her from work that afternoon and she'd eagerly agreed to take care of Picasso while I was away, something about her drawn expression told me she'd changed her mind. Her girlish exuberance about life makes her seem eternally young, while her daily T'ai Chi exercises and macrobiotic diet keep her spritely and trim. But this evening, years had suddenly etched themselves around her mouth and eyes.

"Come in, dear," Millie told me sadly.

"What is it, Millie?" I demanded as soon as she'd closed the door.

"Dear, this trip you're taking," Millie asked as I followed her into her brightly lighted kitchen. Tarot cards were spread out on the table. "Is it important to you? Is it essential that you go?"

"It's a business trip, Millie," I told her, dropping Picasso and sitting down heavily in one of her painted iron chairs. "It's important. But if something's wrong with you, Millie, I don't have to leave. Tell me what it is. Clearly something's the matter."

"Yes," Millie mumbled, turning over a card. "Something is wrong, but not with me. I was working out your chart before, dear. I just wanted to check a few things. Make sure everything was auspicious for you right now in terms of travel."

"And?"

"It's not, dear," Millie told me. Her pale blue eyes, red rimmed with worry, searched mine. "Not at all. And, well, I know what you think of my charts and cards and tea leaves. But, listen to me, Peg—I don't think you should go. I don't want to seem an alarmist, but I see something in your very near future that I don't like in the least."

"And that is, Millie?" I asked with a sigh.

"Death, I'm afraid," she replied gently.

NINETEEN

"LORD, WHAT A VIEW! What a sunset!" Brigitte cried as she and I climbed the ancient, arching steps that led from the Piazzetta di San Marco to the Riva degli Schiavoni. To our left the newly renovated Ducale Palace gleamed in the last rich rays of the sun, while the narrow canal that flowed beneath the infamous Bridge of Sighs glittered darkly, like the fate of so many who had passed above it en route to the prison cells. Across the way, the island of San Giorgio Maggiore cast spidery shadows of Palladian splendor along the blood-red surface of the lagoon. During the few minutes it took us to walk from the *campanile* to the Danieli hotel, night snaked its way down the narrow, echoing streets of Venice, and the pink-lemonade-colored street lamps blinked on one by one along the *fondamento*.

This was my second night in Venice, Brigitte's first. And despite my dark, poorly heated room on the Dorsoduro and the chilly winter mist that hung like smoke above the city, I found the city even more beautiful than I had remembered from my last trip with Theo years ago.

"Someone once said that Venice is kind of like a Renaissance Disneyland," Brigitte commented as we collapsed on the tasseled settee in what many experts feel is the most beautiful lobby in the world. A Byzantine triumph of ornament and material, bejeweled and draped with thick carpets and draperies, the Danieli is where Balzac, Proust and Wagner insisted on staying. And it was one of the few places that Wanda Merriweather deemed "livable" in a city renowned for its meager accommodations and high prices. I kept my eyes on the golden staircase that wound up to the Merriweather suite on the third floor. After some nudging on my part, Wanda had reluctantly agreed that Star and she might join Brigitte and myself for dinner. But she had referred to Merriweather's top designer as that "dumb Swede," and I was beginning to know

Wanda well enough to doubt whether or not she was really going to show.

Wanda, Star and I had landed in Nice the week before after a brief stopover in Paris. From our headquarters at the Négresco, the sprawling wedding cake of a hotel overlooking the promenade des Anglais, we had taken day trips up and down the Côte d'Azur—from Saint-Tropez, Cannes and Cap d'Antibes, to Monaco, Monte Carlo and Menton. The weather was breezy and mild. We woke late, met for a café au lait and croissant in the hotel restaurant and then spent the days in the cherry-red convertible Mercedes that Wanda had insisted on leasing. I found Wanda oddly insistent and assertive about many things: where we would eat; what the day's itinerary would be; how late Star could stay up at night. She came across as a concerned, overly protective stage mother. Only someone who was really looking would see that something wasn't quite right about this particular mother-daughter relationship. And I happened to be looking very closely, indeed.

For one thing, Star willingly did everything Wanda told her. She withstood all of Wanda's parental fussing about her clothes and hair and food. She smiled sweetly when Wanda snapped at her to sit up straight at the table, nodded in fond agreement when Wanda insisted she needed a nap. In short, everything that a normal, healthy teenager would have deemed unfair and uncalled-for parental discipline, Star seemed to lap up like a kitten tasting cream for the first time. For another thing, Wanda wasn't drinking. Her abstinence from booze, and I surmised also from pills, made her snappish and overly critical. And yet, Star beamed proudly at her mother every time she waved away the *carte des vins*.

The more time I spent with them, the more I became aware of how hard they were both working at their roles. I could see what an effort it was for Wanda to play mother…and for Star to act in the subservient role of daughter. Something seemed amiss every time Star murmured, "Yes, Wanda. Of course, Wanda." It dawned on me finally that Star just wasn't used to being mothered. And Wanda, like so many amateurs, was simply overplaying her part. This tension lasted until our arrival in Venice, where, last night over dinner, I had watched

Wanda drink herself into a stupor and Star step into her familiar role as parent.

"She'll be okay," Star had promised me as I helped her lead her mother through the lobby after the meal. "She just needs a good night's sleep. It's all this traveling, you know," Star added as she waited for the elevator. "She'll be herself again in the morning."

And she had been. Only it was the new, unimproved Wanda: whiny during our morning scout of the Rialto and marketplace; complaining throughout the *vaporetto* trip out to the Lido during the afternoon; downright bitchy when I'd suggested she and Star might want to join Brigitte and me for an early-evening tour of the *Campanile* and Basilica San Marco.

"We're not here as tourists, Peg!" she'd snapped at me. "I'm exhausted and so is Star. We're going to take a nap until we have to meet you and that stupid blond cow for dinner. See you in the lobby around eight."

Only now it was nearly eight-forty, and the famous fish restaurant where I'd made reservations didn't hold tables for long. I was just about to ring their room when I saw Star come gliding down the stairs. She was dressed in faded Cougar's Country Jeans and a white cable-stitched turtleneck sweater. Yet for all the informality of her attire, she moved with the studied grace of royalty; an invisible diadem seemed to rest on her head. And every male eye in the lobby followed her as she made her way over to Brigitte and me.

"Hi," she said shyly, nodding at Brigitte, then turning to me. "Wanda is . . . well, we're not going to be able to make it tonight."

"Same problem as last night?" I asked her.

"Yes," Star breathed, her face flushing because Brigitte was glancing from her to me with obvious and avid interest. "It must be a flu or something. She sends her apologies and tells you both to go on. We'll order up room service here."

"But don't you want something more substantial, Star?" Brigitte asked with motherly concern. "You could do with a little more meat on your bones, honey. Why don't you join us?"

"Thanks, but no," Star answered hurriedly, flashing me a nervous smile. She felt she had to stay and take care of Wanda.

That she had to be on call. She was once again taking up the
mantle of responsibility that Wanda kept shrugging off. Her
eyes pleaded with me to understand, not to interfere.

"Okay, then," I said, standing up and pulling on my trench
coat. "I'll see you in the morning. Usual time. Hope she feels
better soon."

"Tell me," Brigitte said as we hurried, high heels clicking
against ancient pavement, through the darkened alleyways that
led to the restaurant, "does she really have a bug? Or is it
something else?"

"What do you mean?" I asked innocently. "What else?"

"Oh, come off it, Peg. Everyone knows there have been
problems. I don't mean to pry. But my heart just goes out to
that poor, beautiful kid."

Mine did, too. As we waited to be squeezed in at one of Corte
Sconta's plain wooden tables, I started to tell Brigitte what I
knew—as well as what I surmised—about Wanda's difficulties. We were seated, served a mouth-watering appetizer of
grilled turbot and a carafe of *Prosecco*, before I got around to
what I considered the main reason Wanda kept falling off the
wagon.

"It's because of Wes, I think," I confided, admiring the
platter of spaghetti with spider crab that had been set before
me.

Brigitte spooned generous portions of the pasta onto each of
our plates and asked as she twirled glistening strands onto her
fork, "What about him?"

"Don't tell me you don't know," I replied, watching her
expression carefully. I thought it was common knowledge now
at Merriweather that Wes played around, but then Brigitte led
a more sheltered and domestic existence than most of the other
people at the office. She was a committed and clearly valued
employee, but everyone knew that Brigitte's home life came
first with her. She always managed to escape by five-thirty or
so and often worked out of her studio in Brooklyn in order to
be closer to her two growing boys. Though bright and talented, she exuded a sense of serenity that made her quite different from the more driven and edgy career women I knew. It
was very likely that she just wasn't on the routing slip for hot
office gossip.

"Well, um, I've heard rumors..." I began hesitantly, then decided it was silly not to go on. "I heard that he isn't, well, particularly faithful. Hasn't been for quite a while. I hope I'm not shocking you," I added, aware that Brigitte had started to blush furiously.

"Oh, that," she replied, glancing across at me with bright pink cheeks. "Yes, I was quite aware of that. He made a pass at me once. Can you imagine?"

"So, you see what I mean," I told her as I helped myself to another spoonful of the pasta. "No wonder Wanda hits the bottle. I would, too, I think, under those circumstances."

"There's simply no excuse for her headlong self-destruction," Brigitte told me firmly. "But I agree with you that Wes's behavior is appalling. I wouldn't tolerate it for a second, believe you me. Marriage, being a parent—these are tough, demanding jobs, Peg. You wait and see. You need a dedicated, strong-willed partner to be successful. I don't know who's more to blame for the disaster that passes for that marriage—Wes or Wanda. But they should both be ashamed."

"Wanda did try to pull herself together," I countered, leaning back as the waiter took our plates away. Steaming trays of grilled fresh sardines were put down in their place. I sighed and picked up my fork. Thank God it wasn't swimsuit season.

"Is that so?" Brigitte replied. "Says who?"

"Well, Wanda did...." I answered, realizing how lame the answer sounded in light of the events played out earlier. "Of course, she slips now and then. But she vowed she was well off the serious stuff. By that I guess she meant...heroin or cocaine?"

"Lord, I suppose so." Brigitte sighed. "Can you imagine? And poor Star having to grow up with all that."

We were served two more courses—a warm salad of highly garlicked radicchio and a huge platter of Venetian cookies—as well as thick espresso and complimentary shots of grappa. The conversation moved on to more personal things: Brigitte's sons and husband, my lack thereof.

"You've met Detective Dante Cursio, haven't you?" I asked her when she asked me if I was seeing anybody.

"You mean that tall, dark policeman with the bedroom eyes?" Brigitte replied.

"Yeah. The very one," I told her with a sigh, and then filled her in on the bumpy course of our romance. She listened with the rapt and focused attention of a college roommate, and I found myself confiding things to her I had told no one but Picasso. "So, you see, what I'm thinking is . . . if I can figure out who killed Berry, if I can beat him to the punch, then he'll see that he doesn't have to commit himself exclusively to his goddamned job. You see what I mean?"

"I think so," Brigitte replied slowly. "You want to prove yourself to him as a person—not just as a woman."

"True. But I also want to shake him up, make him see that love isn't something you can keep at arm's length. It's something you have to embrace, accept, take wholly into your life."

"And you're going to teach him these lessons about life by delving into the facts about Berry's death. It makes as much sense as anything does, I guess," Brigitte told me with a shrug. "But tell me, how are you going to do it? I mean, one of the best homicide detectives in the city is having trouble. . . . What do you have over him?"

"Two things," I answered immediately, because I had already thought long and hard about this very question. "First, I have the element of surprise. Everyone knows what Cursio's after when he comes snooping around. But with me? Well, heck, I'm just plain old Peg Goodenough. Second, I personally—professionally—know just about everyone who could have done it—Wes, Wanda, Dick, Mark, Toni, Sara . . . you."

"I plead the Fifth!" Brigitte answered laughingly, throwing up her hands. The deep, sweet ripple of her laughter made me think of Berry. And friendship. I'd missed having someone to talk to like this, I realized. "Well, I don't intend to pry," Brigitte continued after she'd caught her breath, "but I do hope you'll let me know if I can help in any way."

"Well, there is one thing," I replied.

"Yes?"

"Any idea who did it, Brigitte?" I asked. Two of her closest associates, Toni and Sara, were on the top of my list. The rest of the suspects were people we both knew through business dealings. But I'd learned the hard way from my beloved former boss Ramsey Farnsworth that you could work side by side with someone for years . . . and not really know him at all.

I wasn't surprised when Brigitte answered. "No one I know could have done it. And yet, in a way, I suppose any one of them could."

TWENTY

"ENCORE?" Pierre asked, gesturing to the two porcelain pitchers—one filled with rich, dark coffee, the other with warm milk—that comprised the café au lait. It was after ten in the morning, and the small breakfast room of the Hotel d'Alain, where we were staying in Paris, had all but emptied. Pierre hovered, smiling benevolently down at the three of us. He called us *"mes madames"* and had treated us with unabashed favoritism since our arrival six days earlier.

"Non, merci," Star replied, smiling back at him. *"Et tu, Maman?"* she asked Wanda, who was engrossed in the pages of the *International Herald Tribune.*

"What, honey? Oh. No, thanks, Pierre." After he'd gone, Wanda tossed the paper onto the banquette beside her and said, "So, Peg, what's on the agenda, today? The Louvre again? Back to the Luxembourg?"

The sharper, more demanding atmosphere of Paris had steadied Wanda. She'd crawled back onto the wagon during our afternoon flight from Venice and had stayed there as best I could tell for the good part of a week. And, much to my surprise, it had been an enjoyable time for all of us. Perhaps realizing that she was never going to fit the bill, Wanda had stopped trying to play the role of authoritative mother. And because she hadn't insisted on plotting out our itinerary, I'd managed to get in all the scouting I needed within the first three days. Although I didn't let Wanda and Star know I'd finalized the shots. The idea of work seemed to add some necessary structure to our days.

On the pretense that I was still looking for the perfect backdrop, the three of us spent the mornings drifting across the city, ducking into cafés for tea when the chill, damp air threatened to numb our bones. In the afternoons, we accompanied Wanda as she shopped—at a level of extravagance that would have impressed even Theo—for clothes along the rue du faubourg Saint-Honore and around the place des Victoires, crystal down the rue de Paradis, chocolates and caviar along the place de la Madeleine. We ate raw oysters in Les Halles. *Croque monsieurs* in Montmartre. Chocolate mousse on the Champs-Elysées. I found myself feeling sorry to see our odd, mismatched trip end. Out of necessity, and then out of growing fondness, we had become friends: Wanda, Star and me. The day before, a saleswoman at Hermes had mistaken us all for sisters. And what we shared was indeed the kind of closeness that blurred ages, looks and characters. We had started out the trip walking at different speeds and tempos; we now tended to move as one.

Though we weren't actually leaving for another two days, the news that Toni and Sara had arrived in Paris for a meeting with Merriweather's European distributor had forced us all to face reality again. I'd been surprised and impressed when Wanda agreed—without any caustic asides—to Toni's suggestion that we all meet for coffee later that afternoon.

"It's a lovely day," I said, glancing out at the bright winter sunlight. The latticework on the wall in the courtyard garden glistened with new icicles; the evergreen shrubs were shrouded with a fresh powder of snow. "I'd like to see Notre Dame before we go."

"That hardly seems an appropriate spot for a fashion setup," Wanda replied as she examined her lips in a compact mirror and started to apply a new coat of gloss. Fair-skinned, blue-eyed, Wanda wisely opted for light pink and peach tints in makeup, the kind of subtle, romantic colors I always longed to wear. But pink sat about as comfortably on me as a butterfly on a porcupine. I would wait until I got back up to my room before putting on the only color that seemed capable of standing up to my New York pallor and unruly mass of blue-black hair: a poppy-bright crimson.

"Perhaps you're right," I agreed, though I had no intention of using Notre Dame for any such mercantile purpose. "But I'd like to go, anyway. Let's meet back at the front desk in half an hour or so."

I wore my mink-lined duffle; Wanda her ankle-length lynx with a wide-brimmed fur hat; Star a quilted goose-down jacket. And though booted and wrapped almost beyond recognition, we managed to get our fair share of appreciative Gallic male smiles as we made our way down the boulevard Saint-Germain, along the Seine and across pont au Double to one of the most beautiful facades in the world. Star decided she wanted to climb up to the bell tower and, arranging to meet at the transept half an hour later, Wanda and I pushed through the worn, wooden side door.

"Hey, this is rather impressive," Wanda whispered to me as we walked slowly down the nave toward the chancel. Sunlight, tinted deep red and blue and green, streamed down from a multitude of stained-glass windows. The heavy sigh of an organ filled the transept area, and I stopped with Wanda as she turned to look up at the huge rose window of the cloister portal. In a design that has remained almost intact from the thirteenth century, the stained glass displayed figures from the Old Testament surrounding the Virgin.

"I was raised a Catholic, you know," Wanda confided softly. "I believed all this once. But it was in the same way you believe in Santa Claus or the Tooth Fairy. Now, I don't know, it's really weird. I've started to go to confession again. I can't say why, but it seems to help."

"Whatever works for you," I replied rather lamely, sensing she wanted some kind of response. I thought about the idea of confessing for a second and asked offhandedly, "You go alone? Or...as a family?"

"A family?" Wanda laughed unhappily. "I thought I'd made it pretty clear to you that we *aren't* a family. At least not as presently constituted. But, who knows? I'm beginning to hope again, Peg. I'm actually beginning to think that everything might work out okay."

"You mean with you and Star?" I asked.

"Yeah," Wanda replied, her gaze traveling back up to the stained-glass window. "If I can just get that bastard to agree to a divorce. That's why I went off the deep end in Venice. My lawyer had telegraphed the hotel that Wes plans to fight me for custody of Star if I try to go through with this."

"Oh," I said. Considering Wanda's history with drugs and alcohol, Wes's threat was not an idle one. I was amazed that she seemed so calm about the situation. "What are you going to do?"

"I've already done it," Wanda answered, turning back to me again. "I've hired the best legal advice I can along with an investigative firm that specializes in wayward husbands. They're putting together quite an impressive list of Wes's romantic conquests. I think once that little roll call is read aloud in court, a judge might think twice about handing Star over to her father—even if Star chooses to be with him."

"Sounds like you have a tough time ahead of you, Wanda," I observed.

"It's nothing when compared to what's behind me," she answered evenly. "Nothing much at all."

We had lunch at a small café on the Ile Saint-Louis, then crossed over to the Right Bank for a final forage among the chic new clothing stores that had sprung up along the back streets of Les Halles. I watched in awe as Wanda charged more than a thousand dollars worth of Claudie Perlot designs to her VISA card. We hurried back across the Seine for our five o'clock appointment with Toni and Sara at the lovely Cafe Deux Magots that faces the bell tower of Saint Germain des Pres. We found them sitting silently at a back table: two tired, unhappy-looking American women. Toni, in a Chanel-like get-up that dripped with pearls and gold link chains, seemed overdressed for the occasion. Sara, in faded jeans and a ratty black turtleneck, was anything but.

"Hi, how are you?" Toni cried loudly, as we approached. "How are you doing? You look great!" Her voice carried across the crowded room and people at nearby tables looked over at us disdainfully.

Neither Sara nor Star said more than "hi" to anyone, leaving Toni, Wanda and me to carry on a stilted, desultory conversation about restaurants and shopping that clearly interested no one. I felt badly for Toni, who had instigated the meeting and who was trying the hardest to make the idea work. But it didn't. After all, the one thing these four women had in common was also the one subject they were least likely to discuss: Wes. It was one of the more uncomfortable half hours I can remember.

Without anyone suggesting that we meet up again, we parted in front of the cafe and Wanda, Star and I walked with linked arms back to the hotel, making reservations for dinner along the way. It was a place within walking distance of d'Alain that specialized in hazelnut soufflés. I was just drifting off into a short nap before dressing for dinner when the phone jangled beside my bed.

"Peg?" It was Wanda. "Sorry to bother you, but something's just come up."

"Oh?" I said, sitting up in bed.

"Yes," she said breathily. "It's, uh, about that subject we discussed in the cathedral? You know, that little matter I was having someone look into?"

I supposed that Star was nearby, and Wanda didn't want her to know about Wes's countermove on the divorce. "Right," I said. "I know what you mean."

"Anyway, the thing is," she went on excitedly, "I've got to meet someone about this. And it might take quite some time. Would you mind taking care of Star for me? Would that be a problem?"

"Of course not," I told her. "But isn't this sort of odd, Wanda? I mean, why now? In Paris? Couldn't this wait until we get back to New York?"

"I can't go into it this moment," Wanda replied evasively. "All I can tell you is that it's very good news. You just have to trust me, okay?"

Star and I enjoyed a splendid dinner of escargots, *filet de boeuf, pommes frites* and *haricots verts*, all topped off by the sumptuous, light-as-air specialty of the house. I had an espresso and we talked about Dalton and how her modeling career was going to affect her regular life.

"We'll manage somehow," Star answered philosophically. "Wanda and me."

"And Wes?" I asked. According to Wanda, Star knew nothing yet about the impending fissure in her life.

"I'm not stupid, Peg," Star answered, looking somberly across at me. "I think you know what I mean."

Wanda wasn't back yet when we returned to the hotel, and Star didn't have another key to their room, so I suggested she come back to mine for the time being. She climbed onto the bed and within fifteen minutes was sound asleep. Around eleven, I phoned down to the front desk and left a message for Wanda that Star was with me. I then gently got Star under the covers and climbed in myself. The next thing I knew, sunlight was flooding the room.

I rang Wanda's room, but she didn't answer.

"She must have come in pretty late," I told Star. "Probably still asleep. I say we let her get some beauty rest."

We took turns with my shower, Star climbed into her clothes of the night before, then we walked down the hall to their room and knocked gently on the door. Nothing.

"So, let's have some breakfast," I suggested, trying to keep my tone light and unconcerned. I got Star settled at a table in the breakfast room, and with the excuse that I wanted to look into arrangements for checking out, I went back out to the front desk.

"What time did Ms Merriweather come back last night?" I asked the concierge.

"Pardon?" he replied, his perfectly trimmed mustache forming an ersatz smile. "As far as I know, Madame Merriweather never went out."

"No, she did," I answered. "She left shortly after her daughter and I did—around eight-thirty, I think."

"*Madame,*" he replied with a deep, disgruntled sigh, "as you know, I was at this desk last night. I have been on duty now, except for a very brief break around four-thirty, for nearly fourteen full hours. And, let me assure you, at no time did I see Madame Merriweather either leave—or return."

"You must be wrong," I replied. "She would have called me if her plans had changed."

"She neither left—nor returned," the concierge replied with a self-satisfied smile, obviously proud of his grasp of English phraseology.

"If that is really the case," I told him grimly, "then I am seriously concerned. I want you to ring her room right now, and if she doesn't answer, I insist we open it up."

I could hear the phone ringing, ringing, ringing, before he returned the receiver to its rest. Then he rang the manageress, who came out of her side office, and they had a low, rapid-fire conversation in French, which I couldn't possibly follow. Finally, he fished around in a drawer behind the desk and pulled out some keys.

"The young girl is where, please?" the manageress asked me kindly. She was a thin, middle-aged Parisian who exuded style and élan.

"In the breakfast room," I said.

"We shall leave her there for the time being, yes?" the woman told me.

I followed them as they hurried up the two flights to our floor. The concierge rapped on the door once. Twice. He then slipped the key into the lock and pushed the door open.

"Stay here, please," the manageress told me.

I did. At least until I heard the concierge cry *"Merde!"* and the manageress scream. I found them in the bathroom, the manageress slumped against the wall, her hands over her mouth, the concierge leaning over the toilet bowl.

And, oh yes, Wanda was there, too. Or what had been Wanda, for she was clearly gone. She was curled up in the narrow, half-empty bathtub, her features blurred and bruised looking, her lovely blond hair matted and damp. Panty hose was wrapped tourniquet-style around her left upper arm. And in the curl of her half-open right hand, lay a used syringe.

In bright red lipstick, she had written on the mirror above the sink, "SORRY. CAN'T COPE. GOODBYE."

TWENTY-ONE

"SOMEONE HAD ALREADY rented *Porky's*," I told Star as I locked the front door. The cold air had come in with me, a sharp, fresh smell, clinging to my coat and hair. "So I got *Private Benjamin*, instead. Is that okay?"

"Sure, fine," she answered from her usual spot on my couch. Picasso, looking like an overstuffed and badly wearing pillow, was curled up on her chest, generating the rattly purr he makes when particularly happy. He had good reason to be. Except for the necessary hours I spent at work and Star spent at Dalton, we'd been right there, on the couch, trying to lose ourselves in the celluloid fantasy lives of others. This made for an absolute lovefest from Picasso's perspective; now he could have his choice of two warm, barely moving humans to roost upon. As for me, and even more so for Star, it provided the necessary means of escaping from a world that had grown suddenly, irrevocably, ugly and dark.

Two weeks had passed since that horrible morning at d'Alain. We had been forced to stay in Paris for three more days after that, while the Sûreté and the U.S. Embassy put us through a battery of questions and paperwork. Somehow, during a period that was now essentially a blank to me, I had managed to change hotels, take care of Star, answer to the authorities and arrange for our return to New York. Wes had flown over as soon as he heard the news, but he was as useless as Star, who spent her last two days in Paris staring silently out the window of her second-floor room at the Meurice. My fear that she would jump while I was out dealing with the various bureaucracies had been only partially alleviated by the fact that she didn't have very far to fall. Wes's looming, morose presence the last two days had just made matters worse. And the flight back on the Concorde—financed by Wes, as were the rooms at the Meurice—had been a grim affair.

"It's my fault," Wes had said, sighing brokenly to himself as we ascended to our cruising altitude. With the help of a sedative slipped into her Coke, Star had almost immediately fallen asleep. I had a window seat. And as we flew through the inky blackness above the Atlantic, I heard him repeat this litany to himself at least a dozen times more.

He had changed drastically since the last time I had seen him, in the dining room of P&Q the evening we celebrated the Tantamount triumph. Then he had glowed with self-confidence, preened like a rooster in front of the prettier P&Q secretarial staff, chortled and bossed and joked with everyone within shouting distance. Now this loud, bronzed giant had been silenced and almost physically diminished. He sat slumped in his chair, unseeing when the lovely French stewardess leaned over to take away his untouched tray of filet mignon and expensive burgundy. "It's all my fault," he had muttered again.

Finally, unable to control my temper any longer, I had retorted, "It seems incredibly selfish to me to imagine that you and you alone are responsible. Surely Wanda had some part in the decision, don't you think?"

Wes had looked over at me, startled, as if noticing me for the first time. That was another thing that had changed about him. Before he had been overtly flirtatious; now he seemed to barely register my feminine presence. And although I had been enormously relieved that he had dropped his come-hither approach, I had started to resent the fact that he seemed oblivious to all the practical help I was providing his diminished family.

"You don't understand," he had answered sadly, shaking his glorious leonine head and falling back into the gloom of introspection.

Wanda's small, private funeral, my return to work, even my various phone conversations with Cursio had all passed in a kind of fog. I knew I wasn't focusing well; I wasn't thinking straight. Perhaps that was why I had so readily agreed to Wes's plaintive request at the end of my first week back that I let Star stay with me while he went out to L.A. for a few weeks.

"I've some loose ends I need to tie up there businesswise," he had told me when he phoned at the office. "And the kid has missed so damned much school already, I'd hate to pull her out again. And, well, Peg, she likes you a lot. She trusts you. I sure would appreciate it, and I'd pay you well."

That had done it, as perhaps he had known it would.

"You won't pay me a thing, damn it," I had retorted. "I'll take Star because I'm her friend. I won't hear another thing about being paid for it."

And so another week had gone by, this time with Star at my foggy side. By day, we both went numbly about our office work and schoolwork. At night we became video zombies. We rented comedies mostly—easy, harmless movies that required the minimum attention and the maximum escape. We had started with *Airplane* and *Arthur*, and now we were about halfway through my Video Club listing.

"I'll order up pizza," I told Star as I put away my coat. "Or Chinese, if you'd rather." Our appetites, what there was of them, had been running to the various take-out cuisines available in the immediate vicinity.

"Pizza's fine," Star replied.

Everything was always "fine" with her, though of course nothing actually was. Wes had called only once during the week, two nights ago, to say he'd arrived safely and that he, too, was "fine." Although I only half listened to their conversation, I couldn't help but hear the chilliness in Star's responses, the quickness with which she got off the phone. Wes blamed himself for Wanda's death, and it seemed Star did, as well. But we didn't discuss Wanda, or much of anything, for that matter. Our conversations ran along the lines of me saying "Mushroom and pepper okay?" and Star replying "Fine."

I ordered our dinner and was wheeling the VCR over to the couch when the phone rang. It was Cursio, sounding virile and upbeat.

"So, how are you two getting along?" he asked loudly. He had been calling almost every night since my ill-fated return from Paris. He was worried about me, I knew. And now, concerned about Star, as well. His tone was hearty, well-intentioned. Honest, human feelings that I just didn't have the energy to respond to yet.

"Fine," I said. "We're just about to have dinner," I added, hoping to get him off the phone.

"Great," he enthused. "So, what are you having?"

"Um...well, pizza," I admitted. "With lots of good, healthy vegetables on it."

"Like canned mushrooms, you mean?" Cursio retorted. "Peg, when are you two going to have a decent meal? When was the last time either of you even looked at a lettuce leaf?"

"Thank you for expressing your concern," I told him stiffly. "But we are perfectly capable of taking care of ourselves."

"I don't see much evidence to that effect," he replied bitingly. "And what's on the agenda for the rest of the night? You going to see *The Bad News Bears* again, or what?"

"As a matter of fact, we're going to watch—"

"Don't even tell me!" Cursio cut in. "I really don't want to know. You're beginning to really worry me, you know that? I want you two out of there, doing something, breathing fresh air, seeing people. I mean it."

"I'll have you know," I replied haughtily, "that I'm establishing a very meaningful relationship with the delivery boy from Wonton Palace."

"Please, Peg." Cursio sighed. "Listen to me, okay? I'm getting tickets for the circus this Saturday night. Eva really wanted to go, and I thought it might be a good time for the two of you to brave the world again. What do you say?"

"I don't think..." I tried to invent a decent enough excuse but couldn't come up with one. In the mood that Cursio was in, I realized that he wasn't about to take no for an answer without a fight. And my heart just wasn't in it, so I said, "I don't think we're doing anything else. That would be fine."

"Good, great," Cursio enthused, the relief obvious in his voice. "We'll pick you up around seven-thirty."

"OOOH, LOOK AT THAT!" Eva cried, pointing to the woman on the high wire who had just stumbled, dropping her balancing rod into the safety net hundreds of feet below.

It was a three-ring circus, the original big top, moved inside and made upscale for Madison Square Garden. We had the acrobats in the center ring, a group of clowns piling in and out of a miniature truck on the left and some loping elephants circling around on the right. The spectacle and music and lights were continuous, and, to my mind at least, monotonous. I had

started to get a headache while we were being led to our excellent seats in the second tier.

"Do you suppose that was planned?" Star asked, turning to
Cursio. She had taken to him right away, plying him with soft-
spoken questions about the circus and the people around us.
Though still sad eyed, I hadn't seen her this energetic since the
tragedy. Cursio had been right, I admitted silently to myself.
Star clearly needed to get out in the world again and have some
fun. I wished I could share her interest and at least temporary
pleasure, but the oppression that had been bearing down on me
since Wanda's death continued as heavy as ever. I tried to laugh
with the rest when the clown's truck took off without him, but
I saw Cursio looking at me with an unconvinced expression.

"You okay?" he asked. "Comfortable? Having a good
time?"

"Yes," I assured him, trying to work my mouth into the
shape of a smile. Eva and Star were sitting to his left; I was on
his right on the aisle. I struggled with an inexplicable desire to
run up the aisle, race out of the garden, get home. Instead, I
stretched my idiotic grin even further and added with what I
hoped sounded like enthusiasm, "This is great, really."

"You liked the high wire act?" he asked.

"Wonderful."

"And the elephants?"

"Terrific."

"How about those knife throwers, huh?"

"Wow, yeah," I replied, wishing he would stop. I felt so
tired, and my bones were beginning to ache. If only I could go
home.

"There haven't been any knife throwers, Peg," Cursio informed me quietly. "I just wanted to see if you really were
paying attention."

"That was dirty," I retorted just loud enough for him to
hear. "Underhanded and small-minded. I hope you're satisfied."

"In a way, I guess I am," he replied cryptically, and then
turned his attention back to Star and Eva, who were trying to
figure out if it was a dummy or a real person who had just been
shot forty feet into the air out of the cannon. I half heard Eva's
girlish, eager comments, Star's slower, more careful questions

and Cursio's deep-pitched replies. I tried to force myself to relax, to clear my mind, to drift.... I tried to think of pleasant
things, like Theo and Cal's upcoming wedding celebration, the
surprise bonus that had accompanied my most recent pay-
check, the smell of mingled sweat and after-shave that Cursio
gave off. I let myself remember Cursio naked—the hard, clean
lines of his chest and arms, the delicate, boyish curve of his
shoulder blades. I remembered the two of us kissing, my lipstick smearing...kissing, the lipstick.... Of course, it would
be there, it was bound to have surfaced eventually.

The bright crimson words, as sticky as blood, scrawled across
the mirror in the bathroom.

The bright red smear across the glass. Red....

I jumped, I guess. Maybe I even cried out. The next thing I
knew, Cursio was gripping my arm, forcing me up, pushing me
in front of him down the aisle. "We're just going for some
Cokes, guys," he called back over his shoulder to Eva and Star.
"Don't get into any trouble."

As soon as we were in the hallway, he pulled me to a halt and
wheeled me around to face him.

"Okay, I've had about enough of this," he said. "I've been
very patient, babe, very sensitive and considerate. But you're
not telling me something. Hell, you're not telling me anything! Since you got back, you've cut me off cold."

"I...well, Star and me, have sort of cut everybody off, I
guess," I told him. "I really wasn't discriminating."

"Care to tell me why?" he asked, his dark eyes drilling into
mine. "Why the brush-off? What are you hiding?"

"Hiding?" I retorted. "Jeez, leave it to a cop to mistake a
common, normal mourning period for some kind of subter-
fuge!"

"But you hardly knew her," he pointed out. "And from
what I can figure, you didn't even much like her."

"That's not exactly true," I countered. "We got really close
during the trip. I had begun to sympathize with Wanda, maybe
even understand her a little."

"Oh, hell, come off it," Cursio retorted. "She was a drunk.
A junkie. I can't believe you'd waste sympathy on an addict."

"You're playing real tough tonight, Detective," I replied,
starting to regain my equilibrium. I shook off his grip and

steadied myself against the railing. "Just what is it that you're after? You obviously don't want to hear about the tender friendship that was taking root between Wanda and myself."

"True," he told me, patting his upper right-hand pocket absently. An old smoker's habit; a gesture he made only when he was nervous or upset. "No, it's something a good deal more unpleasant than that, I'm afraid."

"Go on," I told him.

"I've been wondering," he said slowly, "and I haven't exactly been alone in pondering this, about the reasons for Wanda's suicide. We can't get scratch out of the Sûreté, believe me. They've never been big on cooperating with municipal departments in the U.S. So we're left here, pretty much in the dark. But still, I can't help but wonder…" He looked down at me speculatively, his eyes narrowed, his mouth a hard, tense line.

"Yes?" I answered, looking back up at him. "Wonder what?"

"About Wanda's death," he answered shortly. "I've been damn discreet, I think, not asking you this straight-out a week ago, but you seemed so wrought up."

"So, ask me, already," I told him.

"*Was* it suicide? Or was it just made to look that way?"

"What do you think?" I asked coolly.

"I think, sweetheart," he told me with a sigh, "that you know more than you're telling. Give me a break, all right? What the hell really happened over there, anyway?"

"We found her in the bathtub," I began slowly. "You know, one of those small, modern efficiency tubs that Europeans favor? Anyway, she was naked and only partially covered with water. So, it was obvious even then that she hadn't exactly drowned. Also, she had this drug paraphernalia attached to her arm, and later the police found enough heroin in the room to finance a small Latin American revolution—"

"Thanks," Cursio cut in. "This is very, very helpful. So, go on."

"Well, there's not a whole lot more to tell," I told him. "She was dead, apparently of an overdose. The hotel phoned the police. An ambulance came."

"Tell me about the bathroom," Cursio instructed. "What did it look like? Was the light on? Were her things in order on the sink? Try to remember what was there, okay?"

"That's not going to be easy, because there's only one thing I really remember right now."

"Yes?"

"There was something written on the mirror. Her suicide note. It said, 'Sorry. Can't cope. Goodbye.' But what it said isn't nearly as important as how it was written."

"What do you mean?"

"Someone had used lipstick, Dante. A bright crimson."

"So? What's the problem with red lipstick?"

"Wanda wouldn't have been caught dead wearing it."

TWENTY-TWO

"CAN EVA SLEEP OVER tonight, Peg?" Star asked quietly as we were all shuffling toward the escalators after the show. It was nearly eleven o'clock, and although Star looked exhausted, she also seemed excited and pleased. During the evening I had watched how Eva hung on Star's every word. The way the younger girl was already imitating Star's habit of tossing back her hair and nibbling on her index finger in concentration. Eva was clearly a fan, fascinated and awed by Star's beauty and minor fame. She had spent far more time watching Star than the circus. And for Star, being the subject of someone's adoration was not such a bad thing when you were feeling low.

"Sure," I told her, "if it's okay with her dad. I don't mind the couch."

One of the cops on duty outside the garden recognized Cursio and commandeered a taxi for us on Eighth Avenue. It was something of a squeeze in the back seat: Eva sat on Cursio's lap; Star leaned sleepily against me; Cursio's arm found its way around my shoulders. I, too, was half-asleep when the driver pulled up in front of my brownstone on Eighty-sixth Street. I helped the girls out, while Cursio paid.

"You enjoy the show?" I heard the driver ask him.

"Yeah," Cursio said. "It's great for the kids."

"I'm thinking of taking my wife and baby," the driver replied. "Pretty little family you got there," he added as he thanked Cursio for the tip.

"Thanks," Cursio replied, and I felt my heart turn over with longing. Star wasn't the only one in need of comfort and affection.

As I got the girls settled with extra blankets and pillows in my bedroom, Cursio made a pot of coffee. The rich aroma of cinnamon and Kenya AA filled the hallway as I closed the bedroom door behind me. I followed it into the kitchen. Cursio was leaning against my icebox, staring out my kitchen window at the sliver of Hudson that had enabled the real estate broker to claim this apartment had a "river view."

"Penny for them," I said, coming up behind him. He'd gotten out two mugs, the cream pitcher and a package of Pepperidge Farm Brussels cookies, whose ranks he'd already managed to diminish.

"I was thinking about Star," he told me, snapping a cookie in half. "What do you think she knows? You ever talk about it?"

"No," I answered honestly, pouring the coffee. We took our mugs and the cookies into the living room and sat down at opposite ends of the couch. Cursio is a relentless interrogator. I've heard him ask the same question ten different ways to get a decent answer. He tugs and pulls at a problem until it unravels. He does not give up. As we sat there listening to the whispers and giggles coming from the bedroom, I sensed he was simply resting between rounds. The familylike atmosphere that had surrounded us in the taxi had dissipated. Detective Dante Cursio was back on duty.

"What kind of relationship do you figure Star and Wes have?" he asked, fishing out a paper doily from the cookie bag.

"So-so," I told him, debating with myself just how much I should tell him about what I knew and felt. Was it time, I wondered, to close down my personal investigation into Berry's death? Where had it led, after all, except to another murder? I had discovered that everyone had some petty reason to wish Berry dead...but that no one had a motive strong enough to really do it. I had learned more about the emotional content of most of the suspects' lives than I really wanted to, without finding anything out of the usual gamut of human experience. In other words, I probably knew more than Cursio. In fact, the only secret I nurtured was that I was delving into this at all. The whole point of the exercise, I reminded myself, had been to impress Cursio. That I was failing as an amateur was not something, I decided, I particularly wanted to share with the professional.

"What does 'so-so' mean, Peg?" he continued, turning to look at me. "Unfriendly? Combative? Standoffish?"

"I'd pick number three," I told him. "But, of course, you have to remember that I've been observing them under some pretty drastic circumstances."

"Describe how Star reacted to Wes when he first arrived in Paris," Cursio commanded. "Did she run into his arms? Did they comfort each other? What was the mood like between them?"

"He called us from the lobby when he arrived at the Meurice," I remembered, "and we both went down to meet him. He was registering and we walked over and Star said 'Hello, Wes,' and Wes said, 'Hi, honey, how're you doing?' and that was about it. It was, well, all very sad, but also kind of business-like."

"Was it because they were both in shock, maybe?" Cursio pushed. "People often subconsciously suppress their emotions when they're too powerful to deal with."

"That could be," I agreed.

"But you don't sound sure," Cursio noted. "Let me ask you this," he continued, sipping his coffee thoughtfully. "Did Wes seem surprised that this had happened? Did he say things like 'I just don't believe it' or 'This can't be real'?"

"Um...actually, no," I conceded, seeing the truth of my response for the first time myself. "What he did keep saying, over and over again, was 'It's all my fault.'"

"Interesting," Cursio muttered. "Now, what about Star? Was she shocked? Disbelieving?"

"No...." I replied, realizing how odd and possibly suspicious this must seem. "She was depressed, terribly saddened...but not surprised. What are you thinking?" I demanded with sudden alarm. "That Wes and Star *knew* Wanda was going to be killed? That they were somehow involved?"

"Hold on—calm down a second," Cursio warned, glancing at my bedroom door. It was still closed and the girlish commotion had died down. "As far as Star goes, unless she is some kind of genius as an actress, she is not a suspect at all. Did you know she was the only Merriweather I was really able to get through to after Berry's murder?"

"I didn't realize you'd ever really talked to her before tonight," I replied.

"Well, I did," Cursio told me as he pulled another Brussels from the crumpled bag. "I picked her up after school one day in the squad car, and we went for a little drive through the park. We got on well together. I guess she trusted me. Anyway, she opened up a lot to me that day. I had the feeling she needed someone to talk to, and I just happened to be there."

Besides being a world-class interrogator, Cursio also happens to be a gold medalist in the difficult sport of listening. I could well imagine the troubled, lonely Star pouring out her heart to this man. Their session together that afternoon helped to explain her easy, open way with him tonight.

"What was the gist?" I asked.

"That she was worried about her mother," Cursio told me quietly. "It seems that Wanda was planning to leave Wes, suing for divorce on the basis of infidelity and mental cruelty."

"Star *knew* that?" I demanded. "She knew the grounds?"

"Yes," Cursio answered, looking me over keenly. "You did, too, didn't you? And you never told me!"

"You're the detective," I sniffed. "I assumed you'd stumble upon it yourself eventually. Besides which, at the time I found out, I'd also just discovered that you'd been keeping a few things from me. But what else did Star say?"

"I don't know if I should give you all of this for free," he countered grudgingly. "What other vital information are you holding back from me?"

"Keep going," I told him, waving my right hand. "I'll let you know if you've missed anything."

He eyed me coldly before he continued. "Well, it wasn't just the divorce proceedings that worried Star. It was the fact that her mother seemed to be losing her fight against drugs and booze. She told me how hard Wanda had been trying to stay straight. Apparently she and Star used to go to AA meetings together. I mean, Star was really involved with the whole dilemma. And Wanda could confide in her—tell her what a hell of a battle it was, how many times she thought it might be better just to give up. To . . . kill herself. And, Peg, that was only a month ago."

"What are you saying?" I demanded. "That Wanda did commit suicide . . . and just happened to have borrowed someone else's red lipstick for her farewell address?"

"No," Cursio replied, "even without the lipstick business, I'd classify Wanda's death as suspicious because it follows the same pattern as Berry's. Whoever killed these two women knew them, understood their problems, could guess at the way they would do away with themselves if life got bad enough."

"I understand Wanda's method," I conceded, "but I don't see why Berry would want to hang herself."

"Think about it for a minute," Cursio told me. "We finally found out that she was being forced to sell her business, against her will, due to cash flow problems. Her precious company, this thing that was so tied into her ego and personality, was being changed and manipulated by strangers. They were planning to parcel out her name, her ideas. They were going to take her Merriweather signature and attach it to lingerie, linens... panty hose."

"I see," I told him. "A cash flow problem is news to me. Anyone who knew even vaguely what was going on with the licensing projects could guess that Berry hated the idea of diluting her design work in that way. That, in fact, the takeover might be destroying her emotionally. And what a way to go—hang yourself with a pair of panty hose, the very thing that was strangling the joy out of your life!"

"Exactly," Cursio exclaimed proudly. "Aptly put. And for Wanda, well, it was easy enough to choose her poison. I suppose everybody knew she had had a problem with drugs."

"That's true," I responded, "but she promised me that she'd given up the hard stuff a decade ago. Her real downfall more recently was booze."

"That's a nice bedtime story," Cursio told me. "But old tried-and-true police wisdom dictates that once a junkie, always a junkie."

"Okay," I said, thinking over what we had discussed. "Where does all this lead? Or, I should say, to whom?"

"Any number of people, I'm afraid," Cursio responded. "Almost everyone has an alibi... but none of them hold up under heavy scrutiny. Wes claims to have been in Manhattan. Toni and Sara vouch for each other in Paris. Brigitte was en route back to the city from Milan. Mark was at a sales conference in Orlando. Dick was in London. But, as far as we can figure, any one of them could have taken an overnight flight to Paris—and back—that weekend. It's still anybody's guess."

"And what's your guess?" I demanded. "I know you too well to believe you haven't got some theory cooking."

"Statistically," Cursio told me, putting down his empty mug of coffee, "Wes did it. In terms of geography, though, I'm afraid you're our best bet."

"Then I'd better tell you what I know about Wesley Merriweather."

"Such as?" Cursio asked me warily.

"The man is a modern-day Casanova," I replied, "an insatiable woman chaser, a common lech. It seems he had affairs with both Toni and Sara at Merriweather, and God knows who else. He hits on anything in a skirt. Hell, he even tried me."

"So he does manage to display a modicum of taste from time to time," Cursio noted dryly.

"I'm glad you can find levity in the situation," I retorted. "Personally, I think this demonstrates a pretty serious character flaw. One that I would imagine any murder investigator would give his eyeteeth to discover."

"I didn't have to," Cursio replied evenly. "We simply did what we were supposed to—we asked around, gathered evidence, came to the obvious conclusions."

"So you already knew," I said, feeling oddly let down.

"What do you think I do all day, Peg?" Cursio responded, standing up and stretching. He had on the maroon wool crewneck I had bought him last Christmas, and which I noted with fond exasperation was already wearing through at the elbows. He turned to face me, running his hands wearily over his face and then back through his haphazardly barbered hair. The past few times I'd seen him, I had noticed an outcropping of gray around his temples. Damn it, I thought, glancing up at him now. He was the kind of man who would look great at seventy.

"It's my job to uncover that kind of dirt," Cursio continued as he paced in front of the couch. "And, sweetheart, I've really got to tell you that you're playing a dangerous little game digging up this stuff on your own. It's clearer and clearer to me that someone you know, someone in that inner Merriweather circle, is the murderer. And a damn smart one, too. We've been on this case for two months, and though we've collected a hell of a lot of personal information on each of the suspects—like this business about Wes—none of it adds up."

"I wasn't 'digging up' anything," I responded truculently. "I just happened to keep my ears open when Wanda started to pour out her life's story. So, hey, I'm sorry," I added, throwing up my hands. "You clearly know far more than I do."

"Come on," Cursio cajoled, sitting down next to me, "don't be ticked off. But can't you see that I don't like you being so close to all this? I was worried sick when I heard the news about Wanda. I just want you to be careful. Promise me?"

Well, hell, how could any warm-blooded female look into those dark brown eyes and not promise the man the world?

"Okay, sure," I mumbled, trying to get a grip on myself.

"Good." Cursio smiled. "Now let me help you make up this couch."

As I was pulling out extra sheets and pillows from the hall closet, another aspect of Wes's personality occurred to me.

"Don't you think it odd," I observed as Cursio helped me shake out the fitted bottom sheet, "that a man who was planning on suing for custody of his child would up and leave her with a near stranger just days after the mother's death?"

"Custody?" Cursio demanded. "Wes was suing for custody of Star? Where the hell did you hear that?"

"From Wanda," I told him. "She'd gotten a telegram from her lawyer when we first got to Venice that said if she really intended to go through with the divorce, Wes would petition for custody of Star. A pretty serious threat, considering Wanda's psychological background."

"I'll say," Cursio answered thoughtfully.

"But then I guess you already knew about this, right?" I said, tucking in the top sheet. "I mean, one of your men must have dug it up ages ago."

"Right," he told me, busy with the corner of the blanket.

"And so you also know," I continued, sliding a pillow into its cover, "that Wanda had hired a private investigative firm to make up a list of Wes's romantic conquests. That she thought it might just make the judge think twice about Wes's credentials as an only parent if she had the final list read in court."

"Yes, very smart," he responded, straightening up from tucking in the comforter. He looked across at me with a worried, speculative expression.

"So, anyway," I went on gaily, fluffing up the pillows, "obviously you do know everything I know. Including who Wanda was planning to meet the night she was killed."

It was a delicious moment, one that I was allowed to savor for several seconds while Cursio thought over his awkward position.

Finally, clearing his throat, he replied lamely, "Actually, since you were there, I'd appreciate your perspective on that particular question."

"Oh, I'm sure I know nothing more than you do," I told him modestly. "She was very excited when she called to ask me to take Star for the night. She told me that she was meeting someone who had some good news for her about the investigation into Wes's affairs. I guess that's just what you heard, right?"

"Sure," he replied slowly, searching my face to see if I was really as dumb as I sounded.

"I mean, I wouldn't want you to think I was digging around where I shouldn't be, you know?" I added with a wicked grin.

"Damn you, woman," he replied, the truth dawning on him. And with the imposed restraint of a man whose young daughter was sleeping in the next room, Cursio pulled me into his arms.

Afraid for me, indeed, I thought as I felt my worries dissolve under the sweet pressure of his lips. Each of us knows, deep in our hearts, that despite earthquakes and hurricanes, household accidents and midair collisions, we personally are immune to such calamities. Disaster strikes as randomly as lightning, but always somewhere else. Yes, two women had been murdered. True, both had been close to me. But though their deaths had been heart-stoppingly tragic, neither had actually caused the fabric of my life to unravel. As I swayed in Cursio's warm arms, I told myself that I was protected. That I was safe. Who in the world would want to hurt me?

TWENTY-THREE

THOUGH ONLY a half hour away by subway, the quiet, tree-lined streets of Brooklyn Heights seemed a world apart from the hyperventilated pace of Midtown. It was nearly four-thirty on a Friday afternoon in February, an hour that has the main Manhattan arteries jammed with a million commuters, each trying to beat the others out of the city for the weekend. Here, on Montague, a wintry peace reigned. The two-day-old snow cover, though stained a bright doggy yellow here and there under the well-groomed trees, was still a far cry from the slushy substance that was passing for snow in Manhattan. I sighed, breathing in the smell of wood smoke, and saw up ahead the cross street where Brigitte and her family lived. This was the first stop on my two-step social whirl of Brooklyn, the second leg consisting of dinner at Cursio's. Eva and Star were cooking for Dante and me. Star was acting almost like a big sister to Eva—it seemed to take her mind off her problems.

"Come in, Peggy dear—the door's open," Brigitte called from somewhere deep within the house after I'd banged on the gleaming brass knocker. The three-story brownstone had been completely renovated on the outside: brick repointed, new shutters and drainage pipes installed, expensive-looking marble slabs replacing the original steps. The handsome blue fir in the tiny front yard was still hung with multicolored Christmas tree lights. "I'm in the back. In the kitchen," she cried, and I followed her voice down a long, dark hallway that emanated a reassuring aroma of furniture polish and freshly baked oatmeal cookies. To my right, a beautifully appointed living room glowed in the late-afternoon sun: the fireplace laid with birch logs, the comfortable-looking sofas and chairs patterned in a Laura Ashley print and welcoming all comers with dozens of chintz-covered pillows. The study on the left was lighted an eerie green by a glass-shaded banker's lamp on an antique rolltop desk. Though book-lined and handsomely furnished with a well-broken-in leather couch and carved oak chairs, this was clearly not the quiet retreat of the man of the house. Algebra texts and a French primer had been dumped on the floor, and what seemed to be either the makings or the leavings of a chemistry experiment had taken over a good part of the desk area. Something gooey and green and indelible looking oozed from the wicker trash basket next to the couch. I continued down the hall, pushed through a swinging door and stepped into what must certainly be a top contender for a *House Beautiful* feature article.

"Grab a seat. I'll be off in a second," Brigitte told me, her hand over the receiver of a mustard-yellow princess phone. While she continued her conversation from the counter that divided her work area from the back family room, I explored the magnificent ocher-painted, oak-beamed room. Here was the kitchen of every woman's dreams. The far wall, refurbished to uncover deep red brick, was dominated by a genuine Franklin stove in which a log fire was crackling. The floor was covered with blue-glazed Dutch tile, dotted here and there with hand-painted squares of wildflowers and herbs. The cupboards had been stripped down to their original glossy oak and equipped with real brass hinges and knobs. The bay window that overlooked a well-kept, snowy backyard was framed with crawling ivy and unbelievably healthy-looking pots of geraniums. I edged over to the window and reached up to touch one of the plants just to make sure it was real.

"Gosh, sorry about that," Brigitte said, hanging up the phone. "It was one of our suppliers in Singapore. They're having trouble deciphering my cutting instructions on the last order."

"Why Singapore?" I asked, turning back to her and hoping she didn't notice the puddle of red petals on the floor.

"Some of the least expensive labor in the world," Brigitte replied with a sigh. "And I'm afraid that's what it's all about, Peg. Get it cheap and sell it high."

"Well, you must be doing something right," I observed, walking over to the area she used as an office when she designed at home. "From the last sales report I saw, business seems to be booming." The ten-foot-square space was blocked off from the rest of the kitchen and family room by a long oak table and drafting board. Though cluttered with fabric samples, pattern tissues, twill tape and rulers, Brigitte's work area exuded its own aura of homey, creative harmony.

"Heavens, yes!" Brigitte laughed. "Now it's a matter of meeting all those orders. Merriweather's going to have a very good first quarter. Despite Toni's and Sara's dour predictions, everyone managed to survive, right?"

Well, not everyone, I thought silently, but responded aloud, "Seems that way. I guess you've been able to prove to Tantamount that the company's in good hands. You and Toni and Sara should be very proud."

"Yes," Brigitte answered modestly, "it's been quite a haul. But I think we're going to make it. Now, you," she told me, patting a wooden swivel chair next to her three-legged work stool, "sit right here and tell me what's on your mind. You sounded so...I don't know—needful, I guess—when you called yesterday. Come on and tell Mommy Brigitte all about it."

"Thanks," I said, collapsing into the seat and shrugging my way out of my duffle. "I think you're just the person I need to talk to. You're a mother, right?"

"Last time I checked," Brigitte replied, laughing. "You can usually tell us by our prematurely gray hair and our tendency to recite multiplication tables while waiting in the checkout line."

"Yeah, I know," I answered with a smile. "I've been meeting a lot of you guys lately. You know I'm keeping Star while Wes is in California on business."

"Yes," Brigitte answered, "I told him to try you. Can you imagine, he actually called me first? I feel badly for Star, mind, but I just couldn't bring myself to do Wes a favor. And besides, my boys are such a handful. It wouldn't have worked."

It was silly of me to feel let down; still, I felt a pang when I heard that I was the second choice. After all, I was the one who had been with Star through the whole trauma, so why would Wes think to turn to someone like Brigitte first? Surely I was the adult Star felt closest to, wasn't I?

"Peg, honey, I think I've hurt your feelings," Brigitte murmured, giving me a worried look. "I can really be a big, dumb blonde sometimes. Listen, I'm going to make us a fresh pot of herbal tea, and you're going to tell me all about Star and Wes, or whatever it is that's on your mind, okay?"

I am not by nature chatty. I rarely feel compelled to bare my deeper feelings and concerns. Theo despised anything even faintly scented by feminine wiles—gossip, girlish secrets and the like—so I've never really learned the art of woman talk. After Brigitte handed me the steaming earthenware mug of mint tea, I sat there nearly dumbstruck, trying to think of how to begin. I needn't have worried.

"It must be tough trying to fill in as mother to Star," Brigitte began, as if sensing my discomfort. "God, it's hard enough being a mother when you *are* one—I can just imagine trying to cope when you're not."

"She's really been great," I assured Brigitte. "Maybe a little too great. I mean, she's so eager to help around the apartment, so good about doing her homework. But it's odd, you know—it's not like she's a girl. She's emotionally so adult, so collected."

"So, what's the problem?" Brigitte asked. "She sounds ideal to me. If you had any idea of the horrors involved with bringing up normal teenage boys, believe me, you wouldn't be complaining."

"I'm not complaining," I pointed out, sipping the tea. "I'm just worried. She's so sweet and thoughtful . . . and totally superficial. I mean, even before Wanda's death, when we were in Europe scouting locations, I felt I wasn't really getting through to her. Do you know what I mean? There's some kind of psychological wall there. I have no idea what she's really thinking or feeling. It's kind of spooky."

"And totally natural, Peg," Brigitte assured me. "How old is she, after all? Fifteen, right?" When I nodded, Brigitte went on. "God, just being a teenager is bad enough, but compound that with the fact that you're something of a child celebrity whose aunt and mother have just died and, hey, of course you're going to be acting a little strange."

"The point is, she's acting too normal," I told Brigitte. "And the other issue here is I have absolutely no moral or legal rights to help her . . . or advise her. I mean, I'd like to one day just scream at her, 'Star, who are you in there?' I think someone ought to."

"What does Wes say?" Brigitte asked. "Have you spoken to him about it?"

"Wes!" I cried. "He's called twice in the two and a half weeks he's been gone. Both times sounding like he's in a terrible hurry. I put Star on the line to talk with him, and she hangs up a few seconds after saying hello. I have no idea what his plans are, when he intends to come back. I mean, he still sounds half-deranged with regrets and remorse over Wanda's death. And Star is acting like nothing happened. The whole situation is ridiculous."

"You know what I think?" Brigitte asked rhetorically, because before I could answer, she went on. "It's really not like me—you know, I'm usually Ms Emotional Response—but I think you're overreacting, Peg. It's normal for people to act out their grief in different ways. Star is doing it by retreating into a shell and trying to work things out on her own. And Wes is handling it in his usual mature manner—he's running away from responsibilities, trying to lose himself temporarily in whatever he's doing on the coast."

"And just what the hell is it? Do you know?" I asked.

"Something to do with work," Brigitte answered. "That's what he implied, anyway. But who can tell with Wes? Whatever it is, frankly, I wish he'd stay there. The office has been running so much more smoothly without him around." Brigitte misinterpreted my distressed look and hurriedly added, "Hey, don't get me wrong, Peg. One way or the other, Wes *will* turn up back here again."

"Maybe, in my heart of hearts, that's what worries me the most," I told Brigitte.

"You mean Wes taking her back?"

"Yes," I said, not meeting Brigitte's concerned gaze. "Especially if..." But I let my words trail off. I stared out the window. A bright red cardinal lighted briefly on the bird feeder, then fled across the snowy yard. A pile of logs sat stacked in a neat tepee shape against a work shed. A sled was propped up against the back fence, its runners flashing silver in the last light of day. Here, in the warm heart of this well-tended, happy home, murder and mayhem seemed impossibilities. I finished the tea and let the conversation drift into other, calmer waters: Merriweather's fall clothing line, the upcoming trade show in

Paris. Eventually the unfinished thought I'd let hang about Wes faded into the background of the late afternoon. Brigitte's younger boy, Dirk, came bounding in the back door around six o'clock, his fine blond hair, once freed from the knit cap, an electric halo around his cherubic face. Brigitte hugged his wriggling body to her as we talked, gently stroking his hair back into place. The last trace of my "Especially if..." seemed to have disappeared by the time Brigitte walked me down the hall to the front door. I thanked her, said goodbye, and turned into the knife-sharp chill of the night. Into the dark. Back to all the unanswered questions of Berry's and Wanda's deaths and now, perhaps even more important to me, Star Merriweather's young, unhappy life.

TWENTY-FOUR

I WALKED the five blocks from Brigitte's brownstone to Cursio's, arriving at his front stoop the same moment a nearly full moon slid out from under a bank of scudding clouds and cast a magical glow over the frozen cityscape of snowy sidewalks and arching street lamps. Even from the front steps I could hear the subterranean rhythms of rock music played at concert volume. I had to ring the bell three times before the door was finally opened.

It was Cursio, in faded jeans and a worn navy turtleneck, the *Daily News* opened to the Sports section under his arm. He kissed me fleetingly on the forehead as I brushed past him into the living room and surveyed with no small amusement the chaos that had descended on his once-pristine domicile. Star's arrival at my apartment had started a similar tornado of material objects. Though more than willing to pitch in and help when I suggested the place needed picking up, she seemed totally oblivious to the fact that it was she who had dropped things all over the apartment in the first place.

"Not only are your musical tastes changing for the worse," I told him as I took in the clutter of fashion magazines, tape cassettes, schoolbooks, gloves, scarves and candy wrappers tossed around the room, "but you're losing your grip on your housekeeping skills. What is that, Dante, incipient middle age?"

"Hell no," he retorted, leaning over to snatch up a small black Reebok with electric-pink laces. "It's those girls. They cause more noise and destruction than a demolition crew. Listen to that racket! They claim to be making dinner, but I'm afraid to even imagine the state of my kitchen. You go look," he told me with a sigh, collapsing into his favorite chair. "I haven't the heart.... It's been a bad day."

"Anything you want to tell me about?" I asked him. The light from the reading lamp beside his chair sketched his face in high contrast—his cheekbones jagged white, his mouth and eyes valleys of darkness.

"It can wait," he replied, glancing over the top of his newspaper to me. "Don't worry, it's nothing terrible or definitive. Just another ugly wrinkle."

In the ongoing, ever-widening murder investigation, I surmised. After Wanda's death, the newspapers had once again run stories on the many unanswered questions surrounding Berry's homicide. The *Times* had led off a long investigative piece on the huge number of unsolved murders in the five boroughs with a recap of what everyone was calling "The Merriweather Murder." None of this attention was good for the NYPD in general, or Detective Dante Cursio in particular. He was constantly being quoted and misquoted in print and on the local evening news. He prayed daily, he had told me, that the media continued to accept Wanda's death as a suicide. "If that blows," he had warned me on the phone a few nights ago, "the Fourth Estate will divide me up and toss me back with their chasers like so many beer nuts."

But who besides myself and Cursio and maybe a few others at the police department even suspected Wanda had been killed? The murderer, of course, but he or she wasn't about to give out interviews on the subject. He or she. Who and why. Wes out of anger. Toni for revenge. Dick because...who knows? Sara because of jealousy. Brigitte out of pride. Mark for being rejected. Who else could it be? Who else knew both Berry and Wanda well enough to want them dead? These questions were turning into a personal litany, I decided as I pushed through the swinging door to the kitchen.

Well, it had once been identifiable as such. Now there was so much smoke and noise, such a clutter of pans and groceries, so thick an aroma of burning oil and charred meat that I really couldn't recognize the place.

"You're not supposed to be in here!" Eva cried over the full-volume thuds of the E Street Band. She was standing by the stove, pushing small black mounds of something around in a frying pan inch-deep with oil. The black smoke that swirled around her head was obviously tearing her eyes. "This is supposed to be a surprise!"

"I won't look, I promise," I yelled back. "I just thought you might need some help. Where's Star?"

"She went out to buy some ketchup. I don't know what's taking her so long."

"When did she leave?" I demanded, walking over and flicking off the tape. "How far is the store?"

"Hey," Eva objected, "I was listening to that!"

"Well, now you're listening to me, instead," I retorted, leaning over the sink to open up the window. A wave of frigid air rushed in, causing the emotional and actual temperature in the room to equalize. "I said, how far away is the store?"

"I don't know precisely," Eva answered, her voice dripping with haughtiness. "Five minutes or so, I suppose. She's been gone nearly an hour. There must be quite a queue at the store."

"An hour," I muttered, feeling the chill seep into my bones, sensing a cold finger reach into my heart. I'm not an alarmist. I don't worry easily. But then I've never been responsible for anyone but myself before, except Picasso, and everyone knows cats are far more self-reliant than people. In any case, I panicked.

"Dante," I cried, rushing back into the living room. "Star's been gone for an hour—supposedly off to the store. But Dag's is just down the street, right?"

He was out of his chair, shrugging on his jacket, digging into his pocket for his car keys before I'd even finished my tumbled-out sentence.

"You stay here with Eva," he told me in a voice that didn't allow for argument. He turned at the door, looked back at me and said, "We're both overreacting, you know. I'm sure she's fine."

I always thought I wanted to be a mother. I always thought I wanted someone to nurture, to cherish, to bring up with love and wisdom. But as Eva and I sat together in the silent living room, the stench of burned hamburgers hanging in the air, I faced the down side of familial love.

"She probably just got lost," Eva told me as we sat stiffly upright on the couch. "She's not very good with directions, you know. And she doesn't really pay attention."

"You think so?" I asked Eva, turning to her for comfort, though she had no idea of the danger that could be stalking Star at that very moment. It was something I hadn't thought of, either, until I realized Star had been gone too long. The murderer had chosen two Merriweather woman, and now there was only one left.

"She has a lot on her mind," Eva replied. "Like finding out who killed her mom."

"What do you mean by that, Eva?" I demanded harshly. "Doesn't Star understand . . . what happened?"

"Oh, you mean what the papers say?" Eva replied with the slightly strained patience one uses with a silly child. "That she supposedly killed herself?"

"Precisely," I told her firmly. "What makes either of you think it *wasn't* suicide?"

"Mostly stuff that Wanda told Star during the trip," Eva replied, undaunted. "She was getting better, she told Star, every day. She knew she was getting a good grip on herself at last. And she said she was ready to start a new life. I think she even had a boyfriend, but Star is not sure of that."

"My, you two have been talking," I replied, more impressed now than alarmed. They had gotten about as far as the police had, as a matter of fact.

"Well, if she didn't kill herself," I relented, though I refused to be defeated, "any thoughts on who might have killed her?"

"Nothing for sure," Eva replied cagily. "But we're making up a list. There're a lot of people I don't know from Merriweathers. Plus friends and stuff. Star wouldn't put you on, though. She thinks you're great." Eva's tone of voice made it clear she didn't agree with her friend's assessment of me.

"I think she is, too," I replied, and realized for the first time just how much I meant it. In the beginning I thought I felt akin to her because we'd both grown up in unusual households. I saw her as myself, fourteen years ago, standing in the shadow of flamboyant parents, longing for normalcy and order. But now I realized that where I had simply struggled against Theo, Star had struggled for Wanda. I had looked out for myself, and Star had looked out for her mother. No, I realized, we really aren't alike at all. Star was the better person. I felt sick with anger and loss to think it was Eva, and not me, she had chosen to tell her secrets to. What is it about being an adult that makes you immediately suspect to youth? I was so sunk in misery and self-reproach that I didn't hear Cursio's back door slam, but Eva sprang up and raced to the kitchen.

"They're here!" she yelled at me, and I stumbled up and followed her.

"I guess I wasn't thinking," Star was telling Eva as she stood in the middle of the brightly lighted room unzipping her parka. "I must have taken a wrong turn and..."

I couldn't help myself. I went up to her, put my arms around her and cried, "Never, never do that to me again!"

"Hey, I'm okay," Star was saying. "Mr. Cursio just came cruising along and picked me up. What's the big deal? I'm back." But there was a look in her eye—a mixture of fear and relief—that showed me she understood more than she wanted to about what the deal was. She hugged me back.

"And I'm starving," Eva said. "Did you at least remember the ketchup, Star?"

But she hadn't, of course, and in surveying the wreckage in the frying pan, we all decided the dinner as such wasn't worth salvaging. So Cursio bundled us all back into the car and took us to his favorite Italian place in Long Island City. It was past midnight by the time we got back to Cursio's brownstone. We sent the girls straight to bed, and I stayed to help him try to put the pieces of his kitchen back together.

"Lord, for such a neat little person," I told him as I scraped yellowing chunks of onion off a cutting board, "your daughter can sure make a mess."

"Tell me about it," Cursio replied from the sink, his sweater sleeves pushed up to his elbows, his arms deep in grimy suds. "She drives me crazy. Playing that awful music, changing her clothes about sixteen times a day. Rattling on about Star this and Star that. But Gwen called today. She's doing much better and wants Eva to come home in a couple of weeks."

"That's great," I told him. "You must be relieved."

"Yeah," he said. "So why do I feel so terrible?"

What could I tell him? I was just beginning to understand the hidden hazards and rewards of parenting myself. Finally, I said, "While you were out, Eva told me that Star's figured out what really happened to Wanda. Apparently they're conducting their own investigation."

"I know," Cursio replied as he let the water drain from the sink. He turned to face me, drying his hands absently on his jeans. "They came to me with their list of suspects. Wanted to help."

"Dante!" I cried, slapping a dish towel against the counter and sinking into a chair. "I've been so careful all this time not to let on to Star. Why didn't you tell me?"

"Because you didn't ask, that's why," he replied coolly. "The same way I didn't ask if Wes was suing for custody."

"But this is different," I exclaimed, though my flushed face was trying to argue otherwise.

"Maybe," Cursio answered, dropping into a kitchen chair next to me, "and maybe not. As far as I can see, it's just another fact, another piece that doesn't fit anywhere in this awkward puzzle."

"Maybe Star knows something," I thought out loud. "I mean, buried in her subconscious, or whatever. Have you tried to interview her yet?"

"No," he replied, leaning his elbows on the kitchen table and studying the speckled surface of the linoleum. "I told her to come to me if she thought of anything that might help. I don't want to walk her back through all that horror on the outside chance that she saw or heard something helpful. It seems too cruel, considering that what we'd learn would probably be iffy, anyway. And I'm afraid it's going to stay iffy unless..."

"Unless what?" I asked.

"What do you say we be honest with each other for a change?" Cursio said suddenly. Before I could reply, he rushed on, "For instance, I'll tell you the truth. Despite the fact that I have three men assigned to me on this case, despite the fact that I have extensive information networks and research facilities at my disposal, do you know who has been the single most helpful person to me throughout this damned investigation? Do you have any idea who it is?"

He sounded angry and tired and ready for a fight. I decided to keep my head bowed and my mouth shut. But he slid his right hand under my chin and made me look at him.

"Do you know?" he demanded again, more softly, his gaze moving from my eyes to my lips. "Shall I tell you? It's the one person, the very person I want to stay clear of this whole mess. It's the one person in the world that I most want to know is safe and secure. It's the last person I would ever want anything to happen to."

I swallowed dryly and said, "What makes you think this person is in any danger? So what if an innocent stooge pokes around a little? Asks a few harmless questions? I don't see what's so terrible about that. Do you?"

"I don't know," he said sadly, dropping his hand. "I've been debating about this for days. Arguing with myself, trying to figure out another way. But no matter what I do, all the loose threads in this case lead back to Merriweather Sportswear and more specifically to how the company was bought out by Tantamount. What I need to know more about, Peg, is that first connection between the two companies. Who instigated it? When? And why?"

"I'd think that information might be available in the Merriweather account files at P&Q," I replied. "And I don't at all mind checking for you. But can't you demand the files? Can't you—what do you call it—subpoena them?"

"Sure," Cursio replied, "and then the murderer will know how close we are. I've got to keep the cover on this as long as I can. I've got to have facts and figures. Otherwise the entire prosecution will be based on circumstantial evidence."

"The prosecution of whom?" I demanded. "If I'm going to do this for you, I think I have a right to know."

For the first time that night, he smiled at me. He ran his finger along the line of my jaw and then up along my lips. "Don't you understand?" he asked gently. "I really don't know any more than you do. It was one of five or six people, for any of the same number of reasons. I've been working alone in the dark with this. And the only thing I keep stumbling into is . . . you."

He pushed back his chair, walked across the room and switched off the overhead light. Did I believe him? I didn't know. Did it matter? I decided not. He came back and stood above me, his shoulders and head backlighted with moonlight, the contours of sink and cupboards forming pale, ghostly shapes. The only sound in the whole, sleeping neighborhood was the tick-tick of the clock above the sink. He pulled me to my feet. There were so many questions unanswered between us, but now there was only one that mattered: Detective Dante Cursio was turning to me for help. At last. I put my arms around his neck. And I gave it to him.

TWENTY-FIVE

"WE WERE HOPING you could tell us where things stood with Wes," Phillip Ebert declared the following Monday morning.

I'd been called into his office around ten. Mark Rollings and Dick Byser were there, as well. Both Phillip and Mark were wearing the tired, pale expressions common to February. But Dick, despite a recently acquired tropical tan, looked worse than either of them. His eyes had sunk back into their sockets, as if retreating as far as possible from the sights of the world. And his body, usually tense with purpose and stamina, was slack, his arm draped listlessly over the back of Phillip's brass-studded leather chair. Dick looked as though he had recently lost weight, hair and something harder to define. The dynamism that drew you to him, that glanced off him like sunlight on a well-buffed fender, had tarnished. This morning he looked like any other of the thousands of well-groomed cogs that kept the big money machine running.

"I'm sorry," I told them, "but I really don't know much more than you do. He's in California, on business. He wasn't real specific."

"But surely he's told you when he's coming back," Mark pressed me. "It's been nearly three weeks. He can't expect us to hold up producing the Merriweather campaign forever."

"No, I'm sorry, but he hasn't," I retorted. "And to be quite honest, I'm more concerned about what I'm supposed to do with Star."

"Of course," Phillip answered soothingly. "There are many issues here besides the advertising question. We just thought we'd check with you first before proceeding to more formal lines of inquiry."

"How is she?" Dick asked abruptly, and then when Mark and Phillip peered across at him questioningly, he added, "I mean, Star. How is she doing, Peg?"

"Okay, considering," I told him. I wasn't about to add that in fact I thought she'd never been better. Because, finally, she was talking to me. Really talking. To be quite honest, I was having a rough time getting her to stop. I think giving her that hug in Cursio's kitchen was what did it; she knew I cared and that it was okay to care back.

"Does she want to go ahead with the shoot?" Mark asked. "Do you know what her thinking is on that? What her plans are at this point?"

"Yes, I think it's fair to say she wants to continue to be a model," I told them, although that was probably the understatement of the decade. In the past few days, Star had let it all come gushing out: her hope and dream of being the most famous face in the world. How she intended to carry on Wanda's grand plan for her future and become the best, the highest paid, the most admired model ever. Well, that's how fifteen-year-olds think and talk. And boy, can they talk. This particular discussion went on until two o'clock in the morning on Sunday. The ending or postscript to this story is how Wanda's murderer—yes, we finally talked about that, as well—would one day see her on the front cover of *Vogue* or *Cosmo*, and overcome with grief and guilt over what he had done, admit to the heinous act and turn himself in. Hyperbole and coincidence rank high in the teen imagination, whereas reason and common sense don't rate at all. It was a relief to discover, though, that there was a normal girl under the thick layer of maturity Star had been forced to wear.

"Well, that's positive news at any rate," Phillip declared. "Her willingness to go forward is the truly important thing. Now, if we can just round up Wes, we'll be able to proceed. Uh, thanks Peg," he added by way of dismissal. "I think that's all for now."

"Yes, thanks for your help," Mark added unctuously, and I returned his fake little smile with a cool, flat stare. One would have thought that his being named a vice president would have helped check some of his more obnoxious mannerisms. But toadying seemed a degenerative and untreatable disease with Mark. As I was leaving, I heard him confide to Dick in his most self-congratulatory tones, "You see, I *told* you there was nothing to worry about."

IT WAS NINE HOURS later. The cleaning lady had just finished wheeling her cart onto the elevator, leaving me alone in my office and the only one left on the floor. I stretched, tossed aside the back issue of *Adweek* I'd been thumbing through and walked over to the window. By seven o'clock at night on a February Monday, Madison Avenue is a ghost town. The storefronts are hidden behind aluminum grillwork, the sidewalks empty except for the lone, late commuter hurrying downtown to Grand Central. After about ten minutes, I spotted Mrs. Grimwold, the woman who cleans the top floors of Peabody & Quinlan, her head bowed into the wind, hurrying toward the 7:59, New Rochelle, and half a dozen little Grimwolds. I then turned from the window, kicked off my heels and made my way quickly down the carpeted corridor. I could hear myself breathing.

Inhale. I'd reached the long, tidy row of secretarial desks that helped protect the executive offices from unwanted visitors. *Exhale.* I hurried along it to the very end, to the corner where Phillip Ebert's office waited in darkness. *Inhale.* I checked the bank of file cabinets next to his secretary's desk. *Exhale.* They were organized in strict alphabetical order, and none were locked.

God, it was so easy! There, right after Merchant Marine, Ltd. was Merriweather Sportswear, a legal file thick with memos and correspondence, including a typed copy of our creative presentation and marketing plan. Nothing about the Tantamount takeover, though, so I pulled out the file drawer beneath and searched under the *T*'s. Odd. There was nothing. Then I checked under *B* for Byser and *M* again for Merger. *P* for Parent company. *Nada.* Damn.

I stood and leaned against the file cabinets and thought. Well, there was always Mark Rollings's office, I decided. Mark was a notorious note taker, organizer and squirreler-away of the odd piece of information. I heard it drove his secretary absolutely crazy, but he probably had the most complete records at P&Q. He was clearly my next best bet; the only problem was that his office was on the floor below. For the sake of privacy and speed, I decided to take the stairwell that was halfway down the corridor.

The bank of file cabinets lined the outside hall to Mark's office, with half a dozen invading the ten-foot-square space allotted his secretary. No wonder she hated him, I thought, searching along the wall for the *M*'s. There were four full drawers of them. And there were five separate files for Merriweather, each neatly labeled: Account Work, Media, Creative, Marketing, Other. I was just beginning to slide the one marked Other out when I heard the footsteps behind me. *Inhale, exhale.* I tried to slam the drawer shut, but the Other file got in the way. I decided I would just leave it—abandon the thing and run.

"Peg!"

Damn it would have to be Mark, wouldn't it? "Oh, yes, hi," I said, trying to appear that I had every right to be in his office after work.

"What on earth are you doing here?" he demanded, looking from me to the half-open drawer, then back to me again.

In general, I'm a pretty good fabricator. Not that I make a habit of it, mind, but when a good beaut of a lie is necessary, I can usually cook one up. But not in a hurry. Not without forethought, preparation. I stood there, slack-jawed, trying not to look guilty.

"Let me rephrase my question," Mark continued in his most sarcastic snivel. "What the hell do you think you're doing rifling through my files without my permission?"

I clutched at the straw he had accidentally dropped. "Oh, well, I was going to ask you first," I stammered. "But you weren't here, so I thought, well, what the heck, you wouldn't mind, and—"

"Bull!" he cried, leaning over to see where I'd been looking. "Aha! Just what I thought! You were after the Merriweather files! I'm not surprised, not in the least. You're out to get me, aren't you? You've been riding for my hide from the very beginning."

"Please, Mark," I began, "that's just ridiculous. Why in the world would—"

"You just can't stand to see me succeed, can you, Peg?" Mark sneered, his boyish face mottled with a red rash of anger. "You hated it when I was named a V.P. Admit it!"

"That's not true," I told him. "Why should I care?"

"Because you've always disliked me," he retorted, spitting slightly in his eagerness to make my case against him. "You always thought you were better than me because I had to fight my way up the ladder here. And you came waltzing in with your fancy degrees and hotshot mother and—"

"Oh, please, Mark," I broke in, "this is just crazy."

"It is, is it?" he demanded, his face contorting. "Don't you think I notice how you try to belittle me in front of clients? How you try to make me look stupid to Phillip?"

"You don't need my help there," I broke in without thinking. I shouldn't have said it. He was already angry, and now his face took on a look I could only describe as murderous. And then it hit me. What if he was the murderer? Good God, I thought. I took a step back. And he took one forward.

"How dare you insult me like that!" he roared. I noticed that his hands were clenched; two surprisingly large-looking fists curled at his side.

"I'm sorry.... Really, I am," I sputtered. "I didn't come here to spy on you, Mark. Believe me." I didn't know what I was doing, what I was saying. "I'm only trying to get to the bottom of Berry's and Wanda's murders." As soon as the words were out, I could have shot myself. Who needed a killer around when I had myself to do the job?

"What are you talking about?" Mark demanded. "Wanda took her own life. It was suicide. Not murder."

"Well, yeah," I answered lamely. "That's right, I guess."

"There's something you're not telling me," Mark said, his face taking on the strangest expression. In a single second it went from beet red to sheet white, from ugly with anger to almost beatific with—what?—a kind of peace, is the only way I could describe it. Is this how a murderer should act, I asked myself, when he realized the jig is up? Hardly. I felt myself start to relax.

"Um, now remember, this is pure speculation," I warned him.

"That's okay," he promised me. "That's all right. Just tell me what you speculate." It was the weirdest thing, but he looked as if he were getting ready to cry. His eyes welled up. And then he said urgently, "Please, Peg. Tell me what you know."

So I did. And Mark Rollings, the sycophant I thought I knew inside and out, did a most unexpected thing: he hugged me.

"Thank God!" he cried, taking a step away from me. "Oh, I'm so grateful, so thankful. You don't know what this means to me. You just can't know!"

"Well, you could tell me," I suggested, watching tears of happiness roll down his cheeks. What was this?

"Yes," Mark replied, taking a deep breath. "Yes, I could. I will. You see, Peg . . . I loved her."

"Wanda?"

"Yes," he answered pathetically. "Wanda. I've adored her for years and years. I would have done anything for her. I hated to see her so terribly unhappy. I was dying from it, watching her married to that . . . that thug."

"Did she know?" I asked.

"Oh, I'm sure she guessed," he told me. "But I didn't actually come right out and tell her until she confided in me that she was leaving Wes. That she and Star were going to start over again."

"And this was when?" I demanded.

"About a year ago," he said. "I was the one who talked to Dick and managed to get her that trip with you to Europe. Anyone could see she was under too much pressure. That she needed some breathing room."

"But that's not what she got," I observed.

"I know," he replied quietly, then added with more force, "but now I can believe again that she might have been ready to make a fresh start. Don't you understand? If she killed herself, then I have to face the fact that nothing in her life seemed worth living for, including me."

"I see," I added thoughtfully. "The fact that someone might have killed her . . . gives you hope."

"Yes!" he replied, his eyes still glistening.

Hope that a woman now dead might have one day learned to love him. How little most of us have to pin our dreams on, I thought. How often, I wondered, has someone's future been suddenly made worthwhile because someone else—for whatever reason—flashed a smile here, gave a hurried kiss there? "Love," Theo has pontificated more than once, "is never equal and never fair."

"Well, I'm glad for you, Mark," I told him honestly. Then I waited maybe fifteen seconds before I said, "Now maybe you wouldn't mind answering a few questions...."

TWENTY-SIX

ALTHOUGH THE DEFROSTER and heater were both on full blast, the front window kept fogging up and the temperature was so cold that I could see my breath. Cursio had picked us up—gloveless and hatless—in front of the P&Q building within ten minutes of the time I had called.

"My God, Dante," I complained as I tried to warm my hands between my trembling knees, "where do you get these old rust buckets from, anyway? The windchill factor back here is in the double digits."

"Oh, put a lid on it, Goodenough," he told me, catching my gaze in the rearview mirror. His eyes were bright, lighted from within. They slid to his right, where Mark Rollings was hunched in his midnight-blue cashmere chesterfield.

"You can talk to her like that?" Mark asked in awed tones, turning awkwardly toward Cursio. He had his arms wrapped over his chest, his hands warming under his armpits. "I've never heard anyone get away with talking to Peg like that!"

"What can she do to me?" Cursio shrugged, flashing me the kind of smile that Cleopatra sold Egypt down the Nile for. "One false move and I'd haul her in on assault charges."

"So what I've heard is true?" Mark asked, turning just enough to let me know he was addressing both of us. "You two are, well, seeing each other?"

"Saw," I corrected.

"Seeing," Cursio snapped, not meeting my gaze. "I think it's safe to say we're still in the participle stage."

Well, that was news to me! I tried to catch his eyes again in the rearview mirror, but Cursio was careful to keep me out of his line of vision.

"We need a quiet place to talk," he told Mark. "Anywhere in particular you want to go?"

"Not really," Mark muttered, "so long as it's warm and doesn't smell like old cigarette butts." The air in the Chevy was heavy with the odor of tobacco—the sad, stale, chain-smoker variety.

"Hey, I'm sorry, to both of you," Cursio retorted, "but I'm not in one of your glamour industries. This is what you might call a company car. On a night like this, all I ask is that it keeps running."

We finally stopped at a rambling, half-filled restaurant on Third Avenue in the seventies, a place whose clientele preferred the bar to the big round tables and their beer and Scotches to each other's company. A Knicks game was playing on the thirty-six-inch screen above the cash register, and most of the conversation centered on derogatory comments about the home team's performance. We took a table in the back.

"Gotta eat something if you sit here," a young, tired-looking blonde told us, slapping menus down on the table and walking away. We all ordered hamburgers, the least-threatening thing we could find, and draft beer.

"Okay, now," Cursio began after the mugs had been slopped down in front of us. "Peg told me on the phone that you might have some information about how and why Merriweather was bought by Tantamount."

"You could say that," Mark answered with a note of pride in his voice. "I was the one who orchestrated the deal."

Cursio's expression was impassive, perhaps even slightly bored, at this announcement. He poked around in his jacket pocket for his dog-eared notebook and pen, gulped back some beer, and said, "Right." He clicked down hard on his ballpoint. "Why don't you just start from the beginning. When did you first meet Wanda and Wes Merriweather?"

"I knew Wanda way before I met Wes," Mark replied, staring down into the watery depths of his beer. "It was back in the early seventies, I guess. I was a junior account executive for Monro & Gilbert. You know, hardly more than a gofer, on the Bubbles account."

"'Bubbles'?" Cursio asked, jotting something down. His handwriting is perfect for a detective: sprawling, masculine, basically unreadable by anyone but him.

"The powdered laundry detergent," Mark told him. "Had about 20 percent of the market share back then.... That was before the heavy-duty liquid soaps came along and blew the powders out of the water. In any case, I was on that account, television mostly, although we also had a regular print campaign. The focus of the creative was always on some lovely, dewy-eyed young bride type. Every few years, they'd change models, and I happened to be there when they put out a search for the new Bubbles girl.''

"Enter Wanda Merriweather,'' Cursio said.

"You're a quick study, Detective,'' Mark answered, fiddling with his mug. "After about a month of screen tests and test shots and so forth, the Bubbles people went with Wanda.''

"She must have been all of about what, then?'' Cursio asked. "Eighteen, nineteen?''

"Young and fresh and blond....'' Mark's voice had a dreamy quality. He was smiling down at his beer, remembering. "And, you know, kind of flaky.''

"How do you mean 'flaky'?'' Cursio demanded. The hamburgers arrived, big oval plates overly decorated with iceberg lettuce and tomato wedges that looked like they'd been sliced out of pink Styrofoam.

"Wacky, funny,'' Mark replied, taking the bun off the top of his burger, then quickly putting it back on. The patty was charred and used looking. "Sort of like Goldie Hawn in the *Laugh-In* days.''

"Drugs?'' Cursio demanded. "We heard she was using, even back then.''

"Oh, certainly,'' Mark agreed. "But, you got to remember, back then—I mean late sixties, early seventies—everybody was doing stuff. In that sense, it didn't seem too weird.''

"But in some sense it did?'' I asked, hearing a reservation, a note of regret, in his voice.

"Yeah,'' Mark admitted, glancing over at me. "I know life was supposed to be looser, freer then. But I've always been a pretty buttoned-up kind of guy.'' He saw my look, gave a self-deprecating laugh and shook his head. "Okay, so I'm so straight you could run a flag up me. All I'm trying to say is that her, uh, way of life, bothered me. She looked so sweet, so innocent . . . and yet she'd come in for a shoot at six in the morning, having stayed up all night, smelling like—''

"Were you lovers?'' Cursio interrupted him.

"No," Mark answered at once, "but not because she wasn't willing. Wanda would . . . Wanda went to bed with just about anyone who seemed vaguely interested. And she knew that I was more than interested, more than infatuated. I was totally and absolutely smitten. She was *it* for me, you know? And I was just one of the many to her."

"You couldn't stand the thought of sharing her," I observed. "So you decided that if you couldn't have all of her, then you didn't want any. Was it something like that?"

"Roughly, yes," Mark replied, taking a long drag of beer. "Although I like to think of it in a more romantic light. She was such a beauty, but so vulnerable, so unsure of herself. She used men and drugs and booze as a way of bolstering her confidence. My line to her was that she didn't need any of those crutches, that she could be great on her own. And, of course, that we could be great together."

"But she didn't buy it," Cursio observed.

"No," Mark replied, shaking his head, "I'm afraid she didn't. She was the Bubbles girl for all of about nine months. I kept trying to warn her that detergent people don't have any sense of fun or humor when it comes to their snowy-white public image. Especially when the one who's messing with it happens to be their own handpicked, all-American Bubbles girl. I tried my damnedest to protect her, but her name ended up in one too many columns."

"What finally clinched it?" Cursio demanded, at the same time signaling to our waitress to clear away the dinner plates, although none of us had eaten much. We ordered coffee all around.

"I was afraid you'd ask that," Mark said with a sigh when the waitress had moved off.

"Why?" Cursio demanded. "It's nothing I can't find out on my own, you realize. What's the problem?"

"Not what, but who," Mark told us, his voice dropping a few decibels. He looked around the room as if to make sure no one were listening. For the first time, I felt sorry for him. The most painful, most private stuff of his life was being aired for the public record. It hardly mattered who overheard him now. Still, he kept his voice low and controlled as he continued.

"About the same time I was realizing that Wanda wasn't going to heed my advice, she started to fool around with the young, married, Bubbles product manager. They were quite a hot item and the relationship was very much verboten. I mean, Peg can tell you, Detective, client-agency liaisons are just not the done thing. They were playing with fire, but neither seemed to care. They were both pretty high most of the time. At work, I mean—during filming! I tried to warn them. They wouldn't listen."

"You talked to both of them?" Cursio demanded. "Wasn't that a bit noble of you, Mark? I mean, come on, you loved the woman. This product manager was your competition, right?"

"Listen, Detective, I already tried to explain it to you," Mark answered sadly. "The entire masculine population of Manhattan was my competition. That's hard to beat. And besides, I cared what happened to her. And him."

"Okay, you better tell us who he was," Cursio demanded.

"I hope this won't go any further," Mark replied helplessly. "I don't suppose I can get you to promise me that?"

"Listen, I'm sorry," Cursio replied, "but at this point I can get the answer in another way in about ten seconds flat. And you can be darn sure I will if you don't tell me. Nobody has to know where the information came from, though, if it makes you feel any better."

From the look on Mark's face, it didn't, but he gave Cursio a weak smile anyway. We waited while the waitress wearily distributed three chipped coffee mugs around the table.

"I cared about him—" Mark's voice broke, and then he took a breath and went on, "And I still care about him. He was my roommate at Harvard and—"

"Dick Byser?" I cried. "But, my God, Mark, talk about straight arrows! Dick won't even drink quinine water."

"Well, he used to," Mark told us, "and a whole lot else besides. Even at Harvard, I guessed he might have a problem someday. We were roommates and our dorm just happened to be the booze capital of the campus. He'd get stinking just about every night. That was after he finished all the work that put him on the dean's list each semester. Dick was smart, even then, but there was this self-destructive fuse ready to go off, I guess. And Wanda helped him light it."

"Was it just coincidence that you were both working for the same agency?" Cursio asked.

"No, actually," Mark said. "About the time I started at Monro & Gilbert, Dick had gotten the ax from his first job as a marketing manager for a paper manufacturer. He made a joke of it, said there were reams of differences between him and his boss, but later I figured it was because of his drinking. Anyway, I knew some of the lower-level managers at M&G—we all hung out together at conventions and so forth—and they were happy to put a good word in for a friend of mine."

"So you get him a job," I said, "and he takes away your girl. Some friend."

"Yeah," Mark said, swallowing some coffee. "But they were both so messed up, I knew it wasn't going to work out. They had disaster written all over them. They ended up totalling a rented car in Queens, stewed to the gills, knocking down an eighty-year-old Italian grandmother in the process. 'Bubbles Girl Drunk and Disorderly.' It made the headlines in most of the tabloids."

"So Bubbles fired Wanda," Cursio noted. "What did they do to Dick?"

"Oh, he lost his job, too," Mark told us, "and his wife. And custody of his two-year-old son. He went on a nine-month binge after that. He'd come by my place from time to time to hit me up for money to buy booze. Then I lost touch with him for about a year. Seems he hit rock bottom, ended up on the Bowery, even, then somehow found himself at an AA meeting. Says to this day that it saved his life."

"Too bad nothing managed to save Wanda's," Cursio observed softly. "Okay, Mark, fill me in on the more recent history. You claim you orchestrated the Tantamount takeover. How?"

"I, uh, well..." Mark cleared his throat. "A little more than a year ago, Wanda called me. Totally out of the blue. From Los Angeles. She sounded a little worse for wear and very unhappy. Said she wanted out of her dead-end marriage. Said she was trying to go totally straight and begin a new life with her daughter. She asked me—no, she begged me—to help."

"How?" Cursio demanded again. He sounded impatient and vaguely irritated. His tone said story time was over. Mark tensed and started to speed up his delivery.

"She told me that her husband's company, the one he co-owned with his sister, was facing some serious cash flow problems. Although Merriweather itself was turning a handsome profit, it seems that someone had been diverting funds. Berry apparently had just found out and was in a total, though silent, panic. I guess she felt that if she could keep a lid on the problem and sort things out, the company could manage to stay afloat."

"But Wanda saw it as an opportunity to make her exit," Cursio went on, "with a little something for a rainy day. So what was the deal? What did she want from you?"

"Well, she asked me to help her find a buyer," Mark explained. "One who would move swiftly to purchase the company, but who would also agree to feature Star in any Merriweather advertising. She wanted Merriweather to launch Star's career."

"But why didn't she just ask Berry directly?" I demanded.

"Wanda and Berry weren't speaking," Mark told me somewhat hesitantly. He glanced from Cursio to me, back to Cursio again. "I thought you guys knew about that."

"You mean that Berry sent Wes packing back to California?" I said. "Yes, we knew."

"And you know why, right?" Mark asked.

"Well . . ." I began, but Cursio cut me off.

"Sure," he said sharply, "we know."

"So, anyway," Mark went on, "with Wes gambling away half of Merriweather's profits, it was no wonder the East and West coasts weren't exactly on speaking terms. Not that I think Wanda was interested in getting back at Berry, though there was definitely some animosity there. It was more that she finally wanted her due . . . and this was her way of achieving it. After that first call of hers, I immediately thought of Dick Byser. God, he seemed the perfect choice, considering . . ."

I was only half listening at this point, because my thoughts kept looping back to what Mark had said about Wes's gambling. Half the Merriweather profits? I repeated to myself. No wonder Berry had kicked him across the country! But what disturbed me even more was the fact that Cursio didn't seem in the least phased by this extraordinary news. I watched him closely, scrawling his unreadable notes, running his hands through his overlong hair, and my suspicions and anger started to mount.

"Do you think she might have had Dick in mind all along?" Cursio was asking by the time I was able to focus on the conversation again.

The bastard, I thought, observing the practiced, methodical way he was leading Mark along his line of questioning. He had known about Wes from the start, I realized now, and hadn't told me. He had been playing me for a fool, just as he was playing Mark. I was as much a part of this investigation, I told myself, as his grungy-looking ballpoint pen: serviceable, near at hand, easily dispensed with if necessary.

"What I'm driving at," Cursio continued gently, "is do you think there might have been something still between them, Dick and Wanda, and that maybe she set you up to get in touch with him?"

"No way," Mark assured him, slapping the tabletop for emphasis. "At first she was really upset when I told her about Dick's interest. Unnerved, I think, is the right word. She said she just didn't want him in her life again, that there was too much she'd prefer to keep private—"

"Like her drug and alcohol dependencies?" I interrupted. "Maybe she didn't want to hear his rap on AA and all?"

"Maybe," Mark answered doubtfully, turning around to look for the waitress. "But she finally calmed down about it. Saw the benefits of bringing Dick aboard. Realized the incredible opportunities Tantamount offered both her and Star."

"Did she know that Berry had gotten cold feet at the last moment?" Cursio demanded, signaling the waitress over to our table. He pulled a wad of cash from his pocket and paid the girl.

"No," Mark answered immediately. "Of course not. How could she find something like that out?"

"Million ways," Cursio replied. "Maybe Berry called Wes and told him. Maybe Dick knew and had told her. Maybe she talked to Berry directly."

"No," Mark told him. "She didn't do it. I knew her too well—she wouldn't have. And besides that, she and Wes and Star were in Vail when the murder occurred."

"Not verifiable," Cursio told us. "They—she—could have taken a day trip back. All I'm saying, Mark, is that someone with a very vested interest in the Merriweather deal going through murdered Berry. And no matter what you say, it's very possible that that someone was Wanda."

"But if Wanda didn't commit suicide, who killed *her*?" Mark demanded, exasperated. "This is ridiculous! I can hardly conceive of one murderer, let alone two!"

"Ah, well," Cursio answered, sighing. He stretched back in his chair and then stood up. "You're lucky, then. I'm at the stage where I can conceive of just about anybody...killing anybody."

We dropped Mark off at his high-rise co-op on Seventy-sixth and First, then took the transverse through the icy darkness of Central Park to the West Side. I was as silent, as distant and as unapproachable as the frozen lake that glimmered, moonlit, through the trees.

"You're pissed that I didn't tell you about Wes," Cursio announced as he pulled up in front of my brownstone. I reached for the door handle without answering, but his arm shot out and held the door shut. "I'm sorry. I just didn't want you to get involved. I didn't want you in danger."

"Your concern over my welfare, Detective," I retorted, staring out through the frosted front window, "though touching, is about as consistent as Parcel Post."

"Please, Peg," he began in his lowest, most mesmerizing voice, but I cut him off.

"Don't even try me, Dante," I snapped. "You're not playing fair with me, so from now on we're back to tit for tat. I gave you Mark tonight. I want something in return."

"Shit...." he moaned, his head dropping against his arms, which circled the steering wheel. "This isn't a game. Don't you understand?"

"You owe me," I replied simply.

"Okay," he answered, gulping, not looking up. "What?"

"Where is Wes? I think you know, and I think you've known since he took off."

"He's at Santa Anita."

"Where?"

"It's more a what than a 'where,' " Cursio told me.

"And that means?"

"It's a racetrack, Peg. *The* racetrack, actually, in Southern California. Wes has ensconced himself there, playing the ponies. He's an inveterate gambler—has been for years."

"So he gambled away money he stole from Merriweather," I said, speaking more to myself than Cursio. "That's why Berry threw him out."

"Correct," Cursio replied. "It forced her into such a bad financial position that when the Tantamount offer came along, she really had no choice but to consider it."

"Poor Berry," I said, thinking back on our last months together. "And poor Wanda." I sympathized at last with the hard-hearted way she had tried to break free of her marriage.

"And poor Star," Cursio added. "And I mean that literally. You know Wes saw an immediate million dollars from the Tantamount sale, don't you?"

"Yes..."

"Well, I doubt there's much left to see anymore."

TWENTY-SEVEN

IT SNOWED EVERY DAY for the remainder of the week: big, fairy-tale flakes that drifted down like feathers from a low-slung sky. Star, who'd spent most of the past year in the continual summer of Southern California, was thrilled. I bought her a pair of ice skates, and she spent all her late afternoons at the rink at Rockefeller Center. I would pick her up there on my way home.

The weather did nothing to lift my spirits. If anything, the uniform, secretive leadenness of those days darkened my already gloomy inner landscape. My heart was frozen. My mind slow, stripped of ideas and interests. I saw everything in monotones. Cursio had used me; that fact was etched across my brain. And I had let him; little rivulets of shame and anger wriggled through me. Everything I had done to make him see me in a new light, to help him value me as an equal, as a partner...had been lost on him. I was still what I had always been: a warm, willing body at his side. A comfort. A convenience. Oh, he cared about me, I knew that. He respected me. He looked forward to seeing me. But an argument could be made that he felt the same way about the New York Mets. And he wasn't about to commit his life to any of them.

Still, I knew this man in his heart of hearts. And I believed that somewhere in the deepest rhythms of his being, he could admit to himself that he truly loved me as much as I loved him. But I needed to break through to that core, to bare those feelings for him. I had to shake him up hard and shake loose all the excuses, the worries, the fears that kept him from facing the truth. I needed to force him into a catharsis, but there was only one pretext I could think of to manage it. And it was a very dangerous one.

I was thinking all this as I gazed down at Star polishing off a figure-eight in the nearly empty skating rink late Thursday afternoon. In the normal world, it was dinnertime, and the last purply streaks of twilight were being folded into darker night colors. The snow had stopped around noon, and a bleary star peeked out above the Warner Communications building. Star turned, saw me and waved. I waved back, signaling to her that it was time to leave.

"What a lovely girl," a woman standing next to me in a parka and ski cap exclaimed.

"Yes," I answered proudly, watching Star glide backward across the ice with balletic grace.

"You know, I think she's pretty enough to be a model," the woman beside me went on, "don't you?"

"Oh, yes," I told her, squashing the desire to say that she was one—and famous at that. But the unpleasant notoriety surrounding the Merriweather name at the moment made me hold my tongue. Just that week, the *National Enquirer* had carried a story headlined "Shocking Death in a Model Family," with a photo of the three Merriweathers posing for Cougars Country Jeans. And it was in that instant, when I was thinking about Wes and Wanda and Star altogether, that it occurred to me I was probably watching the one person I knew who unconsciously held the key to the murders. She was carefully unlacing her new skates on an empty bench at Rockefeller Center.

I waited until after Star and I had finished scraping the bottom of the Häagen-Dazs macadamia nut ice-cream carton later that night before I said, "You know, Detective Cursio's having a hell of a time. And he's under a lot of pressure to get the investigations tied up before the spring primary elections. I feel badly for him." Only the last part, actually, was untrue.

"Is that why he hasn't been calling much?" Star asked Though she and Eva chatted on the phone at least half an hour every night, Dante and I had been keeping our distance.

"Partly that," I replied, "and also because we had a bit of a disagreement. You see, for a while there, I tried to help him Told him what I knew about Merriweather and Tantamount Kind of gave him the inside track on the business end of things."

"I thought maybe you had," Star replied, smiling knowingly at me. "Eva and I overheard you guys talking a few times."

"Yeah, well, I'm afraid he didn't much appreciate it," I told her. "At least not enough to tell me what was really going on. He's been holding stuff back."

"Like?" Star demanded. At unexpected times it would hit me all over again just how lovely she was: how pale and luminous her skin, how delicate her bone structure, how finely drawn her lips and tigerlike, uptilted eyes. What a gift such beauty is, I thought, if used correctly. What a curse if it isn't. I held Star's gaze for a moment, debating, weighing the odds. Ignorance was bliss, I knew. But what if Star, like myself, was nagged by half doubts, vague suspicions, recurring fears that had a way of crawling into your dreams? Wasn't it worse to let them haunt you, never quite out of mind, day and night...than to turn and face them squarely, however horrible they were? I answered her finally with another question. "Do you know where Wes is?"

"Oh," she said, glancing away and then down, "that. Yes, I was afraid you'd find out at some point. Damn."

"So...you knew he wasn't in California on business?" I demanded. "You've known all along?" A look of such misery swept across her face that I immediately regretted the tone I had used. I added soothingly, "I'm...just surprised, that's all. You never said anything."

"I...I was afraid you wouldn't want me to stay," Star answered brokenly, "if you knew what he was up to. We...we both thought it would be better not to say."

"You mean, you actually discussed this with Wes?" I asked her. "You sat down and talked it over?"

Star stood up, pushing back the kitchen chair, and walked over to the window. We had both gotten into our pajamas before the ice-cream orgy; over her striped flannels she had put on an old plaid bathrobe of mine. Tall for her age, too skinny for her own good, from the back she looked like a slim, middle-aged housewife, slumped and tired after a long day in the kitchen. Though even from the front, it would be impossible for anyone to guess that she was only fifteen years old.

"I can't expect you to understand," she said in a voice as weary as her posture. "But growing up with Wes and Wanda...well...it was like being raised by two children. I mean, they were a lot of fun. And they tried to take care of me.

But they weren't real good at discipline. Their impulses weren't always under control, you know?''

"But, Star," I replied as gently as I could, "gambling away money you've stolen is hardly an impulse. It's a crime."

"You mean the thing with Berry?" Star asked sadly, turning around to face me. "Well, believe it or not, Peg, he didn't *mean* to steal the money. That really wasn't it at all. He told me that he only meant to kind of *borrow* it for a while, until things got better for him. He was going to pay it back, really."

"And you believe that?" I asked her, but from her set expression, I could tell she did.

"Of course," Star answered. "I told you, Peg, they were like two kids. They didn't mean any harm. Especially to each other, you know. Wes loved Wanda—I'm sure of that. And she felt the same way about him. But, well, I don't think they were very good for each other. And finally Wanda saw that if she didn't make a clean break . . . we'd all end up in trouble."

"So she broke free and..." I continued for her. "Star, don't you ever wonder if . . . ?"

"Wes was the one who killed her?" Star replied, flicking the hair out of her eyes. "I did for about a second, yeah. He was really hurt by what she was doing. And you know he still can't see that she was only trying to do the right thing for all of us. But he didn't kill Wanda."

"How can you be so sure?"

"Because I know them," Star told me truculently. "Because I grew up with them. And because I loved them. And they—with all their faults and everything—loved me. It's like we were all kids together, Peg. Yeah, maybe we were sort of bad kids sometimes. But kids don't kill, Peg. You know what mean?"

"I hope you're right," I told her.

"I know I am," Star told me, her upward-slanting gaze meeting mine head-on. "Wes didn't do it."

"Okay," I replied, squeezing her hand before releasing it "Okay. But somehow, kiddo, we've got to find out who did."

TWENTY-EIGHT

"CONGRATULATIONS," I said, standing at the door of Berry's old office. Brigitte, overly erect in Berry's worn swivel chair, sat behind the desk. Toni was poised in a chair to her left; Sara stood at the window. "To all of you," I added somewhat lamely. Just that morning *Women's Wear Daily* had carried the news that Brigitte had been named the new president of Merriweather Sportswear, Inc. Toni and Sara were both promoted to Executive Vice Presidents. Though the titles were clearly a vote of confidence for all three women, I had no doubt that Toni and Sara were disappointed that Brigitte had been handed the ultimate prize.

"Thanks," Brigitte replied. "Come in, Peg, and pull up a chair. We're all three of us still trying to adjust to the news."

"You think they'd have let us in on it," Sara grumbled, biting nervously on her already sore lower lip, "before they told the goddamned press."

"So this was news to you, too?" I asked, sitting down beside Toni.

"Can you believe it?" Toni demanded coldly. "I'm really shocked that Dick didn't have the decency to call first. I suppose," she added with a sigh, "this is just how corporate America works. We'll have to get used to it."

"Actually," Brigitte added sheepishly, "Dick did phone me last night. But it was quite late, and I didn't want to bother either of you at that hour. He said just what I was trying to say before Peg came in. My being president shouldn't really change anything between us. I mean, it was only *logical* that they choose me. I'm the designer, after all. I'm the creative force behind the company now. And everybody knows that a women's apparel line is only as good as its last season. You see, in that sense, I was the one they could least afford to lose."

"Is that so?" Toni sniffed. "Good luck finding replacements for Sara or me. We helped build this company with our sweat and blood, Brigitte. You better not forget it." She looked tired and angry, a combination that made her seem every bit her age. Her forehead was creased with wrinkles, parentheses of unhappiness were etched around her mouth. She had worked so hard only to come in tied for second place. And although I tried to feel sorry for Toni, there was something brittle and ungiving about her that turned back all my sympathy.

"I'm surprised you accepted," Sara added sourly. "I thought it was one for all and all for one. Isn't that what we decided?" She hugged her thin arms, and mumbled without much feeling, "I feel . . . cheated."

"Well, I'm sorry!" Brigitte cried, exasperation clear in her voice. "I'm really, very sorry. But I don't see what the big deal is. I already made it clear that we'll go on as before: a team. But enough already with being mad at me for getting on with Dick and the other Tantamount honchos. It's not my fault I hit it off better than you guys did."

"It's all because I refused to kiss ass," Toni cut in sanctimoniously. "That's the only reason. Isn't it, Brigitte?"

"Oh, please, Toni," Brigitte snapped. "Give me a little credit, okay? I am a good designer, remember, more than good. I loved Berry as much as you did, and I learned a lot from her. But if I went too much longer letting her take credit for my best work—well, I know I would have died."

"Convenient that she did it for you," Sara interjected. For a moment the room was silent as the ugly implications of Sara's remark sunk in.

Hoping to ease the mounting tension, I said, "I know just how you feel, Brigitte. I went through pretty much the same thing with my boss, Ramsey Farnsworth. You'll find, though, in time, that you dearly miss that first real mentor. Ramsey made it all look so easy somehow, so elegant and inspired. I don't know how he managed it."

"Oh, sure you do!" Brigitte snorted, dismissing my sentimental tone. "If you're any good at all, you learn to cope. You did. I did. You just put your nose to the grindstone, and work. As far as I'm concerned, it's just that simple. And, speaking of work, I want to schedule a meeting ASAP with you and Dick Byser to finalize the production schedule for the campaign." Brigitte reached across the desk to her daily planner, flipped over a few pages, and asked, "Is Friday a.m. good for you? Sara will be on the road, but Toni can sit in." Despite what she claimed, her voice did carry a new note of authority and command.

"Friday's fine," I said, finding the perfect segue into a question I'd been hoping to ask. "Sure, with Dick. That's fine. How is Dick, by the way? He seemed a little down last time I saw him."

"Down?" Brigitte asked, scribbling a note on her planner. "We'll meet here, okay? I've a busy agenda that day."

"Fine. Yeah, kinda down, you know," I pressed on. "Sad, depressed. Like the life had gone out of him. You know, I always sort of wondered . . . you think Wanda and he were . . . ?"

"Dick?" Toni retorted. "Wanda? I doubt it. He's into screwing companies, not people."

"I don't know," Brigitte mused. "They always seemed so lovey-dovey during marketing meetings here and at the agency. And, now that you mention it, I remember..." Her eyes glazed over as her thoughts turned inward. I let her think for a few seconds, then broke in with:

"You remember what, Brigitte?"

"I saw them together twice," Brigitte murmured, "outside of work, I mean. Once, up by CitiCorp building, you know in front of that modern little church there? And the other time they were in a coffee shop, let me think, it was somewhere on Broadway, near Lincoln Center. I remember both times I was thinking of saying hi, but they seemed so involved, so intense, I decided just to walk by."

"You only just remember this now?" I demanded.

"Sure," Brigitte responded. "How many times have you seen someone you know on the street or in a store, and don't really focus on the fact?"

"I guess you're right," I said, thinking over the truth of what she had said. Memory is such a strange and murky thing. They say everything you've ever seen and done is recorded in your brain—printed like an LP on the cerebral cortex. And months, years, after something has happened, you can replay whole scenes just as they occurred. You just have to put the needle down in the right place. It was what Brigitte said—about seeing someone you know on the street—that brought the particular memory to mind. And in that moment, I played it all back: the very last night I saw Berry alive. I was walking across town to the Merriweather offices when a tall, handsome, deeply tanned man winked at me as we waited together at a corner for a light to change. He was flashily dressed in off-white leather, fringed cowboy boots. He had a wonderful, toothy smile. And he wasn't supposed to be there at all. Because he was Wes Merriweather, and someone had said that he was skiing with his family in Colorado on the last day of his older sister's life.

It took me a few moments to recover, but luckily everyone was too occupied with their own thoughts to realize what I was going through. At last, I pulled myself together, and asked in a confiding tone, "What do you really think, guys? Did Dick have anything to do with Berry's and Wanda's murders?"

"Wanda's murder?" Toni cried.

"What in the world makes you think she was murdered?" Brigitte demanded.

"Oh, damn!" I replied, biting my bottom lip. "I'm such an idiot. I promised Cursio I wouldn't go blabbing it all over town. Please," I begged, looking from one stricken face to the next, "promise me you won't tell anyone else? I swore on a stack of bibles I would keep my mouth shut."

"Of course, we'll be discreet," Brigitte assured me for all of them. "But only if you tell us *why* they think it wasn't suicide. I mean, Peg, this is really horrifying news."

"To be honest, I don't know any of the details," I replied. "Cursio insists on keeping me out of it—for my safety, he says. But, well, can you all keep another little secret?"

"Sure," Sara whispered, her pale face ghostlike.

"Certainly," Toni added.

"Okay," I said, lowering my voice. "The police have narrowed the suspect list down to two. Cursio won't come right out and tell me, but from what I can gather it's got to be Dick...or Wes."

"But...I thought Wes could account for his whereabouts the night Berry was killed," Brigitte replied.

"Yeah, well, I think some evidence to the contrary has come to light," I said, rising to go. "And I get the feeling it's pretty damaging. But, not a word to anyone about this."

"Of course," Toni replied vaguely. "You can trust us."

It was hardly the moment to argue the point.

I WAS SORELY TEMPTED to ask Cursio, but I knew it would only raise too many questions I didn't want to answer yet. So instead I asked Millie if she would put Star up for the night. I explained I had an unexpected business trip that would take me out of town for a day or two.

"I'd be delighted, dear," Millie had replied, frowning slightly as she eyed me over her half glasses. "I do wish you'd take life a bit easier, though, Peg. You look tired. And worried. Is everything okay?"

"Yes," I answered hurriedly, turning away from her door, but then I saw the look of genuine concern on her face. I turned back to her and said, "Tell me, Millie, all your tea leaves and star charts and tarot cards...they can predict the future, but they can never change it, can they?"

"No, dear, you're right," Millie replied. "Sometimes, though, it is very useful to be prepared for what's to come."

"And other times," I told her gently, "it's a whole lot better not to know until it's too late."

I arranged things at the office, left a note and some money for Star, caught a cab out to Kennedy and made the 4:50 nonstop to Los Angeles by minutes. During our five-plus hours aloft, we were undoubtedly served drinks and dinner and shown a movie, but I remember none of it. Instead, I stared out into the wintry blackness and slowly wove together the last few loose threads of the Merriweather murders. It was a very uneven tapestry of motives and events, but even as I let my mind drift over its rough texture and design, I knew it to be essentially right and complete. I decided that it simply wasn't true that deception makes for a tangled web. In fact, the lies surrounding Berry's and Wanda's deaths were beautifully woven, carefully sewn. The truth, however, was a god-awful mess.

After we landed, it took me thirteen calls from an airport pay phone to find out that Wes Merriweather was registered at the Arcadian Hills Motel in Pasadena, out on Foothill Freeway. I had guessed correctly where his inexpensive motel would be located. It was a little less than an hour from Los Angeles International Airport and slightly more than ten minutes from the Santa Anita racetrack.

I was already exhausted and more than a little unhinged emotionally, so my scene at the dingy front desk of the Arcadian Hills was hardly a difficult role for me. The yawning, bleary-eyed night manager, who came out of a back office after I rang five times, didn't have much of a chance.

"What the hell do you mean you can't give out keys?" I demanded. "My husband told you I was coming in late tonight, didn't he?"

"Uh . . . I don't know," the poor soul answered. "I came on here at eleven. What room is he in? I can call him," the man added, reaching for a house phone.

"I wouldn't advise that if I were you," I warned, fixing him with a menacing stare. "Wes hates to be woken up in the middle of the night. I mean, he loathes it. You've seen my husband, right?" I continued, looking down at the small, helpless night manager. "The big blond guy? With the shoulder span like Mike Tyson? You know the one?"

He obviously did, because without another word he plucked a plastic-coated key chain from the wall and handed it to me.

"Number twelve," he mumbled, turning back to the office. "Round to the back."

My heels crunched on the gravel as I made my way through the darkness to Wes's motel room—a distance of less than fifty yards, but one that seemed to take me hours. The details are still vivid in my mind: the night air warm and humid, thick with the smell of weeds and exhaust from the highway; the western horizon lighted with the insomniac sprawl of Los Angeles; the high whine of trucks on Foothill Freeway and the reedy hum of cicadas in the bushes beyond the parking lot. But most of all I remember the feeling of cold, unquenchable dread when the thought finally occurred to me: what if I was wrong?

I knocked softly four times, then once hard, before I heard someone groan, "What the hell?" Then there was a squeak of bedsprings and a light coming on, outlining two small windows and Wes's bulk in the opaque glass door.

"Who's it?" he demanded.

"It's me, Wes," I told him. "It's Peg. We've got to talk."

"Oh, shit," he muttered, then unhooked a chain and opened the door. He swayed in front of me, a tousled giant, smelling of beer and cigarettes and sweat. The room represented the untended masculine spirit at its worst: clothes in heaps on the floor and chairs, days-old take-out boxes rotting on the dresser, the bed a snarl of sheets and wadded-up pillows. He waved me in, gesturing around the disgusting room. "Welcome to my castle, dearest Peg." He swept a load of papers and empty coffee containers off a chair. "Here, have a seat. I'd offer you some petits fours, but the duchess ate the last one."

"I'm not here for polite conversation," I told him, sitting down on the edge of the hard seat. "As I'm sure you've guessed."

"Yeah," Wes replied, buttoning his rumpled shirt. He'd obviously fallen asleep in his clothes. "I imagine not. What do you want, then? Better spit it out fast—I'm not in much of a party mood." He collapsed on the bed, elbows on knees, head drooping.

"I know who killed Berry," I told him, watching as his head shot up. His eyes, deep blue and red veined, held mine. "And Wanda, too."

He cleared his throat, looked away from me and down at his hands and said, "It wasn't me."

"Jeez, Wes, I know that!" I retorted, standing up in my agitation. "Would I be alone here in the middle of the night if I thought you were a murderer?"

"I...guess not," Wes replied, looking up at me. "But, uh...why are you here?"

"To work out the plan."

"'The plan,'" Wes repeated dully.

"The one that's going to catch the person who did do it," I told him. "Red-handed."

"Oh, no," he answered, his shoulders straightening.

"You can't run away forever, Wes," I told him, sitting down next to him. "One of these days you're going to have to go back and face it. You know that."

He could not meet my gaze. "I know, I know. I just don't... I just can't..."

"Sure you can, Wes," I told him soothingly. "I know you can. We'll do it together."

"Yeah?" he demanded, looking across at me. A tear started to ooze down his cheek. "And how are you planning on doing it?"

"With bait," I told him firmly.

"Oh...no."

"Yes," I told him firmly. "And you're it. Because we both know who was going to be next. Right, Wes?"

TWENTY-NINE

THE GARMENT DISTRICT closes down after six o'clock on weekday nights. Except for spillover traffic from Times Square, the side streets are empty and silent. It was a fact I was counting on.

It was nine o'clock Wednesday night when I nodded to the "security guard" at the front desk of the Zabin Building. Busy thumbing through a dog-eared copy of *Penthouse*, he gave me a quick once-over as I walked in and—I suppose after comparing my various attributes to those of the magazine's models—turned back almost immediately to his reading material.

The elevator seemed even more jumpy than usual, I decided, clutching the guardrail to steady myself. Although maybe it was me. My heart was knocking around in my chest like a badly served paddleball. My armpits oozed sweat. I wasn't breathing evenly. And, after having set this whole thing up, I was no longer thinking very well.

For instance, when the elevator finally creaked open at the eleventh floor, I was panicked to find the reception area flooded with pale light. Was someone still there? Or had an overhead been left on by mistake? I stepped off the elevator and inched my way around the room. The glow seemed to be emanating from the hallway that opened to offices facing Fortieth Street. Holding whatever breath I had left, I peeked around the corner and found myself staring straight into the source of light: the complacent smile of a nearly full moon. Relieved, I made my way as quietly as possible down the corridor. The rounded white face beamed down on me sagely, half-sadly, through each of the windows I passed.

The moonlight streamed through the windows of Berry's old office—now Brigitte's—and I saw immediately that the plan would have to be changed. Considering the light, I could not risk hiding in either of the secretarial modules that flanked the corner office. I finally decided on the small closet at the far end of the room, where rolls of fabric samples were stored. I squeezed between some Milanese wool and Japanese silk, draped myself with a yard or so of bright Indian madras and opened the closet door just far enough to get an inch-wide view of the desk. I positioned the tape recorder I'd brought on the floor beside me—close enough so that I could step down on the Record button with my heel—and waited.

Ever notice how slowly time passes when you're afraid? How the second hand seems to stop when, with the suction nozzle already drying up your mouth, you try to prepare yourself for the dentist's specialized form of torture? Or, if you're next in line to speak, how endlessly long the person before you takes, until your entire part—once put to memory—fades like the print in yellowing newspapers? Later I was able to determine that I waited in that closet for a little under forty minutes. For me, it will always seem—timewise—about the equivalent of my entire primary school education. But when, at last, I heard the elevator swish open and footsteps in the lobby, I realized I somehow wasn't at all prepared for what was about to happen. Five minutes later, I heard the elevator again, voices and footsteps coming down the corridor.

"Don't turn the light on," Wes announced sharply as two people walked into the office. It took me until that moment to realize I'd forgotten about the tape recorder. Damn! As carefully as possible I stepped on the Record lever, but the machine gave off a resounding click, anyway.

"What was that?" she asked.

"What?" Wes demanded irritably.

"I heard something," she said. "In one of the closets. You'd better check."

"The hell I will," Wes retorted. "It's a little late in the game for you to suddenly get a case of nerves, don't you think? It's probably just a rat, anyway. This city is full of them."

"Is that so?" she sneered. "Well, you should know. You've a hell of a lot of nerve running off and leaving me like that, after all I've been through for you."

"Yeah?" Wes said, sighing. I watched him ease himself down into Berry's swivel chair. It groaned under his weight and squeaked as he swung around to face the moonlit cityscape beyond. "Tell me about going through things, okay? What do you think I've been doing?"

"We both know what you've been doing, Wes, darling," she answered, coming up behind him and laying her hands on his broad shoulders. "You've been gambling away the fortune I risked my life to get for you."

"And we both know you're overdramatizing the facts, little gal," Wes retorted, swinging around abruptly and throwing her off balance. She steadied herself against the desk as they faced each other. I watched them and saw what each must have seen in the other when the affair first began. Physically, they were a perfect match: tall, broad, blond, striking. They both also seemed to be in complete control of their lives. When, I wonder, did she start to realize that Wes wasn't much more than an overgrown adolescent? A charming boy who took what he wanted in life, including other men's wives and other people's money. Or had she known all along? Had she realized from the beginning that someone like Wes—someone unable to control his needs and desires—was going to be the easiest kind of person to manipulate?

"Oh, come off it, Wes," Brigitte retorted, hoisting herself up on the desktop and crossing her arms. "We both know what the facts are, dear. You wanted Berry dead. How often did you tell me that over the course of the year that you were supposedly banished to Los Angeles?"

"We've been over this so many times, Brig," Wes answered, sighing heavily. "Wanting and doing are two completely different things. I never would have actually killed her, you know. Never."

"Of course I know that, stupid," Brigitte snapped. "You haven't the nerve. You talk a good line, but it took someone like me—somebody with a little nerve and more than half a dozen brain cells—to carry the thing out. So I actually was the one who did it? What difference does it make? You wanted to as much as me—that's what matters. And, besides which, you ended up being an accessory."

"Yeah, speaking of brains," Wes retorted, "how bright was it to strangle her first and then figure out you weren't strong enough to hoist that rig? Remember how you had to call me at the hotel to give you a hand at the last minute? I wouldn't exactly call that hundred-watt thinking, if I were you."

"Well, that's where you're wrong," Brigitte answered as she started to laugh. "Don't you get it, Wes? I planned from the beginning that you would help me string poor Berry up. Tha way, being more than passingly involved yourself, you'd be less than likely to go to the police. No, dear heart, I worked all this out very carefully."

There was a long moment of silence when Wes turned again to stare out the window. His blond hair haloed in moonlight, his strong hands steepled under his chin.

"But why Wanda?" he demanded just loud enough for me to hear.

"Why?" Brigitte demanded, standing up and walking around to face him. Backlighted by the ghostly light, she cast long shadows down the room. I couldn't see her face at all now, but her voice was strong and carrying. "Why?" she said again, her hands on her hips. "Because you couldn't stop talking about her! All I heard every time we met was 'Wanda this' and 'Wanda that.' The more estranged you two were supposed to be, the more you carried on about her. I was going crazy listening to you! And then, when you heard she was going to divorce you and, instead of rejoicing, you started acting like the damned walking wounded—well, I'd had enough."

"So you did kill her," Wes said evenly. "I guess I've always known it.... I just never wanted to face it before."

"You're such a child!" Brigitte cried, staring down at him. "And, the fact of the matter is, the woman was killing herself. Everybody knew it, Wes. Your pretty little wife was a mess. You should have seen her in Venice. She was so out of it, she couldn't even join Peg and me for dinner. Your precious Star had to stay home and baby-sit her."

"It's true she was up and down, Brig," Wes replied slowly. "But she *was* trying. There were the times this past year or so—when we were in Los Angeles and away from all this—that I really thought she was going to make it."

"And you would have waited around for her forever," Brigitte sneered, "if she had let you. Why don't you just admit it to yourself—you loved her. You never stopped loving her, no matter how many of us you screwed on the side. Isn't that right, Wes?" Brigitte's voice warbled with emotion when she demanded a second time, "Isn't that so?"

"What difference does it make now?" Wes replied softly. "You've got what you wanted—she's gone."

"Oh, like hell she is!" Brigitte cried. "You can't stop thinking about her or talking about her. She's more real to you now that she's dead than when she was alive. And I—the person who has done everything for you—it's as if I no longer exist."

"I never asked you to kill for me, Brigitte," Wes answered.

"What choice did I have, damn it?" Brigitte retorted. "What choice did I ever have?" She started to pace back and forth in front of him, her voice breaking now and again. "I don't think you can begin to understand what it's like for a woman like me, Wes. Until you barged into my life, I had a quiet, organized, perfect little home. Yes, I was bored, uninspired, *unfulfilled*—but I was safe, secure. And then you happened. Then you made me come alive! God, it was ecstatic, marvelous...terrifying! You made everything else in my life—my husband, my children, my friends, my work—meaningless. Worthless. Only you mattered. Only you....

"Only you....." Brigitte continued, her voice choked with tears. "You made all these extravagant promises to me—one you probably don't even remember now. We were going to run away together, remember? Just leave it all behind us and take off to Europe or the Caribbean. You made me *believe*, Wes. really thought that if we could just get some money together...well, then everything would work itself out. God when the Tantamount offer came through, I was so happy! knew you'd make a bundle from it, and we could start our life together. And then Berry confided in me that night that she had decided not to sell. What else could I have done? She was standing in our way."

"But why Wanda, Brig?" Wes demanded. "Why?"

"Because you'd never really left her, damn it!" Brigitte retorted, turning on him fiercely. "Because you still love her...the way you'll never love me."

I saw a silvery flash and heard Wes draw in his breath sharply.

"Put that gun away, Brig," he said carefully. "You don't know what you're doing."

"Oh, but I do, dear," Brigitte answered calmly. "I learned from Peg the other day that the police know Wanda wasn't suicide...and that the suspect list is down to two. But guess who they are, dear? You and Dick! And, personally, I think they're probably leaning over backward in your direction. They just need a little push. Well, as it happens, I have your confession right here in my pocketbook. It's a bit too well written for you but the handwriting is so precisely done I seriously doubt any one will challenge its authenticity. But then I know your hand so well.''

"And what makes you think I'm going to let you get away with it?'' Wes demanded, inching back just enough for me to be able to make out the small, blunt-nosed gun in Brigitte's right hand. She had it pointed at his chest.

"Oh, didn't I explain it thoroughly enough?'' Brigitte replied blandly. "You see, this letter is a suicide note, as well. It explains that you're so distraught over what you've done that you simply can't go on. All in all, dearest, I think you're getting exactly what you deserve.''

"Put the gun away, Brigitte,'' Wes repeated slowly. "You're just making matters worse for yourself.''

"I don't think so,'' Brigitte retorted. "Don't you see? Matters can't get any worse for me. I've nothing more to lose. Not even you.''

Then I heard a click. Then a loud explosion and glass shattering. I found myself tumbling out of the closet, trailing bright Indian madras.

"What the . . . ?'' I heard Brigitte scream. "Wes, you son of a bitch!''

And then I heard another click and felt something hot grazing my upper arm. The last thing I remember was the smell of cordite and something rough scraping my arms, my neck, my cheek as I crumpled onto the carpeted floor.

THIRTY

THE NIGHTMARISH EVENTS of that winter—the murders, m
long hospitalization after my shoulder wound became in
fected, the indictment and hearings—all seemed a world awa
that sun-dazzled Fourth of July morning. From around th
globe, all of Theo and Cal's dearly beloved had gathere
together at Windsong—the island Theo owned off the coast o
Maine—to help join the happy, mismatched couple in hol
matrimony. I, ten pounds lighter and still wan from my so
journ at the hospital, was to serve as the maid of honor. The
resplendent in a hand-blocked sarong, had draped a flowin
silk-screened scarf around my shoulder to disguise the bulk
bandage I was still forced to wear.

"There you go, darling," she exclaimed, standing back t
take in her handiwork. "You look gorgeous. All cheekbon
and black tresses. Like some wildly romantic heroine. Oh, d
try to be happy for me, Peggy!"

"I am, Theo," I told her warmly, "I truly am. I'm delighte
for you and Cal. Honest." And I was. But even Theo's sunn
wedding day couldn't break through the gloom that ha
shrouded my life since winter. Although the rest of the wor
had thawed with the spring rains and blossomed with the su
mer flowers, I had remained frozen somewhere in Februar
Some people, my neighbor Millie for one, believed that my i
ability to recover physically from Brigitte's gunshot was ti
into my unwillingness to face the psychic pain that she had i
flicted. Millie was one of the few people I had allowed to vi
me in the hospital. Star, who had been staying with Dick B
ser's family in Westchester, was another. She kept me abrea
of all the important events: the pretrial hearings, her new hi
school friends, the preparations for the Merriweather shoot
Europe the last two weeks of July. Everyone except me w
convinced that I'd be well enough to direct the location wor
Even now, after Theo left me alone in the garret bedroom
Windsong to finish getting ready for the ceremony, I felt ov

come with weariness—or was it sadness? I sat down on the eyelet coverlet and stared out across the tops of pines to the dancing, whitecapped sea. Sun streamed in the window, warming my pale face. My eyelids felt heavy. I could hear the sounds of laughter and music outside—the string quartet that Theo had culled from the Boston Symphony was tuning up on the front lawn—and then I let my eyes close.

"Why the hell didn't you tell me?" Those charming words were the first thing I heard as I drifted back to consciousness the night I was shot. They were spoken by an ashen-faced Cursio, who stood tensely at the foot of my hospital bed. A day's growth of beard darkened his chin, and his eyes were blue-black with anger. "Why, damn it?"

"You . . . didn't tell me things," I had murmured, realizing for the first time that the whole left side of my upper body was numb. "What happened?"

"Brigitte's bullet missed your heart by an inch and a half," Cursio retorted. "She didn't know what the hell she was doing with that damned gun. We think she meant to hit Wes and got you, instead. Damn it, Peg!" he yelled. "What the hell do you think you were doing?"

"Please," I told him. "I'm tired. I don't want to talk about it. Please . . . just go away." Well, he did. And I hadn't let him come back—despite the loads of flowers and books he sent me as bribes. It was a useless situation and finally I faced it. Cursio and I would go on fighting with each other for another few months, another half a year, but it was over—just as Brigitte's life was over. Oh, she'd be tried and convicted; she'd go to jail. But essentially, the woman I'd known and admired was dead. Or else—and I had to face this possibility—she'd never existed at all. Just the way the love, the passion I had once felt for Dante Cursio might have been an illusion. It was certainly gone now. That was the kind of tough thinking I did in the hospital. Tough and honest—and just terrible. I guess when people like me—usually so optimistic and happy—hit bottom, well, we really crash.

Yes, it had been a dark time. I'd gone back to work the beginning of June, deciding to put in half days until my strength came back. Only it hadn't. And it wasn't. It was almost as if the infection that had spread through the wound—forcing me back into the hospital a few days after I'd first been released—had oozed into my soul, as well. My mind was listless. My heart

leaden. I could sleep for fourteen hours at a stretch and still b
tired. I'd felt so lousy a few days before the wedding that I ha
asked Millie to come up to Maine with me—for physical ar
moral support.

"I'd be honored, dear," she told me. "Who else is comin
Peg. Anyone I know? Aren't the detective and Cal goo
friends?" Along with Star, Millie had been relentless abo
trying to get me to see Cursio again. I tried, on many occ
sions to explain to both of them that the relationship was ov

"Yes, as a matter of fact, there'll be several people you kno
there. Dick Byser's bringing Star up. Phillip and Mark are i
vited. And I asked Toni and Sara, thinking it would do the
both good to get out of the office for a time. They've be
putting in unbelievable hours since being named co-presider
of Merriweather. And, yes, Detective Cursio will be there, to
He's a good friend of Cal's, as you know. But please, Milli
promise me you'll let sleeping dogs lie?"

"Sleeping dogs, yes," she'd replied. "But sleeping peop
who don't have the sense to see that—"

"Millie!" I'd cut in. "One more word and forget about t
wedding. I'll make it on my own."

"Okay, dear, fine," Millie had responded soothingly. "I
never mention the man again."

She hadn't. And neither had Theo, Cal or anyone else in t
wedding party during the two days I'd been at Windsor
Maybe I'd been wrong, I thought drowsily as I glanced do
at the crowd milling on the front lawn. Maybe Cursio was
coming. Perhaps he felt I didn't want him there. And I didr
of course, not personally. But his absence would most c
tainly hurt Cal and Theo, I told myself. And it was, after
their day.

"Peggy, dear, whatever are you doing!" Millie cried, l
voice breathless from climbing the stairs. "The ceremony sta
in half an hour. You aren't half-ready yet."

"Yes, I am," I contradicted, wincing as I got up from
bed. The doctor had assured me that my shoulder was entir
healed and that I was only imagining the stabbing pain I fel
moments like these. "I just need to put on a little lipstick."

"And fix your hair and put on some blush and..." Mi
bustled around the little attic room, her heavy violet toilet wa
filling my nostrils with what smelled to me like the swe
haunting aroma of sadness. Though her own bleached c

fure was a frightful balancing act of French twists and supple-
mentary falls, I let her tinker with my hair. I hadn't gotten
around to cutting it in the past few months, and now it tum-
bled in an unruly mass below my shoulders. Millie pulled it
back off my face with two diamond barrettes and brushed it
until it glowed. Then she made me put on the dangly Peretti
earrings Theo had given me for my last birthday and enough
blush and eyeshadow to almost disguise my wintry pallor.

"There you go!" she announced victoriously, taking a step
back as we both stared at my reflection in the mirror. "As good
as new."

"No, Millie," I told her, shaking my head. It was hard to
recognize the woman with the darkly haunted eyes, jutting
cheekbones and full, unsmiling lips who stared back at me.
"I'm afraid I'm not anywhere near new.... I've aged, can't you
see?" I sought out Millie's eyes in the mirror.

"You really want to know what I see, young lady?" Millie
snapped at me. "Someone who believes she's the first person
to find out that there's ugliness in this world. What do you
think, that you discovered violence? Do you think the rest of
us aren't touched by the same things you are? That we don't
hear sirens and cries in the middle of the night, too? Heavens,
Peggy, I thought you were smarter than all this."

"Well ... I'm sorry," I replied brokenly, a tear trailing mascara down my cheek. "I'm afraid I didn't realize ..." I knew I
was on the verge of one of my big crying jags. I took a deep
breath and went on, "I haven't really ever had to face it before. I mean, what Brigitte did—she destroyed something in
me."

"But that's good, dear," Millie replied confidently. "Don't
you see? All Brigitte did was take away your silly innocence. It
was time someone did. You've joined the ranks of the disa-
bused, that's all. You've grown up. And, if you ever manage to
see beyond your nose, maybe you'll wise up, as well."

"What do you mean, Millie?" I sniffed, reaching for a
Kleenex. The string quartet was beginning to perform in earnest, and the crowd had hushed.

"Heavens, we're going to be late!" Millie cried, looking at
the window. "Hurry Peg. I promised Cal I'd have you down in
the kitchen by ten-thirty. We've less than a minute to make it."

Skirts and hair flying, I followed Millie as she raced down the
three winding flights of back stairs. Though almost eighty,

Millie was as nimble as a teenager. I just managed to keep up with her and then stop her as we reached the landing that led down to the butler's pantry.

"Tell me," I demanded, my breath coming in short gasps, "what you meant . . . about wising up."

"Oh, that," Millie answered distractedly, trying to put her hair back into place. With a bobby pin clenched between her teeth, she answered, "It's quite simple, really, dear. You know anyone with half an eye can see what's wrong with this world, the way you have. The hard part is finding the gumption to try to make it better. The trick is that once you see what's what . . . you must manage to carry on."

Without another word, Millie pushed me in front of her down the last few steps, through the butler's pantry and into the kitchen, where Theo and Cal were waiting amongst a gaggle of friends and servants.

"Everyone outside, now!" Nattie Zellerman, Theo's long-time agent and today's master of ceremonies cried, shooing people through the screen door.

Millie melted away with the rest of the guests, and I stood alone in front of my mother and her husband-to-be. Theo's wedding march began. No, not the traditional "Wedding March" by Wagner—this was the Beatles' "When I'm Sixty-four," performed with charming seriousness by the distinguished orchestral musicians.

I don't know where he came from, but suddenly Dante Cursio was standing next to me, dressed in a beautifully styled black tuxedo. I stared up at him. A new haircut accentuated his thick, expressive eyebrows. He looked tired and sad . . . and ridiculously handsome with the white collar and perfectly cut bow tie sculpting his face. He held out his arm. It took me a second to realize what was happening.

"I'm sorry," he said as we walked slowly through the kitchen door that Nattie was holding open for us. "But Cal asked me months ago if I'd be his best man. I couldn't let him down."

It was, in the best Theodora Goodenough tradition, an unusual and eclectic ceremony. A female federal judge did the honors. A fellow women's rights pioneer with Theo, Judge Whitestone's approach was straightforward, no-nonsense and—to my eye, at least—perhaps not entirely appropriate. I guess the way the judge saw it, one of the cause's great leaders was going over to the enemy. You had to know Cal better to realize that the ERA movement wasn't losing a daughter but gaining a son.

Brahms and Blood, Sweat and Tears. Mozart and Peter, Paul and Mary. The music, like the gold-and-blue striped canopies set up on the beach below, was buffeted about by a mild sea breeze. Gulls called from the jetties and the waves crashed against the rocky shore. How long did the service last? I really don't know. I tried to track the judge's stern admonitions about cleaving "in sickness and in health," but I found my thoughts turning instead to Millie's earlier chastisement . . . to the truth of what she had said. And, okay, I admit it, my attention kept wandering to the man standing a few grassy steps away from me.

At some point, Dante had slipped on dark glasses against the bright sun; they lent him a distant, almost dangerous appeal. God, he did look wonderful in that tux, I thought, knowing but suddenly not caring that he'd probably rented it from the cheapest joint he could find. For the first time in many months I found myself wishing that things were different between us. Damn it, all he had to do was take a look at Theo and Cal, with twenty years of differences between them, to realize that almost any obstacle could be overcome if you cared enough. If.

All at once I realized that Cal was kissing Theo, and the quartet broke into the Stones' "You Can't Always Get What You Want."

The reception lasted through the afternoon. A Dixieland jazz band replaced the quartet on the front lawn. The buffet under the canopies resembled an old-fashioned clam bake: whole lobsters steamed on beds of seaweed in the sand; fat ears of fresh corn grilled on the open coals; clams, steamed in their shells, briny with sea salt. Champagne flowed. Nattie and half a dozen other friends gave speeches. Even Felix Northfield said a few kind words. I was surprised to find myself talking with something almost like pleasure to people I have avoided for months. Phillip and Mark. Dick Byser, who had been kind enough to take care of Star after Wes was arrested. Along with a number of other younger guests, Star had gone swimming off the rocks, leaving Dick and me to talk alone together for the first time since Wanda's death.

"What do you think Wes's chances are?" I asked, squinting behind him into the sun. I'd been trying to keep Cursio in my line of vision most of the afternoon.

"Not good," Dick admitted. "I think both he and Brigitte will be away for a long time. We're going to have to talk about Star at some point, you know. She misses you terribly, Peg."

"I know," I told him, and we both turned to watch her dive off the crowded dock. Already a group of young men were following her around like homeless pups. "I miss her, too."

"Couldn't you take her in?" he demanded. "That's what she really wants, I think. She needs love...and friendship. God, I'd hate to see her end up like her mother."

I'd learned through Star that Dick and Wanda's renewed relationship during the last few months of her mother's life had had nothing to do with passion. Dick, a recovering alcoholic himself, had convinced Wanda to seek help for her problems. Yes, Brigitte had seen them more than once. But Dick wasn't Wanda's lover...he was her sponsor at AA, and he made a point of seeing that she made her weekly meetings. That's probably when Brigitte spotted them together.

"I don't think so, Dick," I replied. "She needs a father more than anything, I think. She needs a real family. And, well, I'm just not in the greatest position right now to take care of her."

"Yes, of course," Dick said. "I understand." Though I'm not at all sure he did.

The reception drifted on into the evening. People started to dance on the lawn. Japanese lanterns and fireflies blinked together under the stars. I spent a long time talking to Sara and Toni about their new ideas for Merriweather. And in doing so I felt the first vaguely familiar stirrings of interest in their advertising plans.

"I need a word with you," a voice called from the shadows as Sara and Toni moved off. Cursio was standing under the large cedar tree that looked out over the ocean.

"Yes?" I said, walking slowly across the lawn. I was conscious of my bare shoulder and my wind-tossed hair.

"I've been thinking," he said abruptly as I came near. It was difficult to make out his features in the gathering dark. "You know, I've had a lot of time to think since Eva went home."

"Star told me she'd gone back to England," I replied. "I understand her new brother is doing just fine."

"Yes," Cursio replied bitingly. "Everyone's just fine."

"You don't sound very happy about it," I observed, studying his profile.

"I miss her," he said, "and Star. Laughing too loud. Messing up the house. I miss having people I love around, Peg. I...I miss you."

I didn't give myself time to think. I told him the truth. "I miss you, too."

"Do you?" he asked, turning to me. He grabbed hold of my shoulders. "How much?" he demanded, and before I could answer, I felt his lips on mine.

"Hey!" I cried at one point, coming up for air. "I think you really *have* missed me."

"Yes," he said roughly, running his hands down my arms. His fingers stopped at the bandage. He caressed my skin. It occurred to me briefly that my shoulder didn't hurt anymore. "You know, weddings have a way of doing this to me," he murmured, his cheek warm and rough against my skin.

"Then you should go to them more often," I told him teasingly.

"As a matter of fact," he answered, but his voice was gently serious, "I was just about to propose that very thing." Then he leaned over and kissed me again. First my lips. Then my shoulder. Then the spot where Brigitte's bullet had entered, an inch and a half above my heart.

It's funny how a life can change in a second. I mean, someone suddenly says, "You've won the prize" or "You've got the job," and your whole world screeches to a halt, takes the turn and rattles off in an entirely new direction.

"What exactly are you trying to say, Detective?" I asked him, and at that instant I was just another slowly despairing working girl in her late twenties.

"Marry me, Peg," he said. And in the next instant, my life opened before me, boundless, strange and beautiful. And I realized that, for better, for worse, nothing was going to be the same again.

"Reid Bennett is one of the most interesting series who-dun-it
heroes of the decade."

—*Chicago Sun Times*

WHEN THE KILLING STARTS
TED WOOD

When a wealthy mother hires Reid Bennett to find her rebellious son
who's run off with a mercenary unit called *Freedom for Hire*, he
suspects trouble.

Bennett is annoyed with the outfit's sadistic commander, Colonel
George Dunphy, especially when the ex-British paratrooper declares
war on him in the Canadian wilderness—complete with ex-SAI men
and automatic weapons. Bennett brings the boy home. But that's
when the trouble really begins. It seems that the woman who hired
Bennett *isn't* young Jason's mother after all, and now Reid is being
framed for murder...

Can you keep a secret?

You can keep this one plus 2 free novels.

"This fast-paced mystery contains a rich trove of sharply
edged supporting characters. Of course, mom steals
the show."
— *Publishers Weekly*

WORLDWIDE LIBRARY

A NICE MURDER FOR MOM

James Yaffe

For a New York City homicide cop, Mesa Grande, Colorado,
was like another planet. But Dave liked his new job as Chief
Investigator for the Public Defender's Office, although he
did miss his mother's cooking. He also missed her amazing
knack to solve his most difficult murder cases. So when Mom
comes for a visit, Dave knows what she'd really love is a nice
murder.

Luckily, there was a corpse to oblige. A pompous college
professor is bludgeoned to death in his living room. Soon
some very bizarre twists and turns leave everybody guessing.
Except, of course, Mom.
